PENGUIN CANADA

BELLE FALLS

SHERRI VANDERVEEN's short works of fiction have appeared in several Canadian literary journals. She currently lives in Toronto with her husband and daughter. This is her first novel.

Belle Falls

Sherri Vanderveen

PENGUIN
CANADA

PENGUIN CANADA

Published by the Penguin Group

Penguin Group (Canada), 90 Eglinton Avenue East, Suite 700, Toronto, Ontario, Canada
M4P 2Y3 (a division of Pearson Canada Inc.)

Penguin Group (USA) Inc., 375 Hudson Street, New York, New York 10014, U.S.A.
Penguin Books Ltd, 80 Strand, London WC2R 0RL, England
Penguin Ireland, 25 St Stephen's Green, Dublin 2, Ireland (a division of Penguin Books Ltd)
Penguin Group (Australia), 250 Camberwell Road, Camberwell, Victoria 3124, Australia
(a division of Pearson Australia Group Pty Ltd)
Penguin Books India Pvt Ltd, 11 Community Centre, Panchsheel Park, New Delhi – 110 017,
India
Penguin Group (NZ), cnr Airborne and Rosedale Roads, Albany, Auckland 1310, New
Zealand (a division of Pearson New Zealand Ltd)
Penguin Books (South Africa) (Pty) Ltd, 24 Sturdee Avenue, Rosebank, Johannesburg 2196,
South Africa

Penguin Books Ltd, Registered Offices: 80 Strand, London WC2R 0RL, England

First published 2007

1 2 3 4 5 6 7 8 9 10   (WEB)

Copyright © Sherri Vanderveen, 2007

Epigraph by Edna St. Vincent Millay from the Steepletop Collection.
Reprinted by permission of the Edna St. Vincent Millay Society

Manufactured in Canada.

LIBRARY AND ARCHIVES CANADA CATALOGUING IN PUBLICATION

Vanderveen, Sherri
Belle falls / Sherri Vanderveen.

ISBN-13: 978-0-14-305113-8
ISBN-10: 0-14-305113-X

I. Title.

PS8643.A49B44 2007   C813'.6   C2007-900022-3

Visit the Penguin Group (Canada) website at **www.penguin.ca**

Special and corporate bulk purchase rates available; please see
www.penguin.ca/corporatesales or call 1-800-810-3104, ext. 477 or 474

For Michael, who would have been so proud
and will not be forgotten.

PARIS APRIL 1ST, 1922

A mile of clean sand.
I will write my name here, and the trouble that is in my
　　heart.
I will write the date & place of my birth,
What I was to be,
And what I am.
I will write my forty sins, my thousand follies,
My four unspeakable acts …
I will write the names of the cities I have fled from,
The names of the men & women I have wronged.
I will write the holy name of her I serve,
And how I serve her ill.
And I will sit on the beach & let the tide come in.
I will watch with peace the great calm tongue of the tide
Licking from the sand the unclean story of my heart.

—Edna St. Vincent Millay, Paris notebook

*P*edalling down the sidewalk, his helmet lopsided and sticking to the back of his head in the heat, Brennan Allister stops suddenly and leans forward, the front tires of his bicycle inches away from a squirming dark line. Today—a day after his sixth birthday (the cake, he can still taste the cake and the frosting and the way it melted in his mouth)—he's alone, his mother hidden somewhere in the house, allowing him a sort of freedom. As he dismounts, his bicycle clatters onto its side. He pauses for a moment, wondering if he should set it upright again, then shrugs, moves forward in a crouch. Extending a curious finger, he pokes at the wriggling line, giggles as the ants scramble, frantic. Right now, with the sun beating down on the back of his neck, with his new bicycle and the ants, there is nowhere else he'd rather be. A long great summer stretches behind him, endless days of Popsicles and swimming pools and bare feet on his front porch after his evening bath, warm air blowing across his forehead and hair slicked behind his ears.

At the end of the street, a city bus stops, emitting a grey-blue cloud from its tailpipe as the driver steps off the brake. Brennan shakes his head in disapproval, the way his kindergarten teacher had when she talked about *pollution* and what it was doing to the *environment*. But then he sees the crazy lady, left behind as the bus lurches on. Worse, she has seen him and is smiling that crooked grin. She shifts, tightening her grip on the plastic bag she carries, then begins to cross the street toward him. She walks funny—all the kids think so—as if she were a crab shuttling side to side.

She's famous, almost. Everyone whispers about her, or at least the kids do. Brennan tries not to listen to their scary talk, but he knows what they do, sees the way they dare each other to peer in her dirty windows and write *witch* with trembling fingers in the dust. And why shouldn't they be afraid? She has that look about her: shiny rolling eyes that sometimes look right through you and pretend not to see, hair like tangled dirty cobwebs, and *things* (bits of leaves or torn newspaper and once a slender twig) caught and dangling. Today a happy face smiles out of a bright yellow T-shirt tucked into a long skirt, with white socks and dirty sneakers on her feet. When Brennan's shoes look like that, his mother throws them in the washing machine and out they come all white and glowing (one time he put them on when they were still wet to hear the *squish slosh* with every step he made). The crazy lady never washes her clothes, not that he can see. The laces of her left shoe have come undone and flop around her foot.

He looks to his right, and thick air presses against the side of his face, spreading heat and sending a rushing sound through his ears. He's right in front of her house, the wheels of his bicycle tainted by the touch of her walkway. No lights shine from her windows, but none ever do. She lives without power—no heat, no electricity, no water. At night sometimes there are candles, but mostly just dark shifting shadows. *What kind of woman lives like that?* he heard his mother say to his father once, using her angry voice. *Disgusting.*

The last time he saw the crazy lady, his mother had been here to protect him. She still walked him to school, though he had begun to notice that other kids, kids the same age, walked by themselves. And he had felt the first stirrings of shame to be seen with her then, his small hand cupped in hers. She walked with too much bounce, jolting his arm at every step. But now he wishes she were here.

"There's the crazy witch," he'd whispered to her that time, expecting to be comforted, not really afraid, not with her there, her body protecting his. "She eats little kids." He dug his small fingernails into her palm.

"She does? Who says so?"

"Everybody knows that, Mommy."

And his mother had laughed and told him not to be silly, making him feel better and protected and safe.

But now she's not here. His breath rises in his throat and catches; he swivels his head from side to side in a silent cry, an appeal. *Help me!* He looks across the street to the safety of his house, which used to be beige (*dirty*, his mother always said) but is now bright white with dark green shutters that match the tall hedge winding around the house. (This year, Brennan tasted the hedge, crunched bitter seeds between his teeth. His mom said he was lucky he didn't get sick.) *Mommy*. There aren't any kids around except Corrina Armstrong, who once fell off her bike and split her tongue open, blood and guts spreading out in a pool on the ground, but she's way over there at the end of the street so that he has to squint to really see her. She won't be any help.

He pretends to study the ants more closely as the crazy lady draws near, that strange smile lighting up her eyes. He wonders if she'll stop when she sees the ants or simply step on them on purpose, squishing and killing them all. Instead, she falls, one of her feet hooking into the wheel of his bike, the new bike that he has left in the middle of the sidewalk. Just like his dad always says: *Don't be so careless, Brennan!*

He's instantly cross with the crazy lady. Why can't she walk around it like a normal person? Why does she have to fall like that, her bag torn open and spilling out candy canes over the sidewalk? And why is her leg bent funny? Why does her face twist up like she's going to cry?

NONE OF THE CHILDREN on the street know where he is, though some pause, considering, before shaking their heads, snotty crust edging their nostrils. But then the little Armstrong girl points hesitantly toward Belle Dearing's house, with its broken windowpanes and dangling wires—a dismantled house of neglect.

"In there? He went inside her house?" Trina Allister wants to shriek, grab the girl by the shoulders *(why didn't you stop him?)*, and shake, shake. Didn't she know that something like this would happen? Didn't she warn David, seven years ago when they'd first moved into the house? Oh yes, she had. That crazy woman, ruining the good name of the neighbourhood, her yard a waste-land of rusted toys and a washer and dryer, soggy scraps of garbage and deflated tires. And the weeds—sickening, choking, the kind that spread from house to house on the slightest of breezes. Trash, she's nothing but trash. You'd think they could charge her with some kind of pollution offence, wouldn't you? There must be bylaws against this kind of thing. But the officer who'd shown up to listen to her complaints had rolled his eyes.

"She's entirely harmless," he said. "Thinks she's living in another world."

Looking toward Belle's house, Trina sees something and wonders why she missed it before: Brennan's bicycle, tossed on its side on her walkway. And scattered about, a few candy canes. Oh God, oh God—did she lure him to her house with candy?

"No, no," the little girl says, pointing to the silver trailer almost concealed by a weeping willow at the edge of the driveway. "In there."

He would have found it irresistible, the combination of candy and shiny metal. The probable scene replays slowly in her head (door closing behind Belle and Brennan, the tires of his bicycle still spinning as it lies on its side), but then the door of the trailer opens and Brennan streaks down the walkway (screaming, he's screaming) in his underpants.

Trina stands frozen, her vision narrowing in on that door and what lies behind it: a small table and cushioned bench upon which Belle Dearing, resident crazy lady, object of much derision and distaste, sits. And she imagines (though she can't possibly see this in such detail, not from this distance) that Belle is smiling.

Hermit Arrested in Kidnapping

A local woman was arrested yesterday on suspicion of assault and sexual interference in Ludlow's affluent Roseland neighbourhood. The six-year-old boy was missing for several hours before he returned home to his frantic mother. Noticing bruises and what appeared to be bite marks on his shoulder, his mother, who remains anonymous in order to protect the boy's identity, called police. The suspect, 51-year-old Belle Dearing, was taken into custody late last night. *The Lighthouse* recently published an article about Ms. Dearing, who lives without power in a dilapidated house described as "disgusting" by neighbours in the Roseland area. Better known as "the hermit," Ms. Dearing and her house are considered a disgrace by some, bringing shame on and lowering the property value of the exclusive neighbourhood.

ONE

I will admit that I was drunk when they arrested me. I knew they would come, eventually. I did remember the little boy, how he'd run from my trailer. And I knew his mother across the street, her pursed lips and the kind of blond hair I always wished for when I was a little girl.

Of course, I know what they think of me, all of those shiny people with designer clothing and desperate, blank lives. The kids throw rocks or run past my windows, shrieking. At Halloween there is always a burning bag of shit, eggs dripping rank yolk, or soaped-up windows. But the adults are almost worse, with their insincere pressed-lip smirks, their hands tightly holding on to their small children and jerking them away across the street. At summer barbecues, I imagine they all look sideways at my house and wonder how I could live the way I do, their voices pretending wonder but just barely containing their own version of nastiness. But I'm used to it.

I was never like most people anyway. When I was seven months' pregnant, I stripped down to my winter boots and woollen socks and posed nearly nude for the man who was not yet my lover. With quick broad strokes, he outlined me on paper, then leaned forward, squinting, to fill in the details. Once, he carved me out of a piece of wood, rounding my belly, my breasts, smoothing the rough edges with sandpaper before preserving me with a coat of shellac.

I saw him on the bus, years later, or at least I thought I did. He wore a brown corduroy jacket over a blue hooded sweatshirt, a green fisherman's cap pulled down to cover the tips of his ears. He sat in front of me, two seats up, the back of his head looking the way I remembered.

He reached up to pull the cord for his stop. As soon as his leg slid out from the seat, I knew it wasn't him. That's how well I thought I knew him, that I could recognize the shape of his leg, his knee, beneath a layer of winter clothing. He smiled at me as he passed; I wanted to wrap my fingers around his neck and squeeze, willing his face to change into another. I looked down instead, somewhat surprised to find that I could still feel disappointment.

When the police arrived, they knocked at my door, polite and smiling on the doorstep. But as soon as they came in, as soon as I told them my name, they grabbed my arms and wrenched them behind my back (though they deny this now). *I'm not a Barbie doll*, I told them. *You can't just pop off my arms and put them back on again*. But yes, I was drunk. I couldn't walk in a straight line, almost fell as they walked me down my front steps.

You have the right to retain and instruct a lawyer without delay. You also have the right to free and immediate legal advice through the provincial legal aid program.

In the police car, I leaned my head against the window and watched the trees flash past, counted the seconds between lamp-posts. I was tired all of a sudden, tired of life, of being me. Once upon a time it all used to be different, once upon a time I cared. I used to be funny, in a stupid way, I used to be *unique*, some would say.

Do you understand?
Do you wish to call a lawyer now?

The police station is in the east end of Ludlow, where all the poorer people live. Where I should live, I suppose. Here are people who look just like me: lost, ragged. They must all have their own stories, their own lineups of dead photographs, one, two, three. But you see, living in houses that lean so close to one another, no one cares to listen to them.

You need not say anything. You have nothing to hope from any promise or favour and nothing to fear from any threat, whether or not you say anything. Anything you do or say may be used as evidence.

I had no purse, nothing of my own that they could take away and keep from me, not even the gold wedding band I used to wear. But I was photographed, fingers rolled in ink and pressed against smooth paper by an expressionless woman with short sharp fingernails. They told me my charges, watching my face closely to see what I would say. I pretended to be confused, hazy with my memories. I knew my rights. They said: *You molested him*, only they said it with words like *sexual interference* and *assault*. They wanted me to break down, confess all in a torrent of jumbled words and tears.

As if I could. I've only ever cried a few times in my life. Not because I'm mean or cold-hearted, though some would say so. I think there's something wrong with me, with my anatomy; something blocks the corners of my eyes so the tears can't come out. People always wondered why I could never feel things the way normal people could. Or at least that's how it seemed.

I smiled at them instead.

The bars of my cell are moist with condensation. I try to stay centred in my bed in the middle of the night, try not to roll; the walls are damp, and other faces have been here before mine, other cheeks have been pressed against this same wall, leaving indelible marks.

It's hard to make a jail cell feel like home, especially when you're not used to so much empty floor, barren wall. Where are the maps, the photographs, the carvings? Where are all the *things* that make up a person's life, her memories? Without them, I'm afraid of falling into a deep pit. I have to use other clues to ground me in reality: the guard who brings me my meals on steel trays, the front pocket of her shirt bulging with packets of sugar for the instant coffee she makes down at the end of the hall; the feel of the scratchy wool prison blanket on my calves when my pants ride up during the night. And the same guard who walks by my cell every fifteen minutes to make sure I haven't killed myself yet.

I CARRY THEIR WEIGHT on my shoulders, I see that now. I should never have gone in the trailer again, where they all live, my ghosts. A time capsule of events meant to be buried for decades. Years ago, a young man knocked on the front door of my house and asked if I would consider selling. The Airstream's a collector's item nowadays; *vintage* is all the rage.

Tomas Phillips
Proprietor, Blast from the Past

Antiques and toys for all ages

I tucked his card in my pocket, watched him circle the trailer and run his hands over its dulled silver surface. My skin prickled.

He declared it miraculously preserved, his eyes aglow and glassy and hair sticking up in tufts.

"Amazing," he said. "I can't believe the body isn't in worse shape, sitting underneath this tree for so long. Weeping willows are bad, but it's like a cave under here."

He offered me cash on the spot. I studied the uneven streaks of colour on his cheeks, the nervous dancing movement he made with one leg twisted to the side, like a ballerina. I closed the door in his face, threw his business card in the junk drawer in the kitchen, hiding it beneath pencil stubs, rubber bands, spare batteries, and assorted papers. And then I stared for a long while at the trailer parked in the driveway, the branches of the weeping willow dropping over its aluminum sides like nature's own tears.

I NEED ALCOHOL. A long fire burns down my throat; my tongue sticks to the roof of my mouth. *Tap, tap, tap, tap.* Long fingernails on steel bars. I ignore the sound for as long as possible. Crazy Naked Lady in the cell across from me presses forward so hard the bars must leave indentations on her cheeks.

Lady might be too generous. Though there are four cells for women here (the rest reserved for the men who spill in on Fridays from bar fights and domestics, men in tank tops and hairy fat chests or T-shirts with yellow stains under the arms), she's my only neighbour, and lucky me.

She's ugly enough with all her clothes on; naked, her skin hangs in grey folds, jiggles and shimmies when she moves, pockets of indentation catching in the fluorescent lighting. They make an effort to keep her dressed, but as soon as their heavy footsteps disappear, she disrobes again. What's worse, maybe, is the way she looks at me when she does it, as if I'm *liking* the show. Once she's finished her striptease, she wraps both hands around the bars and just stares, sometimes bending forward and shaking her behind a little, sending her pendulous breasts swaying from side to side.

When I turn my back and lie down on my bunk, cold steel digging into my spine, my heels, the back of my head, she gives up and simply mutters to herself, fingertips yellow and singed from burned cigarettes, cheeks pitted and drawn. That first night, she bursts into startling snatches of song and begins to laugh; her pale arms thrust through the bars, hands bloodless, lifeless.

"They used spoons," she says. *Please, please, just one drink.* I cross my arms across my chest, curl up into a ball, and close my eyes, but she's relentless.

"Did you know that?" she asks. "They used spoons to dig themselves out of Alcatraz."

"I have a headache," I say. "Please stop." *Tap, tap, tap.* Shards of fluorescent light from the bulb in my cell creep under my eyelids.

"You and I are the same," she says.

Long minutes pass until I think she must have forgotten the conversation, must have been distracted by a random thought misfiring in the empty spaces of her mind.

"There's only one difference between you and me—you know what that is?"

I shift my weight, hip aching from the pressure of the hard steel bench, and pray for her to disappear, fall into a coma of sorts.

"I let it all go, everything," she says. "But you—you still pretend. You keep your clothes on. But we're the same, you and I. We both have nothing left."

She's wrong; I have let it all go. On the way into the police station, I saw myself reflected in the glass doors, noted my dirty, sweat-stained shirt, my hair loose and grey and knotted. *There goes a woman who's let herself go*, I thought.

They take Crazy Naked Lady to court in the morning, and I almost miss her. At least when she was here I could ignore her, she could stare at me, and we were somehow busy doing both of these things. Just before she leaves, she licks her lips and smiles at me, but her eyelids twitch in fear. One thing I have learned is that no matter how much craziness shows on the outside, something much smaller and younger and scared lies hidden inside.

Two

When I was little, I used to sit with my father by the ocean, just the two of us, my shoulder pressing against his elbow or my head resting on his chest. In my memories, it's always cold, and he always wears a thick grey sweater that scratches against my cheek. He would put his arm around me and pull me close, and we would just sit and think there on the boulders that steadied the rising cliffs, my lips slightly parted the way his were, my tongue tapping against my upper teeth. We'd watch the tide pull in clumps of seaweed and recede, leaving glistening pebbles oddly patterned with white stripes, as if carved by cavemen and tossed back into the sea.

He died when I was sixteen, and I lost my only ally, the only person who understood what I thought or meant without me saying a word. Not that I was all alone; I had Gardie and my mother, after all. But they were almost twins, both pale and fair and little, their heads bent over their knitting or books and other things I didn't much care for. I looked more like my father—big-boned, or *sturdy*, my mother would say, with dark tangled hair, only my blue eyes linking me to my mother and Gardie. Cat's eyes, we always declared, peering close into the mirror and blinking in unison.

It used to bother me, my looks, the way I was taller and bigger than every other girl and even some of the boys in my class. Every year, our school put together a bunch of themed plays at the end of the year, right before summer. Everyone came—mothers and fathers, grandparents and cousins. Getting a lead role was critical if you wanted to be a star, so we all held our breath waiting for the announcements. I remember one year—grade four, I think—we all acted out different fairy tales, and our class had *Little Red Riding Hood*. I wanted the lead desperately, knelt down by my bed every night to ask for God's help (in whispers, so my mother wouldn't hear). I wanted to wear a red cape, wanted to skip and prance and tremble before the wolf.

The morning Mrs. Drindle stood with her list at the front of the classroom, I slouched in my chair and tried to make myself as small as possible, hunching my shoulders forward and doing my best to look fragile, all for nothing. Sheila McNaughton— cute, dainty, blonde—landed the role. I waited and waited, as the choice parts were handed out. Grandmother, wolf, rabbits and birds.

"Belle Dearing," Mrs. Drindle read, then looked up and smiled at me. "You'll play the biggest, scariest tree in the forest."

A *tree*? I think I cried then, not in class, but later, on the way home, small Gardie trailing behind me, asking what was wrong. She must have said something to my father, because he came to find me that afternoon, put his arm around my shoulders and pulled me close.

"Trees are wonderful," he said. "They put down roots."

"I don't want to be a tree," I wailed.

My father tucked my chin into his palm, forced me to look at him. "Listen to me, Belle. You're strong, like me, and that's a good thing. Fragile people are too easily broken."

I did it to make him proud—I stood on that stage, my face poking out of an oval cut into painted brown cardboard, my arms stretched out and leaves stuck on the tips of my fingers. I imagined roots growing from the bottom of my feet and digging down, down, pushing through rock and mud until the whole of me spread out beneath all of Newfoundland.

I USED TO BELIEVE in God and miracles, in the power of prayer. I used to believe that good things happened to good people, and vice versa. We went to church every Sunday, sat in the pews like true believers, hymnals open on our laps, not fidgeting or kicking the seat in front of us or pinching each other on the legs and giggling behind cupped palms. We were good.

When my father died in February, the worst of months, I let my religion go. It slipped away in one fell swoop, in the middle of a hymn, swallowed whole by open, gaping mouths showing wads of gum tucked against the sides of cheeks and yellow and brown teeth stained by tobacco and tea and the hard life. Voices loud and full in the crowded church, off-key.

Through every age, eternal God,
Thou art our rest, our safe abode;
High was thy throne ere heav'n was made,
On earth thy humble footstool laid.

And just like that, God disappeared, at least to me. I stopped singing, my mouth closed in a steely grip, lips pressed tightly together, searching for that devout feeling that would bring God back, searching for faith in the light shining through the stained-glass windows. Instead, I saw the dirt behind the ears of the man who sat in front of me, the way the seams of his coat pulled and stretched, shiny, around his shoulders. My mother pinched my leg lightly, but I wouldn't budge or unhinge my jaw. Her eyes looked small in her pale face; dark circles stood out like shiners.

The singing stopped, an abrupt silence filling the space. Gardie stuck her elbow in my side and stood, stiff and erect (*like a soldier*, my mother directed), her eyes glowing blue. She wore her best dress, sent by Aunt Hannah from Eaton's in Toronto before she married Uncle Erik and moved to the States. Blue velvet, with white lace around the collar, hem, and sleeves, the dress was the most beautiful thing I'd ever laid eyes on. Aunt Hannah sent me a sensible skirt and cardigan; I was too old for velvet. Still, I wished, I wished. Just to have it, to touch it once in a while. No one wanted to stroke wool.

In the church, someone coughed, waiting, the echo hitting the walls and bouncing around the room. I looked over my shoulder. A man behind me shook his head, sad eyes filling with the heaviness of his grief. He was my father's friend, a miner. There were a lot of miners that day, scrubbed clean and come to pay their respects all the way from Conception Bay. If you looked closely, you could probably see the iron ore under their fingernails.

There was a photograph of all of the miners, old and slightly cracked, but one of my father's favourites. Nine men, all with work overalls and cloth caps instead of hard hats or electric lights. Too young, all of them, frozen faces stunned and staring at the camera, blackened noses and white blank eyes. Two men had tucked pipes in the corner of their mouths. And there was my father, just a boy, a shovel propped under his arm, the only smile in the photograph.

We lived in a fishing village in Placentia Bay, but my father— like his father before, like the McCargo boys and men, who lived a few houses up the road—shovelled iron ore almost two hundred kilometres away. Our house was nestled in a cove sheltered on two sides by ragged, powerful cliffs, as if dropped from the heavens. I never wondered why we lived so far from the mines; it's just the way it was. We lived in the same house my father grew up in. *Preserving our history,* he used to say. I think my mother felt differently, saw it in the way her neck stiffened when my father went off to work for weeks at a time, but she never said a word against him. He stayed in mess shacks overrun with lice and bedbugs, and came home on the weekends if the weather was fine. During the winter, he was sometimes gone for long stretches until the roads cleared for travel. He spent most of his life down there in those pits, in that damp darkness, and what kind of a life was that? He told us that he came out bathed in red dust so thick his eyelashes were heavy, throat dry, back aching.

There were accidents, deaths. One man blown to bits, right in front of my father's eyes; one man run over by a cart thirty or forty times, back and forth, before anyone found him. I saw my father cry, saw his shoulders sag as he sat and stared, eyes glazed. It's no wonder there were so many blank faces in the photographs.

Death, like an overflowing stream,
Sweeps us away; our life's a dream,
An empty tale, a morning flower,
Cut down and withered in an hour.

It didn't take him that long. Not an hour. The doctor said it was fast, but he might have said it so he didn't have to look much longer at my mother's face, red and horrified and stunned. He gave her a shot.

We had two brothers at one time, but they died. All of the men die in our family. Our older brother drowned two years before; he must have slipped from the rocks and went out with the sea. They found him the same day, his face buried in a tide pool. My father held him against his chest, wrapped him in a blanket, but he was long gone. My younger brother died when I was only two, of whooping cough or pneumonia or some such thing. In life, we were in death.

Teach us, O Lord, how frail is man;
And kindly lengthen out our span,
Till a wise care of piety
Fit us to die, and dwell with thee.

My mother and sister and I sat in the front pew so that (I suppose) we couldn't fail to see his coffin at the front. It was the smell of flowers that I couldn't stand, everyone sniffling and blowing noses around us until the sound nearly exploded in my ears. Since I no longer (suddenly) believed in God, there was no reason for me to stay. I stood, struggled to push my arms into my heavy coat, glad to disrupt the weepers, who stared with runny eyes and noses.

His shift was over. Over. As he walked back up from the pit into the open air, he removed his helmet to let the air cool the hair that stuck to his scalp in the heavy heat. Maybe he smiled. Part of the ceiling collapsed.

Outside, I leaned against the side of the church, then hunched over from the sudden pain in my belly, wondering what on earth we were all going to do now.

"You gonna throw up?"

"Huh?" I looked up. Worthy McCargo (eager, wide face, brown pools for eyes) peered down at me. For a while, Worthy and his dad used to drive up each week to the ferry in Portugal Cove with my father; like a lot of miners' sons, Worthy went to school until he turned fifteen, then started working the family trade. Now he was nineteen, a sad puppy with ears that folded over at the top. His father had died of a heart attack a few months earlier, and the weight of supporting his mother and younger brother fell hard on his shoulders.

"You look like you're gonna throw up, all hunched over like that."

I pushed myself up, hands on my hips. "Go away," I said, mean.

"I'm sorry about your dad," he said. His face spasmed, lips pulling up, then down.

"Stick your sorry up your arse," I said, then felt bad for the way his face looked after I said it. "I don't mean it." I took a deep breath and felt Worthy curve his hand around mine, his skin warm.

"Come on," he said. I followed blindly, not sure I cared where we were going, concentrating on the effort it took to place one foot in front of the other. We walked across the road, down past the graveyard marked by a rickety wooden fence that overlooked the ocean, Worthy's arm strong and steady around my shoulders when I stumbled. And there was a place there, a cave of sorts, where we could sit sheltered by rocks from the wind, watching the water crash against the shore in angry white sprays. I crouched on my heels and wrapped my arms around my knees, pulling down my heavy coat and new skirt from Toronto. I could feel him, my father, there in the wind that blew down my neck and crept in to find the strip of bare skin between my boots and coat, there in the churning, roiling sea and the taste of salt in my mouth. Worthy didn't say anything but let me cry, patting my back, his eyes dark and veiled.

THE FLOORBOARDS in our house in Newfoundland were old and cracked from too many years of cold and rain. They creaked uneasily under our feet. Long ago, my mother knitted slippers for us, bright blue mine were. I hated that colour—too bright, too happy and sunshiny—but my father's were thick and grey. I slipped them onto my feet when we heard the news and didn't take them off for three days. People came and went, and I just pressed my forehead against the window, those grey slippers tap tapping on the creaky floorboards in front of me.

"We could move," my mother said. "Aunt Hannah and Uncle Erik said we could come anytime. They'd put us up." I barely remembered my aunt. I knew she wore a lot of wool scarves around her neck and long, flowing skirts like a prairie woman, and she smelled like fresh-cut lemons.

"No."

"You'd like to move there, I think. The States. Lots of things to do for you. Not like here. I could maybe get a job—"

"You can get a job here," I said, my voice sharper than I meant. I wanted to pull back in, duck down, but I wasn't a child anymore. Things had changed. I wanted to stay in this house I knew so well, where each room had a history.

"Sure, there's no jobs here, you know."

"Then you can ask the government, after all he did, breaking his back like that."

She didn't say, *It was his head that broke.*

We didn't have much choice. My mother's parents no longer spoke to her and lived far, far away in New Brunswick. My grandfather—Father's father—died before I even knew him, around the time that my mother and father married. My grandmother lived with us for a long time, but there was something wrong with her brain, so that she recognized us hardly at all and muttered to herself as she sat staring out the window. Sometimes at night I'd hear her cry out in her sleep, and the bedsprings next door in my mother and father's room would creak, creak as they shifted. When I thought of Grandma now, I couldn't remember her face but could smell the old mustiness of her room, see the skin hanging from her wrists when she just stopped eating, no matter what any of us did. She wasn't even that old when she died, my mother told us, but she'd just given up on life. *Imagine that*, Gardie marvelled later, when we were alone and sure that they wouldn't hear us. *Imagine just giving up like that.*

When my father died, we were alone, no one to help out for long, not enough to keep us going for the years that we would need. And something was happening in our cove, whispers about people in Bonavista Bay who'd been paid by the government to leave their villages.

You watch, my father had said. *It'll happen here too. Come back in twenty years, and nothing will be left of this place.* Turns out he was right, but we weren't around to see it happen. We moved into the farmhouse in Vermont in April of 1966.

THREE

This I know: your heart doesn't break all at once, like a childhood valentine torn in two, ripped down the middle. Instead, imagine your heart frozen and hurled to the ground so that it shatters and chips in tiny fragments. That, my friends, is a broken heart.

After my father died, my mother stopped hugging us, as if it was too painful, our skin too much a memory of what she was missing. But she and I were never close, and I know why: I was too different—sloppy, boyish, opinionated. I never cared what people thought, always did whatever I wanted.

Sometimes I wished I were more like my mother. It never mattered what she was doing at the time; even bent over the tub washing Gardie's slippery, fat limbs, the sleeves of her dress rolled up to her elbows, strands of her hair curling in the steam from the bath, even then she seemed perfect.

The deaths of the men in her family carved the beauty from my mother's face, leaving only tired lines etched deep into skin framed by strands of grey hair. I suppose she was still beautiful to others on the outside, those who didn't have the memory of *before* to compare with *after*, but I could see it, especially if I put her side by side in my mind with my aunt, four years younger at thirty-three and newly married. But that wouldn't be a fair

19

comparison. My mother had already lived through a hard life; my aunt was just beginning.

One thing everyone noticed about my mother was the way she dressed, for she never wore slacks, ever. She thought they were unfeminine. She always wore dresses or skirts with stockings, even in the summer. I'd seen my mother's bare legs just once, when we went on holiday with my father in Nova Scotia. Only then had she consented to forgo the stockings, and as she settled herself onto a blanket we'd spread out on the beach, her sun umbrella casting a shade over all exposed skin, I'd caught my father looking at those bare legs with an inscrutable expression.

I was nothing like her, but she never said a word. I never wore skirts or dresses, never wore stockings, but slopped around in the same old overalls or the dungarees I'd stolen from my older brother and had worn since he died, cuffs rolled up five inches to display my ankles, a pair of beat-up sneakers on my feet. What did I care? In Newfoundland, it didn't seem to matter much; in small-town Vermont, it did. My mother said it would take some time to make friends in the States. To my aunt, she said that sixteen was a difficult age, especially for a girl like me. By that I suppose she meant someone different, someone who stuck out, someone who didn't try in any way to become like all the others.

They put me in grade ten when we moved to Lily. When the teachers found out how little I knew, they held a mini-conference and invited my mother. She showed up in her perfectly pressed skirt and stockings, her leather shoes carefully buffed, listening as they tiptoed around the word *dumb* and suggested that I be put back a grade the following year. *No point in moving her now*, they said to my mother. *School's out for the summer in a month.*

My mother looked at me, slumped in my chair, pretending to not care, the tips of my ears red from unstoppable embarrassment. She looked back at the teachers, all men sitting up straight with their hands folded in their laps and condescending, patient smiles pulling at their plastic faces. If there was one thing my mother hated, it was condescension.

"No," she said firmly, lips pursed. I wanted to cheer. She told me later that it was hard enough to be new; better not to be new *and* stupid.

On the ride back to the farm, she lectured me the entire way, saying that I'd have to study this summer, to get my grades up, to really impress those men at the school who thought I wouldn't amount to anything. Mostly I didn't say anything back, partly because she wouldn't let me even edge one tiny word into the conversation, but also partly because I was still amazed that she was able to drive my uncle's pickup truck.

"We'll blow their socks off," she said, smacking the steering wheel with her palm and jerkily shifting into third. After listening to her for almost twenty minutes, I caught her excitement, her enthusiasm. Not for knowledge itself, you realize, but for the sole purpose of proving men wrong.

I HATED THE FARM, which Uncle Erik inherited when his parents died. I hated it for what it *wasn't*, rather than for what it *was*. Aunt Hannah led us outside and talked and talked—about the beauty of the rolling green land in the summer, the open blue sky, and the colours of the leaves in the fall—her arm cutting through the air in broad strokes. It was like a paint-by-number painting, she'd said, with twenty shades of red and orange and gold. That was my aunt, a hippie of sorts in long flowing skirts, a scarf always wrapped around her neck (wool in the winter, cotton or silk in the summer), and strands of beads entwined around her left wrist and halfway up her arm. She wore her hair long and parted in the middle; she also smoked my uncle's pipe.

I thought she was dashing and large and so much brighter than my tired, washed-out mother.

But in Lily at the end of April, only patches of brown showed beneath the snow, and bare tree branches arched into a grey sky that seemed too big. There were no neighbours, no little outcroppings of houses, and no sea. There was only a creek that wound its way through acres and acres of bare land, and a big lake to the west. Back home, we were rooted by salty air and rocks jutting out over the ocean; in Lily, we were lost, dropped from the sky to land in the middle of nowhere.

My aunt and uncle tried their best to help us adjust. Up a narrow flight of wooden stairs, my room was lavender and white, with a dark dresser and night table. Gardie's was lighter and sunnier, with dusty rose walls and pine furniture. My mother slept down the hall in a four-poster bed that must have been my aunt's before we arrived, so that we could all sleep on the same floor, the Dearing family together. My aunt and uncle moved into the bedroom downstairs, opposite the formal living room with its plastic-covered chairs and sofa, into the least comfortable room (drafty, small) in the house. No one ever sat in the living room unless visitors came by for tea or coffee. Instead, we crowded into the warmer kitchen, sat at the table or on the bench against the wall facing the mud room, where our coats and hats and boots jumbled together in heaps. Just like home, my mother would say.

But I never felt lonely back home in Newfoundland. I had my father, when he was home, and there were always people sitting around in our kitchen, always doors opening and closing and chatter filling up the rooms. When my father was working, everyone took the time to drop in, for often there wasn't much else to do. And they'd talk, or Gardie would find bits of clothing and scarves, oversized boots, and other kids would join in with their own costumes, a miniature play springing to life right there in our kitchen. In Lily, it was different. No one came to visit my aunt and uncle—that's not the way things were done here. There were only the five of us, always two (Aunt Hannah and Uncle Erik) plus two (Gardie and my mother) plus one (me).

Here was nothing recognizable, and I missed my father. His absence ached, large and empty, in my heart. I missed his sly jokes or the way he would place his warm hand on my shoulder and squeeze when he was happy, the scratch of his cheeks when he didn't shave, the thick sweaters he wore that caught and held his scent. I missed the constant rush of waves against rocks, the way the fog rolled in thick during a storm and the wind took the breath straight from my mouth. I belonged there, not here in this farmhouse where the rooms were large and drafty, with wide wooden floors and slanted walls. There were too many doors, cupboards, and corners. My skin felt too big, too loose in these rooms. I'd been displaced.

LILY WAS TOO SMALL for its own high school; we all bused in to Freeman, a twenty-minute ride smelling of dirty feet and bubble gum. Although some of the girls had boyfriends with cars, the parents in Lily were tight-lipped and conservative. Too many bodies pressed in too tightly, the radio blaring, those in the back seat leaning over to talk to those in the front, skirts riding up, bare knees pressing against other legs. No, too dangerous, those cars. I didn't mind; with all of us piling on and off the bus, moving together as a group into the school, I wore a suit of armour, protective gear.

It was hard to be me in a small town like Lily. We all stood out that first summer, mostly because we were new and from some strange faraway province with slanted ways of saying ordinary words so that sometimes you could barely understand them. But of our family, I stood out the most. All the other girls at school were small and dainty, with blond hair carefully curled, angora sweaters, and thin gold bracelets around their wrists. They carried their books in front of their chests and spoke to boys in tones that implied boredom and maturity. Even the farm girls wore dresses with bows at the collars and hair pulled back into a braid or high ponytail.

Gardie fit in easily, at least on the surface. She'd always liked to dress up in other clothes, costumes that didn't fit, and here was no different. She brushed her long hair in front of the mirror in my mother's room every night, stroke after stroke, counting to one hundred. And then she'd place the brush—antique silver with fancy scrolls—carefully on the vanity and study herself. Lips puffed out in a pout, head tilted first to this side, then to the other.

"Which side looks better?" she'd ask me.

"What?" Sometimes I just couldn't understand her, that one. And she'd sigh, all dramatic, and roll her eyes.

"Everyone has a good side, don't you know that? I'm just trying to find out which side is my best. For all the photographs when I'm a rich and famous movie star."

"You don't have a good side, Gardie."

"At least I make an effort, Belle." Her blue eyes stared hard, looking me up and down in a way I hadn't seen back home.

She took her place with the other girls, her blond hair pulled back, books held high against her imaginary bosom, face secretly flushed with hints of my mother's makeup. And then there was me, a giant among ants, hair with multi-shades of red and blond and brown that could never be tamed, no matter how much it was brushed or braided or wet down. I didn't wear skirts or fuzzy sweaters (too itchy), slung my books over my shoulder in an old leather satchel my father used to carry the Bibles he sold when he tried to escape the mines, wore dungarees and overalls that didn't nearly fit me properly. But most of all, my mother would say, I had a bad attitude. *You'll never make friends if you don't make an effort,* she said, shaking her head (and Gardie, standing in the background, nodded in agreement). *It's good to be independent and not care what people think of you, but you have a chip on your shoulder that does you no good at all.* I didn't have any sort of chip; I simply never thought of girls as any use. What did I care about movie stars or boys or the proper way to stick out your chest so that men noticed?

But even popular girls have their moments, I suppose. In those first few weeks in Lily, I heard Gardie crying late at night. I knew she stuffed her face in her pillow to muffle the sound, but the walls between our rooms were flimsy. Sometimes I heard my mother's door open, the sound of her bare feet padding down to Gardie's room. A fresh burst of tears, the *shhh shhh* as I imagined my mother rocking her back and forth, and then silence.

I FOUND THE MAPS at the back of Dillard's Dried Goods and Sundries, the store closest to my aunt's farm and a fixture in the small town. Everyone came to Dillard's, not just to shop but also to gossip on the wide front porch or sit back in the wooden chairs George Dillard had set up on the stony grass spreading patch-like around the store. Many of the people who hung about were old, with long lines criss-crossing their faces and folds of skin under their chins, people who had been born and would die in Lily without ever stepping foot anywhere else.

Dillard's carried a bit of everything: food, clothes, rolls of twine, work gloves, boots, and dusty figurines of bunnies and women in old-fashioned dresses. The maps were stacked on shelves near the back of the store; they were the kind you unfolded pleat by pleat and could never quite fold back the proper way. Or at least I couldn't. You could tell that no one had touched them in a long time, save the odd lost tourist on his way through the town, heading somewhere else, somewhere not here.

Though I didn't yet know it, those maps would give me a home, ground me with a sense of the familiar, no matter where I ended up. The first time we visited the store, while everyone was busy at the front, I grabbed one of the maps, smearing dusty fingerprints across the others, and stuffed it down the front of my pants, where its corners dug into my thighs and made swooshing noises in time with every footstep.

I walked up and down the aisles casually, pretending I had nothing but my privates in my underpants, touching the worthless knick-knacks on the shelves. I made a game of moving things, trying to place them back in exactly the same spot, careful not to breathe too close for fear of erasing the outlined place mark of each object.

"Belle!" My mother waited impatiently by the cash register, her purchases bundled in brown paper bags, Gardie standing beside her, practising her wide smile on Mr. Dillard. Just to be ornery—because I am, my mother always said—I scowled and shuffled forward, forgetting for a moment the map in my pants.

My mother grabbed my arm hard. "What's this?" she asked, thrusting her hand beneath my waistband, slapping the map down on the counter. Four heads bent simultaneously. I hadn't taken the time to examine it before shoving it down below.

"Hmm," Mr. Dillard said. "Mongolia." I could tell by his strangled throat sound that he was trying not to laugh. People were always laughing at me, and I hated it. Made me uncomfortable and maybe not so smart as I thought I was. My mother wasn't laughing, just looked at me, her eyebrows pulled forward so hard that creases showed between her eyes.

I shrugged, like I had a darn good reason for wanting that particular map, that it was worthy of *stealing*, which definitely would have been a sin if I still believed in God. But I didn't even know where Mongolia was, though I sort of knew it wasn't in Canada or even here in the good old U.S. of A. There was once a kid at school we used to call a mongoloid, and I half wondered if it was the same thing. I meant to say something smart, like that I had a school research project. Instead, my head dropped down, my voice shrinking until only the tiniest speck of myself remained.

"I like maps," I lied, feeling stupid again.

"Stealing is wrong," Gardie said, crossing her arms across her chest and lifting her chin in motherly disapproval (her eyes shifting once, twice, to make sure that my mother and George Dillard noticed her wisdom and maturity). I rolled my eyes and pinched her, quiet and swift. She was the worst, most annoying thirteen-year-old I'd ever known.

Everyone got really quiet as they pondered what to do with the likes of me. I knew my mother would be embarrassed, being new in town and Canadian to boot. The Americans already thought we were dumber, somehow, and now I'd gone and proved them right.

Mr. Dillard studied me with soft brown eyes. "Don't worry about that old map," he said. "Not many people care much about Mongolia around here. You might as well take it." And maybe it was the kindness in his smile, or his quick grasp of this moment's importance—here with me on one side, my mother and Gardie on the other—that made my eyes burn and my throat swell so that I couldn't say anything, could only look away and hope that he saw my gratitude.

"We couldn't let you do that," my mother said, her face flushed. She tugged at her earlobe, something she always did when she felt awkward and unsure, and smoothed wisps of hair from her face.

Mr. Dillard stared at her earlobe, curving above the delicate line of her jaw. He let his gaze drop down to her left hand, which still bore its gold wedding band, then, inexplicably, blushed. "How old are you, Belle?" he asked.

"She's sixteen," my mother said, as if I hadn't heard and couldn't answer for myself. "Be seventeen in June."

Mr. Dillard nodded slowly. "Tell you what," he said. "I've been thinking of hiring myself a helper around here. How about you come to work for me a couple afternoons after school. You can have all the maps you want. What do you say?"

I wanted to say no but knew I couldn't, not there with my mother's lips set in a firm line, Mr. Dillard's offer an easy way out of the trouble I'd caused. But a job in Lily meant *permanence*, and I still wanted to believe that this town was just a simple stop along the way to something larger, better.

Four

In court I sit bleary-eyed, my hands shaking so much I clench my fists and hide them under the table. Words wrapped in cotton candy bounce off me, muffled and incoherent. I tell them all that I have no money—not exactly the truth, not at all, since I worked in the factory for over twenty years and almost never spent a dime. It's all there, but I don't feel like wasting it on lawyers. I'd rather represent myself, to tell the truth, but no one seems pleased to hear this. They set my bail at two thousand dollars and advise me to find a lawyer. I say I'll think about it. And now I have a new court date in a few weeks to look forward to.

Off I go to the Ludlow Remand Centre, a red-bricked, stately old building that looks more like an old school or factory than a jail. I have no voice here. I'm only one of many—a nutcase, crack job, a woman with stringy hair and no past of interest, one blank face in a blue uniform among hundreds of others.

I never realized how much time there is in a single day, especially when you're sober. It's been twenty-four hours since I last had a drink, and let me tell you, I can feel it now. The worst is a headache that pulsates and pounds and colours my vision red and grey-blue. I steady shaking hands by wrapping them around the cool bars of the cell, but they slip slowly down, leaving slick trails of sweat. *I can't, I can't, I can't.* I curl on my cot, bring my knees up to my chest, don't answer the guard who calls out to me then bangs on the bars to get my attention. *It's coming. Oh, God, it's coming.*

THAT FIRST SUMMER in Lily, I carved out a space where I could breathe a little easier. Uncle Erik didn't bat an eyelash when I told him my plans for my new cottage—an old chicken coop over eight feet high and twelve feet wide. Truth was, I knew I'd found a special place and wanted to claim it for my own before Gardie had the same idea. My mother always said I had a good eye for potential. I cleaned out the coop so that it practically shone, scraping every last remnant of chicken from the wooden floorboards and walls. My aunt gave me an old pillowcase and matching sheet, which I stuffed with straw and made up into a kind of daybed on one of the planks that lined the walls. The other planks I used as shelves to store candle stubs and interesting things I found around the farm: a stone shaped like a bird, a broken piece of pottery (which I was sure came from caveman days), and a strip of rubber I imagined I could make into shoes, if only I knew how.

Uncle Erik helped me paint the cottage the perfect shade of red with white trim. For a while he didn't say much, just sweated and stroked his brush over the planks, eyes squinting under the July sun that weekend. I was never sure what exactly he *did* every day; my mother sometimes whispered unkind things about him when Aunt Hannah wasn't around. I knew he gambled with cards and often lost a lot of money. I also knew that he sometimes drank too much and knocked over tables returning home late at night smelling of cigars and whisky. But mostly he was good and nice to all of us and worked in a lumberyard doing something with wood. And he had to be a nice man, taking in a family of strangers so soon after marrying my aunt.

We always wondered if Aunt Hannah would ever marry. She left their small town in New Brunswick for teachers' college in Toronto a few years after my mother married my father (*as soon as I could get out of that house*, she would tell us). My mother believed then that Aunt Hannah left to not only get away from the family but also to get her M.R.S. (*her missus*, I explained patiently to Gardie, who stomped away screaming that she knew already, I didn't have to keep going over everything when everybody knew that Belle was the dummy in the family). But year after year passed and still Aunt Hannah lived alone in a row house with her skirts and scarves, climbing ever higher to old maid status.

Two years ago, just like that, Aunt Hannah sent the telegram saying that she'd married and was moving to a place called Vermont in the States. My mother cried—not because she was sad for Aunt Hannah, she said, but because she hadn't the money to go visit her and had missed her only sister's wedding. I could tell my father felt bad about it, as if he were to blame for not making enough money; he walked around for days not meeting my mother in the eye.

We all thought maybe my aunt was *in a family way*, but here she was, stomach still flat, with Uncle Erik. I studied him as we painted, trying to guess what it was that made my aunt drop everything and marry him. He wasn't ugly; he had nice green eyes and clean ears and never picked his nose in front of us, like some boys I knew back home (not to name anyone or point fingers, Dicky Brummley, but you know who you are). But for the years she was married before I met him, I always pictured him as a kind of bright hero, rescuing my aunt from old maidness and gossip—wearing maybe a white suit and dashing about gallantly, like Errol Flynn—when in fact he was just an ordinary man, like my father. It was somehow disappointing.

I didn't know much about love back then, didn't know that sometimes the ups came with the downs or that sometimes you married and then wondered why you had. While we were waiting for our second coat of paint to dry, I asked him why he married my aunt and if he was in love. I was always asking things that embarrassed my mother; my mouth just couldn't stay shut when I wanted to know something. Because Uncle Erik was slow and quiet, I liked to talk to him. He never ignored me, but didn't talk much himself, just grunted every once in a while to show he was listening. But this time he looked at me right away, a shy smile creeping across his face.

"I needed a wife," he said. One of his good friends had married a Canadian, a woman from Saskatchewan. Since he liked the look of her, with her strong bosom and child-bearing hips, he assumed all Canadians would be from the same hearty stock. He'd never been in love before, had grown up in Lily with the same people all his life, watching as they married, divorced, or died, one by one, until there was no one left for him.

"I always figured I had lots of time," he told me, shrugging his shoulders in a way that meant he'd just never thought much about having a wife or family.

He put an ad in newspapers in Montreal and Toronto, figuring that if he got no response, he'd move west across the country (he ignored the east coast completely).

Eligible bachelor, 32, with farm in Vermont seeks wife of similar age. Must believe in true love. Send letter plus photograph.

His friend, the one with the Canadian wife, had persuaded him to add the line about true love. On his own, Uncle Erik would never have thought of it. *You'll get good women,* the friend had said.

Uncle Erik received three letters, all from Toronto, all from women who had moved there from somewhere else, somewhere small, barely dots on maps. Two of the letters were mostly the same: *I am responding to your ad in the Toronto Star. I am a single woman living on my own in Toronto, aged 35. I love animals, children, and taking long solitary walks. I don't mind hard work.* The enclosed photographs were similarly dour and sad, black-and-white head shots of women attempting to smile and look young.

In her letter, my aunt admitted that she was completely unsuited to farm work, had horse allergies, but was nonetheless convinced that she was meant to see his ad. *I believe that when two people are committed to a life together, that's true love,* she wrote. I'm not sure that the letter alone could have swayed Uncle Erik, but the photograph she sent—a nude—did.

"It was what you call an artistic picture," Uncle Erik said, his face pink and angled slightly away from mine. With the shadows and careful lighting, you couldn't see much, but if you looked closely, maybe you imagined the outline of a nipple, just one. (He never told me this, would never be able to say the word *nipple* in front of anyone, never mind a teenage girl like me. Later, Aunt Hannah showed me the photograph, proving that she'd been the kind of woman who took risks and moved life forward instead of waiting for it to happen.)

Uncle Erik wasted no time in visiting Aunt Hannah in Toronto, spurred on by the thought of that glimpse of skin. He liked her version of true love; moreover, he thought that any woman daring enough to send that photograph would at the very least be interesting.

"Belle," he said, "when we met, I just knew she was the one for me. And I think she felt the same way."

After he told the story, I did notice certain things when they were together: the way his hand would reach down and just brush hers, the way her eyes grew rounder when she looked up at him, the corners of her mouth upturned slightly. It made being at the farm more bearable, somehow, this proof of love, as if their happiness could spread like germs, as if there was hope for me yet.

Gardie always wanted what she couldn't have, especially if what she wanted was mine to begin with. I saw from the shine in Gardie's eyes that she liked my cottage and had plans of her own. I had to act fast.

"It's mine," I told her. "You can't come in here whenever you like. It's all mine." I knew my mother would disapprove, and she did.

"Now, sure, you can share, can't you?" she said, frowning. Gardie preened at me in that ha-ha way she had. As in, *Ha-ha, I knew you would have to share.* And *Ha-ha, I can have everything you have.*

"But it's mine," I said. "I found it, and I cleaned it out."

When my mother just shook her head at me, I turned and pressed my face against the wooden wall, my arms stretched out as if to hug the little house to myself. The loneliness of the last few months swelled around me until I couldn't stand it anymore.

"I know you think I'm selfish and a mean person," I said, my eyes closed, face still pressed against the wall so that my words came out squashed sideways. "But I just wanted a little place to myself for a bit. A teenager needs a private place so as not to go crazy."

After a long silence, my mother made one of those choking throat sounds and told Gardie that *Belle is right, she needs her own place,* and *Hasn't it been hard on her, moving away from home and no friends of her own here yet?* And for once, it didn't matter how much Gardie pouted and screamed and shouted that it wasn't fair. I think I even heard the slap of my mother's hand against her arm. The cottage was mine.

EVERY COUPLE OF WEEKS, Worthy McCargo sent me a letter from home. Everyone thought it was cute the way his letters arrived on schedule, my name (*Miss Belle Dearing*) painstakingly printed in wobbly letters, *U.S.A.* written large at the bottom, as if it would never make its way out of Newfoundland otherwise.

"You have a boyfriend," Gardie said. She was always the one who brought me the letters, holding them aloft in her hands like a gift. "Read it," she'd urge. "Read it!"

Worthy's letters all began the same. *Dear Belle, hope you are well (I'm a poet and I know it)*, they'd say. He signed each one differently: *yours truly, yours in friendship, cordially yours, your friend*, and, sometimes, *your true friend*. The lines in between varied, depending on his mood. At the beginning of summer, his letters began to get longer and longer. His mother wasn't well, he wrote. They were talking about closing the mines for good, and he and his younger brother, Oscar, were worried. *Everyone always asks how you and your family are doing, Belle. I told them that you wrote to tell me all about your life.*

In truth, I'd written only once, asking him to stop writing. He was making me nervous. *I'm an American now*, I wrote, though it hurt my soul to write such words. *And as such, can no longer correspond with you.* I'd thrown out that letter instead of sending it, picturing his puppy-dog disappointment. I wrote instead that we were all well, that America was the same as Canada, and that I didn't mind it as much as I thought I would.

WORKING AT DILLARD'S STORE that first summer in Lily, I finally earned the attention and respect of the town girls by giving them free bottles of soda. Teenage girls in Lily didn't work, not back then in 1966, but I liked my job arranging merchandise and ringing up purchases; it gave me power. The other girls came into the store to stare at me with wonder and (I liked to believe) a certain amount of jealousy.

"Oh, Belle, it's so hot, we're absolutely *dying* with heat. But we don't have a *cent* on us," they'd say, all the while eyeing the icebox where we kept the sodas.

"Please, just this once, loan us a soda? We'll pay you back, swear."

I always said no to them at first (*Mr. Dillard doesn't allow me to hand out free sodas*), feeling good that I had at least stuck to my morals, something my mother always said was more important than anything else. *It may feel good at first to do something bad,* she'd said, *but it always feels bad to compromise your morals in the end.* I think she was talking about sex, though she'd never come right out and say so, but I believed this could also be applied to stealing sodas for your friends.

In the end, it wasn't such a tough decision; after I stole for them, they let me into their group. I think they put up with me *because* I was different, not in spite of it. They'd never met a Canadian before, even though Vermont was on the border, and they'd certainly never heard of Newfoundland. They wanted to know if everyone had my accent and asked me if I slept in igloos. I told them all kinds of lies, about how we had dogsleds instead of cars, ate beavers for dinner, and wore wolves on our feet for boots. They began taking me to their parties as a conversation piece.

By the time school started again in September, it was now okay for me to be strange and tall, to wear overalls and sneakers, to have a funny accent and unruly, unfashionable hair. I was one of them now.

And school was more fun with friends. In class we made lists of what we wanted in our future husband. Mine said:

Devastatingly handsome
Tall
Dark hair with curls at the neck
Good sense of humour
Rich
Nice hands

I looked at the other girls' lists and realized that I hadn't put down any of their qualities (kind, generous, good with children and women), as if I didn't care what lay below the surface. I added them quickly to the bottom so that I wouldn't seem so shallow.

I never brought these girls back home to the farm. Around them, I was different: I became funny on purpose, exaggerating my accent and pretending to be dumb but wise. And now that I had friends, I felt raised in the eyes of my family, as if I had suddenly earned my place, become important. I pretended to care about what the girls said, began to use the collective *we* when I had an opinion. It's too hard to be an individual in a small town like Lily. Better to be one of a crowd, even if you stuck out oddly, like me. I convinced myself that this new version of me was better than the old.

But with the arrival of each new letter from Worthy in Newfoundland reminding me of the way things used to be, I'd steal another map from Dillard's and tuck it out of sight in the chest of drawers in my room. I spent hours just lying on my daybed in the cottage dreaming of faraway places and cursing myself for pretending I was something I wasn't, crushed by an overwhelming sense of homesickness.

I kept a jar of my father's ashes hidden under my bed. He was going to go beneath my long underwear with my maps, but I didn't think it was fitting, somehow. And they weren't really his ashes; he was buried in the cove in Newfoundland, his feet facing the ocean. But a few weeks after his funeral, when it looked like we had no choice but to move in with Aunt Hannah and Uncle Erik, Worthy showed up at the house, a beautiful old-fashioned glass jar, the kind with a heavy stopper, cradled like a child in the crook of his arm.

"I found it around the mine," he said. "And I thought you'd like it." As he held it out, I looked at his solid fingers wrapped around the glass, pictured him pulling it free from the earth and scrubbing it clean, all for me. My face felt too hot as I took it, the muscles of my throat burning and swelling. We walked to our special place where I'd cried, and sat down, spreading out newspaper Worthy carried in his back pocket, the sharp edges of jutting rock digging into our backs and newsprint smearing across our bottoms.

"What should I use it for?" I wondered out loud, holding up the glass so that the sun poured through. And Worthy had the best idea I'd ever heard.

"You should take some Newfoundland with you," he said. "That way you can think of it whenever you want." He scrubbed the rocky ground beside his leg, lifting up a handful of dirt and emptying it gently into the bottle.

I had my own idea a few days later when I said goodbye to my father. The ground around his gravesite, freshly dug and only partly frozen, crumbled and slid down the neck of the bottle easily. When I inserted the stopper, I imagined my father's soul mixing with the earth, sky, and sea. He would be happy with that.

In my cottage, I placed my glass bottle on a plank, turning it this way and that way until it was just right, sunlight through the little window landing on the stopper and sliding down its neck so that it glowed, and I imagined my father's soul speaking to me. I opened up the map of Mongolia and tacked it onto the wall next to my daybed, wedged myself in, and ran my fingers over the lines and dots, wishing hard that something would happen to take me away from this place so far from home.

FIVE

You have a lot of time to think behind bars. About your life, those wrong turns that seemed so right at the time, about your body's ability to just shut down, as if someone had flicked a light switch so your bulb wouldn't burn out so quickly. No one is ever happy, not really. There's always something going on, some darkness kept hidden behind the eyes. Riding on the bus to and from work every day, I'd look down into each car as it passed, wondering with vague boredom what worries the people inside carried, what lives they lived. There, the child with the bowl-cut hair and brown eyes rounded as she peers out of her window: what is she afraid of when she closes her eyes? Or that man, hunched over his steering wheel, the cuffs of his shirt showing wrinkled and stained: is he having problems with his wife; is his brother speaking to him?

I wandered around my neighbourhood late at night sometimes. I may have been drunk; probably I was. On summer nights, when you could hear the constant hum of electricity through the wires, when the moon lit up strange, idle objects (a torn piece of paper against the curb, a poster about a lost cat on a telephone pole), I almost felt that I could wrap my arms around the heavy air, bundle it up, and take it home with me, full of memories and halted pockets of time.

ON THE ONE-YEAR ANNIVERSARY of my father's death in February, my mother couldn't get out of bed in the morning. Aunt Hannah kept Gardie and me away from her room when we tried to bring her a tray with tea and toast.

"It's not food she needs," Aunt Hannah said. "It's your dad." My chest burning, I fled to my cottage, shut the door, and tried not to cry, my breath coming fast and pluming outward in great puffs from the cold. I had forgotten.

A small scrape at the door, and there was Gardie, biting her lip until I saw blood on her teeth, blinking her eyes, the tips of her eyelashes wet. We sat on the planks not talking, feeling the draft under the door and around the window creep under the hems of our flannel nightgowns. By the time my mother came to find us, our lips were blue, our fingers icy and numb.

"You missed the bus," she said dully. Her eyes, red-rimmed, looked too small, too dark against her pale skin. I remembered the funeral, the circles under her eyes then, and all our pretences (*get up and dressed smile and eat and move your mouth to say words you don't mean don't think or remember or make mention of what you have lost*) hit me with such force I couldn't breathe. And then she touched us—light hands on our shoulders, her face pulling down, the skin folding in grief—and we followed her into the farmhouse, let her tuck quilts around our legs and hand us cups of hot tea. I let the steam rise up, put my head down so that the warmth seeped into my skin.

Later in the afternoon, Gardie and I put on our coats and hats and mittens and wound scarves around our necks before cutting a diagonal path through the acres of farm toward the woods that enclosed our little space of land in a tight box. The sky that day seemed bigger than ever, threatening to swallow us whole, our faces turned upward, arms outstretched. I liked to think of my father, caught captive just above the clouds, his elbows resting in white wisps of cotton, looking down on us both.

I think of that day often now as the last day Gardie and I were at peace with each other, real sisters, you might say. We'd never been the best of friends, no sisterly bond that made us kinder to one another. There was always something between us, too much competition for an imaginary crown. *Who do you think is prettier?* Gardie would ask, flicking her hair over her shoulder and looking sideways at herself in the mirror before glancing at me with a small, secret smile, as if to say, *We both know the answer; I'm asking you to be polite.* Always, always, I came out the lowlier sister. *I'm the queen of the castle, and you're the dirty rascal!*

But that day, the anniversary of death, everything was all right between us. The snow balanced on the tips of the trees insulated us from the wind and the black thoughts in our heads. We stopped in the middle of the woods and brushed snow from a fallen tree, sat down (careful to tuck our woollen coats beneath us to keep from freezing), and began to reminisce. *Remember when—?* one of us would begin, the other filling in the forgotten details. Remember when Father caught you kissing Jimmy Gallo in grade three? And you were so scared that you peed your pants all over his shoes? Remember when we went to Nova Scotia on that trip and we all got lost and Father refused to stop for directions and we wound up in New Brunswick? Remember when he laughed, cried, lived? When he breathed in the same air we did and held our hands tightly?

And there was a moment when I looked at Gardie, laughing open-mouthed, a piece of her hair caught in the corner of her mouth, and for the first time was overcome by the irrefutable permanence of our connection. The knowledge that no matter what happened, she and I were strung together by thin strands leading from my parents to us. Her eyes met mine, then dropped. She clasped her hands, played with her fingernails.

"I miss him," she said.

"Me too."

"But you had him more," she said. "He was yours."

I didn't know what to say, wanted to touch her hand, put my arm around her shoulders, but how to cross that line, undo old habits, trample down the sudden satisfaction to hear her say *he was yours*? When she looked at me again, I saw regret swelling, spilling down her cheeks. I said nothing.

By the time we returned to the farm, we found a new warmth there: my mother, eyes swollen but open, setting the table, my aunt by the stove, wooden spoon in her hand, steam rising over the pot and clouding the windows, thickly sawed slabs of fresh bread piled on a plate in the centre of the kitchen table. Uncle Erik in the living room, a newspaper spread out on his knee, reading glasses sliding down his nose to rest on its tip, making him seem less like a sturdy lumberman and more a retired professor. Gardie and I smiled at them, secure with our pocketful of memories and shared stories, our father's image a solid—if desperate— photograph in our minds. Neither of us could admit that we'd already moved on, had already begun to let him slip away.

SOMETIMES I THINK of my brothers—the two lost when they were young. Julian died when I was two and he was only a baby, not even a year old. He died of an infection or the whooping cough, or something else that simply grabbed his chest and refused to let go. Whenever I try to remember him, my memories jumble and mix with those of Gardie, born a year after his death, and that's a shame, as if he's been cheated of more meaning. There's only an image of a baby, a white nightgown, tiny feet and toes cold against my arm.

Jacob was eighteen when he died, fully grown; his were the overalls and dungarees I wore, his was the smell that I tried to preserve, to sink in through my own skin. His face now is vague, blurry; I only remember tufts of dark hair falling over into his eyes, a delicate nose, a mouth always smiling. He must have been tall, but this is what time can do to a memory: distort and fade, shrink and confuse. What I also remember: my father's hands, shaking, pressing Jacob's head against his chest, pushing and wringing pockets of water from his clothes.

My mother floated and hovered for nearly a year after Jacob's death, a thin ghost, her skin so pale you could see the blue-green veins along the sides of her face, in her neck, crawling up the backs of her hands and wrists and disappearing into the buttoned cuffs of her blouses. My father walked with a stoop, as if someone had punched him in the stomach so that he couldn't straighten up, and he didn't look anyone in the eye when he talked. Though neither of them did much talking anyway. The first few days after the funeral, there were always others in the house who filled up the silence with words and stories and even laughter, always the smell of something cooking, but after a while these people drifted back out, leaving us alone to settle back into our routine, rearranging ourselves to fit the new shape of our family.

I don't think I ever tried to take Jacob's place, not outright. His edges were round, while mine were sharper. I couldn't tease my mother or make her blush and flutter her eyes, I didn't have the same ease with Gardie, couldn't call her *my little baby doll* unless I wanted her to pinch the flesh of my upper arm until I cried out. But I tried to quiet myself into a more mature version of me. I was the oldest now, and that held some kind of responsibility, didn't it? I smiled down at Gardie as if I knew better than she did when she tried to pick a fight, aligned myself with my mother—older, wiser. And I wore Jacob's overalls, his jeans, far too big but cinched at the waist with a long scarf my aunt once sent to my mother but which she never wore because it was *too loud*. I pressed my head against my father's shoulder and copied his body—legs pulled up, arms wrapped around knees—as we sat and watched the ocean pull in and out, as if breathing.

What a family we would have made, had we all lived. A mother and father, two girls and two boys; equal, balanced, complete. I thought a lot about our losses throughout that winter, must have let the grey cold chip away at my layers until I was stripped bare, a skeleton of *needs* and *wants* that I couldn't quite define. I suppose that's why I wrote to Worthy in March of 1967. I hadn't heard from him in a long time, not since before Christmas. And even though I hadn't wanted him to write to me in the first place, I felt (perversely) that I'd lost something I wanted back, my one connection to the way things used to be.

I'd just started the letter in class when one of the Lily girls passed by, the breeze from her wide behind whipping the note from my desk and sending it up in a graceful ballet of fluttering paper. When she handed it back, she happened to look down and catch the first line—*Dearest Worthy*, I'd written, *I miss you*— and raised her eyebrows.

In the hallway, the girls surrounded me, their words toppling over themselves in haste.

"Why, Belle, you have a sweetheart—"

"Can't believe you didn't tell us—"

"We didn't even know you liked boys—"

I didn't tell them that I wasn't writing to Worthy to tell him I missed *him*; the sentence in my head waiting to be written was *I miss your letters—they made me laugh*.

The girls made me think it was an accomplishment, this having a boyfriend, even a fake one like Worthy. I began to write

him in earnest. *I'm dreadfully sorry I never wrote before but once,*
I told him. *It was hard to settle in here and we were all so busy.* I
pleaded with him to tell me how he was, what he was doing with
himself. Had the mines closed? Was his mother still ill? How was
his brother, Oscar? Was he working at the mines too?

I'd expected him to write back immediately, and when he
didn't, it was a shock. There's nothing like supposed rejection to
get a girl's blood going. I wrote furiously, steadily, for two
months. I carried his old letters with me to stack in my locker at
school, where they'd fall out whenever the door opened.

I changed details to make it all more exciting, of course. My
cottage where I wrote the letters became a small room with
slanted ceilings, bright shafts of sunlight through a window, and
historic, dark furniture. I settled Worthy down to fight in some
distant war, gave him a uniform with brass buttons, boots that
laced up to his knees, a round helmet. He grew taller and more
handsome, his face longer, the skin stretched taut against chis-
elled cheekbones. He held my letters and read by the light of a
match in a muddied trench until the pages became spattered
with blood.

I was on the verge of giving up when his letter arrived that
May. Strange how excited I was, when I could barely remember
what he really looked like (although I could still feel the imprint
of his hand on my bare, goosebumped flesh). His writing was
more hesitant than it had been before, more polite. He wrote
that he was not so good but didn't say why, had moved to
Ontario for a new job, and no, thank you anyway, his mother was
still not well. He was holding back, and it drove me crazy. My
letter-writing campaign knew no boundaries: I woke up thinking
about what to write in my next note, and fooled myself into
thinking that Worthy was a prize to be won.

LOOKING BACK at your life from an advantage of age, you can often pinpoint exactly when everything changed, when your life altered its course, veering from one direction to the other. When Worthy McCargo appeared in Vermont, my life settled onto a path that felt orchestrated, unchangeable. It makes me wonder what kind of person I would have become, how different my life could have been. And I wish sometimes that I could stop time and reach down, a pointed finger firmly planted on the top of my head, and move me in a different direction. Other times, I'm not sure I would have done anything differently at all.

Everyone teased him that he'd ridden all the way from Ontario on his bicycle, though he protested he had not. The people of the town were more thrilled with the *idea*—imagine! riding a bicycle all that way to see Belle! what dedication!—than with Worthy himself, standing dejectedly on the porch, his brown eyes hopeful and earnest.

He looked different—shorter and stockier than I remembered—and my fantasy of my imaginary boyfriend shifted and began to slide. His face was wider, his forehead large and shiny. Tiny pimples crept along one side of his jaw.

"Belle—" he said, and then couldn't finish, swallowing hard around words lodged deep in his throat. He did have a bicycle, propped against the side of the house, his bag tied on the back. He said he'd found it in a town just north, lying unused and wasted in the tall weeds beside the road.

It rankled him that word about his momentous ride would spread with long fingers throughout the town, especially when the bicycle metamorphosed into a girl's bicycle with a front basket. *He rode straight up to her door, that basket just full of wildflowers he'd picked for her along the way!* His blush then was unattractive, splotches of hot indignation colouring the bones in his face.

And what did I feel? My first thought was of popularity, for if there was one thing that made a girl truly popular in those days, it was a boyfriend. I already had a measure of status with my armful of polite letters, but now a live boyfriend—if that's what Worthy was—had materialized in the flesh. My second thought was, *Is he mad?*

But what did I *feel?* I can't remember, but it must have been something close to panic. Worthy had taken me too seriously; he believed we were meant to be together. Why would he think those things? Because I had written letters telling him so.

"What are you doing here?" I eyed him up and down, hands on my hips, a scolding mother hen. His mouth gaped open, then closed, fingers playing with the woollen cap he held. And then, as if he'd managed to pull free the stopper in his throat, the words rushed out.

"I love you, Belle!" Only he said, I *loves* you, the way I used to talk too, back home, but no longer did. He lurched forward and clasped me to him, his head tucked down against my neck so that his hot breath blew moistly on my skin. I blinked. It was one thing to have a pretend boyfriend, but quite another to have a love-spouting puppy clinging to your neck. That was too much responsibility.

OVER DINNER, we talked about everything except why Worthy had come. My mother inquired about people we knew back home. (*How many children do the Dunns have now? Eight? My goodness, imagine, eight children. You remember the Dunns, Hannah— Oren Dunn went to school with us.*) Uncle Erik worried about the Vietnam War and the possibility that he would be drafted. And Gardie just stared until my mother noticed. (*For Pete's sake, Gardie, close your mouth! We don't all want to see what you're eating while you're eating it.*) Worthy spoke quietly, telling us how everyone was disappearing from the coves back home, the government moving people out family by family, the empty skeletons of homes dotting the shoreline.

"There's nothing left for us now," he said. "Everyone's gone. And I had no job when the mines closed for good last summer."

"Your poor mother must be worried sick," my mother said, shaking her head. She rose from the table and began clearing plates.

"She was worried sick," Worthy said, his finger tracing unknown patterns on our plastic tablecloth. "She died just before last Christmas."

My mother held plates aloft, a frozen statuette, her eyes softening, then tearing up. "Oh, Worthy," she said, the plates clattering back onto the table. "I'm so sorry."

He swallowed fast—once, twice, his Adam's apple bobbing—before he pushed aside his chair with an apology and stiffly headed for the front door.

We eyed one another helplessly after he left, not sure what to say, until Gardie smacked her open palm down on the table.

"You'd better be nice to him, Belle," she said, the colour of her eyes melting and shifting through her tears.

I FOUND WORTHY admiring my cottage, hands on his hips.

"It's very fine," he said.

I nodded, pleased. "It's mine," I said. "It used to be a chicken coop." I showed him inside, all the while talking at a fast pace, afraid that if I stopped I'd have to say something serious. I told him what we'd done, how I'd found the paint, how Uncle Erik had helped me by building the furniture and giving it a window, how—

"Belle." Worthy stopped me, took my hand in his. He looked around the cottage, his hands following to touch everything his eyes first touched: the table, the bed, my maps, my treasures and, finally, my father's ashes.

"You still have this?" he asked. I just nodded. "Remember when I gave it to you?" His eyes were changing, becoming deeper and darker as he stepped toward me. I nodded again, backing up until my heels thudded against the wall. When he pressed himself against me, I could feel his heart beating as if it were on the outside of his chest. I gave in when he kissed me wetly, my head tilted back. His kisses made me feel as if all the blood had drained from my body.

"Remember when I did that?" he asked, his lips seconds away from mine. "Or this?" He reached under my overalls and touched my breast. I remembered. I remembered looking at his fingers wrapped around the glass, remembered the great gulf of sadness that he'd done this for me, remembered running into our house for a blanket, something soft we could spread out, something we could wrap around our freezing skin afterwards. Remembered the abandoned house by our special place, the smell of cedar and fish and the fear of splinters in my back. I especially remembered this feeling that turned tough Belle with her hard mouth into a soft little girl.

I wanted him to touch me forever. I liked this version of Worthy, the Worthy who took a kiss when he wanted, the Worthy who reached under my layers to touch the bare moistness between my legs until I was nearly crazy.

HE WANTED ME to come with him and his brother to Silver Falls, a town in northern Ontario, where he had a job with a mining company.

"I know you don't love me like I love you," he said, not

looking at me, "but I think we'd be happy anyways. I have some money saved up—we could get married, and I'd take care of you real good."

I didn't love Worthy. I wasn't even sure what love was supposed to feel like. I looked at the maps on my walls; escape was close, palpable. I squeezed my eyes shut and tried to imagine my life if I stayed in Vermont, then took another path to see a future in a place with a name like Silver Falls. What if Worthy was my only chance?

I told him I'd think about it. Over the next few days, his eyes would burn with the question whenever he looked my way, so much so that I was sure others would notice. I thought of my mother telling me *you have to make an effort with people.* Maybe I could love Worthy if I tried. Maybe I *should* love Worthy, maybe he was meant for me. My mother was settling in here in Lily, talked about getting a job, Gardie was smart enough for college after she finished high school. What would I do here after everyone had moved on with their lives?

That night at dinner, I leaned in to Worthy and whispered in his ear, "That'd be okay, I suppose." He puffed and swelled, his face a red balloon of pleasure.

MY MOTHER shook her head. "You will not."

I shrugged, kept washing the dishes. She knew I would pay her no mind.

"Belle, I didn't know you felt that way about Worthy."

"We've been writing letters," I said.

"I know." She made us tea and sat me down in the kitchen, talking to me woman to woman in a grown-up tone of voice that made me feel inches taller. "Belle, marriage is serious. And you're only eighteen. I think that's too young."

"You were married when you were sixteen," I said.

"Yes, but—" She bit her lip, looked at me closely. "You haven't been messing around with Worthy, have you?"

I blushed, shrugged. "A little," I admitted.

My mother took a long, slow sip of her tea, her eyes never leaving mine. "You're not pregnant?"

"God, no!" We hadn't done the deed yet, Worthy and me, but not because I didn't want to. *Wait until we're married*, Worthy kept pleading. I didn't see much point in waiting, but what could I do?

My mother sighed, blowing out a lungful of air, relieved, I imagine.

"I won't stop you," she said. "But I think you should wait. Finish out high school. If Worthy's the right person, he'll wait for you."

I knew Worthy would wait for me; I just wasn't sure I could wait. I feared that if I didn't leave then, that instant, if I had too much time to think about things, I'd change my mind and lose my one and only chance. That prospect scared me more than anything.

In the end, Uncle Erik took Worthy aside and suggested that it might be best if Belle at least finished school, while Worthy went back home to Silver Falls, saved some more money, and built a home for us. Worthy announced the plan that night at the dinner table; he'd decided, he said, that Belle should graduate, since he never had.

"She'll be the smart one in the family," he said. Everyone paused after the announcement.

"Well," my mother said. "That's good news, then."

"Congratulations." My aunt came around the table to kiss us both.

I expected Gardie to laugh out loud or roll her eyes, but she sat very still, not looking at any of us.

Worthy was full of self-importance now that he was almost a married man. Even the way he walked changed, with chest thrust out and shoulders back, head held high. He took my hand in front of everyone and kissed me on the cheek every night before heading to sleep in my cottage, his choice, the only place (he said) he could possibly sleep.

Gardie moped around and didn't look so good anymore—pale and tired, dark shadows like smudges of coal beneath her eyes.

"What's wrong with Gardie?" my mother asked me. "What did you do to her?"

Even then, it was obvious to me that Gardie had a crush on Worthy. I watched her face, saw the way her eyes followed him around, tracked his movements. When he was in the room, she thrust her skinny little chest forward and lifted her chin, angling it in profile to her *good side*, the pose she practised endlessly in front of the mirror. She giggled too much and blushed. Of course, I know now that it was more than a crush, but none of us could imagine how far she'd taken it.

ONE NIGHT, after we'd all gone to bed, Gardie came into my room. She stood in the doorway until I noticed her, a ghost in white, arms and hands limp by her sides.

"What do you want?"

She said nothing at first, then padded in, her bare feet slapping against the floorboards. She stood over me in the bed, face blank.

"You can't do this, Belle," she whispered.

"Can't do what?"

"You can't marry him."

I pushed myself up, leaned back on my elbows. The bit of light coming in through the window fell on one side of her face.

I'd left the window open to catch a breeze; the night was too hot, my legs tangled in my nightgown, already sweaty.

"Why not?"

"Because you don't love him." Steady, unblinking.

"And how do you think you know that, missus?" I mocked.

"Because you never even look at him. You never touch him, never smile like you should if you were in love. It's just a game to you, like those stupid letters you wrote, pretending to feel something you didn't because you liked the idea of it. Worthy's not an idea, he's real. And you're playing with his feelings."

Of course, she was right, I was a sham, but *how dared she?* My back and neck muscles tensed, ready for a fight. And this I can admit now, after all these years: I enjoyed it. I had something that Gardie wanted, and that made me clench my fists and hold on tighter than ever.

"When you marry somebody, you're supposed to be in love," Gardie said, her voice tight and high and sounding almost like she would cry. And then I said something mean, something to make her stop talking to me like that and disappear.

"You're just jealous because you don't even have a boyfriend," I said. "You wish that Worthy asked you to marry him."

And it did stop her. Her expression changed to something I couldn't quite make out in the half-light. Surprise? Rage? Hurt? Her chest rose once as her breath stopped.

"You don't know anything," she whispered. "Father would be so disappointed in you." Her own parting shot, aimed where I would feel it most. I closed my eyes until the sound of her bare feet faded back down the hall.

How different it would all be if my father were still here. *He would be so disappointed.* But was that true? He knew what it was like to be trapped; he knew all about escape. He tried to get out as well, didn't he? Sometimes in the evenings, when the light was fading from the sky, leaving the room in shadows and soft kerosene light, he would tell the story we loved to hear most. *The story of falling in love*, Gardie would say.

In 1945, a young man with a mission strode up a gravel road, a leather satchel slung over one shoulder. He wore a black suit and tie, a white shirt so stiffly starched he could feel the blood in his neck pulsing against the collar. The road was too narrow for his car, which he had just bought with his Bible money. Sweating slightly in his suit on that July day, he trod with purpose toward the white two-storey house. It seemed to hold promise at first, unlike many others in the small New Brunswick town on the coast. He squinted as he walked closer; was it him, or did the porch seem to sag to one side? And when he put one tentative foot on the first step, did he only imagine the creak? His spirit dropped further when he noticed the paint flaking off the side of the door. He twisted his head sideways to survey his image and smooth back his hair. He patted his bag, which held Bibles that, in Catholic towns, he would swear to his customers were blessed by the parish priest (in Protestant towns, he would say nothing), reviewed his sales pitch, and cleared his throat, twice. As he raised his hand to knock, the door opened to reveal peacock-blue eyes and the purest blond hair. His gaze slid down to her lush lips, the brown shoulders peeking beneath her sundress and, below that, the hint of cleavage. By the time she asked what he wanted, he had forgotten his mission.

Just like that, I was in love, he would say then, snapping his fingers.

We would nestle under his arms and pull a thick blanket over us on the daybed. I'm sure that my mother sat with us sometimes, but in this memory she sat at the kitchen table, mending socks and smiling. I remember watching the light from our one lamp resting on her hair and making her face glow.

I always tried to imagine them in those days. I played it out like a movie in my head, made the drama grander, more exciting than it must have been. But what really happened would have cut through the layers of my mother's skin until it reached her heart. Her family was appalled by the appearance of the travelling Bible boy, more so when he admitted that Bible peddling was just a diversion from the mines in Newfoundland. When they discovered that he wasn't even Catholic but a dirty Protestant, they banned him from the house.

And this is the part I always tried to imagine: they ran away together. He pulled up in his car after midnight, his headlights off, pulled into the lane where she waited with a battered suitcase, praying to God, asking Him to forgive her sins. I liked to add details in my version of the memory: a full moon lighting the way for my father, the quiet sounds of a summer's night, a slight wind rustling through the leaves of bushes, the crunch of tires on the gravel road, and the way my mother's heart must have sped up.

When my mother told us this part of the story, her eyes would darken and deepen in her small face.

"They never forgave me," she would say. And then, after a pause: "I never saw them again." Of one sister and two brothers, only Aunt Hannah understood, only Aunt Hannah sent secretive letters to my mother in the cove. *I'm leaving home*, she wrote one December. *I've been accepted at teachers' college in Toronto. There's nothing here for me anymore.* And then she too was banished from the family.

"Hannah was the only one who stood up for me," my mother would say. They would cry later; I saw them both. They wrote home every few months; no letters ever came from New Brunswick. I suppose you could say it was a sign of their characters that they never gave up, never stopped writing, as if they were all still connected. I would have given up long before them. In fact, years later, I did.

Shortly after we arrived in Vermont, a single envelope came bearing my aunt's maiden name written in large, looping letters. Opened, a small clipping fell: an obituary for Jonathan Carlisle, the grandfather I never knew. He had died after a long illness, surrounded by his wife, Elizabeth, and two children, Paul and Robert. I pored over the announcement later, secretly, hoping to see my name in print. Gardie and I weren't mentioned, though Aunt Hannah and my mother were, along with eight cousins I'd never met. There was nothing else inside the envelope, only the cold black-and-white square, hard news. I believe the absence of a letter struck my mother and aunt harder than the death itself. (Four years later, Gardie would tell me, another envelope, another square clipping. My mother threw a plate against the wall. *Damn them to hell!*)

What would it be like to disappear from someone's life like that? My mother was only sixteen when she met my father, seventeen when my brother was born. My father would always finish the story the same way: *We all lived happily ever after*. But it wasn't true. He had tried to escape his destiny and the destiny of all the men in his family, but he returned to the mines, returned to his fate. And that, in the end, hardened my resolve: at least one of us should escape.

Six

The idea was just there, suddenly, hanging empty with potential, a game. Why not just get married on the sly? Why wait? I suppose neither of us thought it through. And maybe—just maybe—neither of us wanted too much time to set in, time to think rationally, time to change our minds. Gardie's accusations stuck in my head, repeating themselves over and over until I was blue with anger. The nerve, how dared she? And then: *I'll show her*.

Worthy had some money. We snuck away in the middle of the night like criminals, told no one our plan, caught the bus to Montreal, then the train to Ottawa. We applied for a marriage licence and then toured the city, giddy and childish in our excitement. We'd never been in a city this big before—so many people, real sidewalks, and official, imposing buildings. I clung to Worthy's hand as we walked along the canal, taking everything in, wondering what it would be like to stay here forever, the top of my head hot from the sun, our cheeks and arms sunburned at the end of the day.

When we married, I wore the same blouse and wool skirt I'd worn to my father's funeral, Worthy in a suit that was too small and rose above the cuffs of his shirt. None of it felt real, not then. Worthy quivered beside me, his leg brushing mine as he wobbled; I suppose he felt the weight of reality more clearly than I did. Everyone in the building wore a solemn air. The judge barely looked up, simply congratulated us with his head bent low.

We stayed at the River's Edge Inn, which was meant to be quaint but just seemed dingy and sad, for all its expense, butter moulded into the shape of small flowers, and mints on our pillows at night. But the wallpaper buckled in a corner of the room, and the bedspread was thin and scratchy.

After we were married, Worthy tried to carry me over the threshold, the way he'd seen it done in the movies. I was afraid that his arms would snap when he lifted me and my big bones; though he looked sturdy, he never seemed particularly strong to me. He gave up after two tries, and I walked into the room myself. For all our messing around, we'd never actually done it or seen each other fully naked, and I wasn't sure what to do now, the proper etiquette. Did I undress in the washroom or right here in the middle of the room? Or did I wait for Worthy to peel my clothes off, piece by piece? The buckling wallpaper and sad darkness in the room made everything awkward.

Worthy took off his suit slowly. Before he got to his pants, his hand on his belt, he paused, then turned around so that his back was to me.

"Don't you want to use the toilet?" he asked. Suddenly nervous, I said yes, went to the little bag I had packed, and carried it with me. Because I didn't know what else to do, I drew a hot bath and soaked for a long time. When I finally emerged, hair brushed neatly back and behind my ears, skin rubbed with my mother's lavender oil cream, skin wrinkled raisin-like, Worthy had fallen asleep with his mouth open, leaving me intact, a virgin still on my wedding night.

I WENT BACK to Lily on my own. Worthy figured there was no point in spending the money on his ticket to the States when he'd just be turning around again to return to Silver Falls. Outwardly I agreed with him, but the long ride home made me nervous. My mother would be furious; I wished I'd forced Worthy to come with me so I didn't have to face everyone alone.

I'd been gone for a week, and stony silence met my return, as if I'd murdered someone and come home to confess. Only my aunt stepped forward.

"Well then, congratulations," she said, kissing me on both cheeks before wrapping her arms around me in a hug. "You worried us sick, I'll have you know, but I guess it turned out all right in the end." I took all I could from her warmth, frozen by Gardie's icy glare and my mother's quiet disappointment as she crossed her arms in front of her chest.

"Oh, Belle," she said, before unwrapping the apron from her waist and sinking into a kitchen chair.

"It'll be all right," I said, cheerfulness forced into my voice. She just shook her head again, then turned away almost before I could see the tears in her eyes.

IT WAS ALMOST as if it never happened. In September, I went back to school, hardly able to believe that something of this much importance—a marriage!—could show so little on the outside. How could I walk the same, sling my pre-marriage bag over my shoulder just as usual? How could my braided hair fall to the same place against my back? But I knew it wouldn't be a secret for long, not in a town like Lily. In small towns, stories have ways of migrating from ear to ear on their own. Within one hour of Worthy's initial arrival in town, everyone knew, as if I'd driven down every street holding a megaphone, shouting out my news to one and all. And it seemed funny to me how some of the details—

a girl's bicycle, a basket of flowers—managed to pop into the story, to make it more interesting for both the *teller* and *tellee*.

But now it wasn't so funny. The thought of all those girls pressing in with their detailed questions filled me with dread. *What's he like? How did he ask you to marry him? Was it romantic?* They'd remind me of my list (or worse, would have a copy of it) and ask me, *Is he terribly handsome? Tall? With dark hair that curls at the neck? Is he funny, rich, and does he have nice hands?* And how could I tell them Worthy was no Prince Charming, that he was average height and had light brown hair that fell in wispy strands into his eyes? I couldn't really remember his hands, except for the way they felt on me, and I would never call him handsome. At least I'd listed those other qualities; Worthy was kind, generous (here I pictured him handing me the glass bottle), and—as far as I knew—good with women and children. But the more I thought about it, the worse I felt.

Before the week was out, they all knew I'd gotten married. The girls at school regarded me at first with a kind of awe: I was practically a rebel, sneaking out of town as I had. It's not as if mine was the only young marriage they'd encountered. But I was already an anomaly, a bit of a freak, in my overalls or dungarees and sneakers, and my adjectives (tall, strong, striking) that weren't popular in a girl.

The boys shuffled their feet and looked away before offering their congratulations. And they would give me the once-over, trying to be sneaky about it (as if I wouldn't notice), wondering if maybe they should have paid more attention to me before. The girls were nosier, wanting every last detail of our surprise elopement.

Even our night at the River's Edge Inn was bathed in romance, so much so that I couldn't bear to tell them the truth. But every once in a while, I caught a secretive look passed from one girl to another. *How did she get a husband?* they seemed to ask. No one noticed it was all a joke. For one brief moment, I was the undisputed expert on all things romantic.

And then I think they saw through me. I didn't act like a newlywed; I didn't blush or giggle or make sly references to our wedding night or what must have occurred in that small, tired room at the inn. After a few weeks, everyone stopped talking about it, and then, finally, stopped talking to me altogether, as if I was already gone.

Worthy wrote from Silver Falls in October, November, December, but the letters were stilted, short. My own efforts to write back stalled, no matter how hard I tried. I would settle myself down at the kitchen table, determined, blank sheet in front of me, but ink would explode over my hand or make unsightly smears on the paper, and the sight of those mistakes would send a streak of panic down to my toes.

Shoving my feet into Uncle Erik's high winter boots, I wandered the fields and woods behind the farm to calm my fears, telling myself that everyone was nervous about a new marriage, everyone worried and feared leaving home for the first time. At night I couldn't sleep well, tossed and turned until I felt smothered by pillows and blankets, my nightgown twisted, binding my knees together. Even my cottage solitude couldn't help; the walls with their maps swallowed me and sent me spinning.

It was spring before I had any real news from Worthy, and it came by telegraph.

Found home. Stop. Waiting eagerly for your arrival. Stop.

I stared at the absence of the word *love.*

In June, he sent an envelope with money for the bus and train and a short note, telling me that he'd pick me up at the station, the job was good, and hurry, hurry, he missed me. He also sent me a map of Ontario for my wall. Stuffing his money and letter into my back pocket, I spread the map out over the kitchen table for everyone to see.

"Where's Silver Falls?" Uncle Erik asked. That's what we all wanted to know, me especially.

"West of Sudbury," my mother said. "Just find Sudbury." We looked and looked until Gardie (eyes rolling so far back I was sure they'd be stuck there forever, a fate I warned her about whenever I could) stuck a long finger onto a dot to the northwest.

"Now we look west," I said, and ran my stubbier finger to the left. Silver Falls was a tiny dot partially smudged by a wiggling blue line named Owatanagan Lake.

"What kind of name is that?" my mother asked, squinting her eyes to get a better look.

"It's Indian," Gardie said. "You'll be trespassing on Indian land."

I'd never met any Indians before. Standing there at the table, I had to squeeze my thighs together to stop my legs from shaking.

THERE WERE THINGS I had to do before I left. I debated about the contents of my cottage and whether or not to take them with me. The little things I could leave with no qualms, but what about my maps? Would I need them? When people escaped, did they still need to keep the means? In the end, I folded them carefully and placed them at the bottom of my bag. Just in case.

In a gesture of goodwill, I gave Gardie my cottage.

"Unless I come back," I warned. "Then I'll need it again." She shrugged as if she didn't care, but I could tell she was somewhat pleased. I wanted to say more now that I was leaving, but the words wouldn't come, stayed jumbled in my mind. Everyone sensed Gardie's moodiness but blamed it on me.

"She's just sad that you're leaving," my aunt said. "Deep down she cares."

"She's going to be left behind while you go off on your adventure," my mother said more realistically. "Put yourself in her shoes."

I shrugged it all off, as I always have.

I GRADUATED in June. The whole family came to the ceremony, to watch me walk across the stage in my royal blue cap and gown. My grades were terrible; how I'd managed to squeak by was a mystery to me. I felt like a fraud, so much so that I imagined the principal withholding the diploma from me, our arms both outstretched, me trying to pull the paper from his grip, a tug-of-war of sorts. And when the roll slid easily into my palm, I imagined him stumbling back from the force, his smile revealing small fangs at the sides of his mouth.

And then it was over. I didn't go to the graduation dance, had nothing in common with any of the boys or girls anymore, no purpose, no need to fit in by standing against a wall all night while others secretly tilted their pelvises toward one another or made out in sweaty dark corners under the bleachers.

I certainly didn't want a party at the farm, but my aunt and mother insisted, inviting all the kids in my class. They came out of curiosity, though they'd stopped speaking to me weeks before, and brought presents of new pots and pans, sheets, and other wifely items. The girls found my cottage dubious, wrinkling their noses and claiming they could still smell the remnants of dead chickens; the boys examined the workmanship and debated the properties of different wood.

I slipped away from them easily, out of place and unnoticed at my own party. Up in my lavender room, I opened the window and peered down at the crowd, that swirling, giggling, flirting mass of hairspray and lipstick, Brylcreem and acne.

"Hey!" I called down, watched questioning faces turn up toward me one by one. I waited until they fell silent, let the curiosity stretch until I knew I had their complete attention. They had no cares, no worries; they'd probably never leave Lily, would marry, have kids, and die right here, all without setting foot in someplace different or even wondering what the rest of the world looked like. And I almost envied them, the simplicity of a life mapped out like that.

"Dare me to jump?"

Down below, my mother froze and raised her face, a small white oval, her hands holding a tray of bacon-wrapped sausages beginning to shake. Someone laughed, but most just looked horrified. A few of the girls glanced nervously at one another, then back at me.

"Just joking," I muttered. I slammed the window, paced in my room. I wasn't one of them, never would be. How could I have fooled myself into thinking I could pretend my way through a marriage?

"It's only cold feet," my aunt had said the night before. "Everyone feels that way."

I wrapped my arms around my knees to stop them from shaking. "Something terrible will happen if I go," I said.

My mother sighed. "Oh, Belle." She had little patience for me, I could tell, and I could see why—I had gotten myself into this mess. She had tried to warn me, tried to delay my determination months ago, and I had refused to listen.

She exchanged looks with my aunt: *Look what Belle has done now.* But then she touched the back of my hand. "You don't have to go," she said in a soft, sad voice.

That night, my aunt came to my room, knocking slightly, hesitant, a round cream hat box under her arm.

"My memory box," she said, settling on the edge of the bed, her weight sinking down into the mattress, rolling me onto my side. I sat up, watched as she sifted through photographs and letters until she found what she was looking for.

"Here," she said, thrusting a small square into my hands. Her nude photograph, the profile in black and white, the hint of nipple. She put her hand over her mouth and giggled. "Can you imagine I sent this to Erik before I even met him? He had an ad in the paper, and this is what I sent." I pretended I'd never heard the story, let her live it again through the telling. She took the photograph from my hands, stared at it a moment before setting it back in the box with a sigh.

"If I hadn't sent that photograph, if I hadn't answered that letter, I don't know where I'd be today, Belle."

Her hand touched my arm, her palm cool and smooth, her fingernails small tapered ovals. "I have another story for you," she said. "Let me tell you something about your mother. When she ran away with your father, she was pregnant with Jacob. She never told you, but she was, and maybe you and Gardie have figured it out for yourselves anyway. But what you don't know is how terrible it was for her to make that decision at the time. Our family called her every name in the book. She was sixteen, and they told her to burn in hell with her dirty Protestant boyfriend and never come back to *shame the family again.* She gave every-thing up to be with your father, to have that baby." She paused.

"She wrote letters and sent pictures of Jacob, but they never wrote back, never a word to say they understood and forgave, never an apology for the hurtful things they'd said to her. Their first grandchild! The terrible things people do to one another." She looked down at my hand, squeezed. "I defended her," she said. "They said I could choose between them and your mother, but I couldn't have both. You know what I chose. But your mother and I—we never felt right about it. Always felt there would come a time when we would be reunited as a family. But there comes a point when you just can't cross back over the line. Always a point when it's too late to go back." She stopped then for a moment, drifted off into some other space in her head, a curtain falling down over her eyes. I felt that I should say something, anything, to show that I was a compassionate person, that I understood the depths of despair my mother must have felt.

"Poor Mother," I said, the words slipping out lamely. It wasn't enough, and I knew it, but my aunt didn't seem to notice. Her eyes snapped back into focus, and she smiled, took her hand from mine to tuck my hair behind my ears.

"If you asked your mother right now if it was worth it all, even now, after she's lost your father and Jacob, she'd say it was. For you girls. So, Belle, go to Silver Falls if you want, if you truly love Worthy and think he will make you happy. Because you must be in charge of your life; you must make your own happiness. If you wait for others to do it for you, you're bound to be disappointed." She leaned forward and kissed my cheek.

"You'll make the right choice," she said.

Now, standing at my window, hearing the party down below, I closed my eyes, pictured myself staying in Lily, facing the sly glances of my old friends. Girls could be mean, I knew; I'd never live it down. *Poor Belle*, they'd say. Or, in gossipy whispers: *Divorce!*

To hell with them. I could do whatever I pleased. I filled an antique jug with water, carried it to the window.

"Me again!" I called down, waved to get their attention. "I just want to say one thing before you all leave." I watched them smile their fakeness, mentally aiming at two girls below with white, smooth necks and fragile, jutting jaws. I lurched, pretended to stumble, and tilted the jug at just the right angle so that the water poured down in a single torrent, then pressed my hand to my mouth in mock horror as the girls shrieked and stood with arms outstretched, dripping hair stuck in their mouths.

"My goodness!" I said. "Oh, my goodness!"

BEFORE I LEFT on the bus that would take me to the train station in Montreal, my mother gave me her wedding gift: matching wedding bands for Worthy and me.

"Mine and your father's," she whispered. I thought of the effort it must have taken to slide that gold band from her finger, to lay it side by side with my father's, which she'd kept in an envelope in her jewellery box ever since he died. She didn't have an engagement ring, no photographs except the old mining group shot, nothing else to remind her of him. I told her I wouldn't take them.

"Please," she said. "It would make me feel better with you so far away. Take them with you." She reached out her hand with the two bands that seemed to hold so much power. At the touch of my fingers on her palm, she caved inward momentarily, her mouth pulling down, before she straightened again and forced a small smile. I saw then that my leaving would take much more from her than the removal of a simple band of metal.

I gave something in return. Not because I felt I should—one gift deserves another, and all that—but because I couldn't leave her like this. It wasn't right; without anything to anchor her to me, to her past, I felt she would just drift away, becoming, after a while, just a bobbing speck in the distance, a smudged dot on a map.

She held the glass bottle up to the sunlight, as I had done when Worthy first gave it to me, then shook it gently, her eyes silent question marks. And I couldn't explain it to her then, what the contents meant to me; it was too embarrassing, too awkward here at the bus station.

"Just promise you'll keep it," I said instead. She nodded. I took away with me the memory of how she looked standing there, smiling past her sadness for my sake, and tucked it inside with my memory of Gardie in the woods on the anniversary of my father's death. Those two images stay with me today, reminders of all that was good and genuine.

Seven

orthy picked me up from the train station when I arrived in my scratchy wool skirt and the blouse I hoped showed no perspiration stains under the arms. The open door of the train let in a stinking warm burst of air, a noisy exhalation of bad breath. Out of my window, I saw him searching the faces of all the passengers, eyebrows raised, waiting. My legs shook as I stood and made my way down the narrow aisle. I took that last step down and then froze, just looking at him. Neither of us knew what to do, really. Then he smiled, awkward, stepped forward, and hugged me, his arms bending stiffly, as if his elbows needed grease.

"Hi," he said. His face had turned deep red. When he bent down to grab my bag, I noticed small folds in the back of his neck for the first time, saw how he sweated along his hairline.

In the car, he handed me a small blue box.

"I was going to wait until we got home," he said. "But maybe you'd like this now." Inside, a thin circle of gold blinked at me. I thought of the rings my mother had pressed into my hands, looked at Worthy's eager face, and felt my skin tingling from the heat. I opened the passenger window, breathed more easily. Worthy pushed the ring onto my finger, frowning and grunting a little when it stuck on my knuckle.

"I guess it's a little small," he said. I stared at the way my skin puffed up around the ring, imagined the dent it would leave when removed.

"It's fine," I said. I smiled to show I meant it, and Worthy's face smoothed out.

"Let me take you home," he said.

Home. I stared out the window as he drove up Main Street, silence gathering between us, building up until Worthy felt he had to say something. *That's the post office*, he said then, or *Best eggs in town, there*. He always smiled with each declaration; he wanted me to like this place, wanted me to give some sign that I would stay. My skirt had ridden up so that my thighs stuck to cracked burgundy leather seats. Worthy kept his window shut, despite my internal begging and the rivulet of sweat inching down the side of his face. He drove too slowly for any breeze; I wondered what he would think if I suddenly stuck my neck and head out the window and opened my mouth for air.

After a few minutes, he took my hand and ran his fingers over the ring, something he would do often in the next few weeks, as if to convince himself that I was his. I couldn't wait to soak my aching finger in cool water, couldn't wait to take off the ring, even for a moment in dark solitude.

We passed a church and two schools, crossed the train tracks, and left the centre of town behind.

And now I could see the mine shafts in the distance, and, closer, a cluster of houses that were exactly the same, row after row of identical boxes, only the paint of the clapboard siding and the flowers in the gardens changing from house to house. We turned left on Silver Road, then right onto Garland Street.

"Here we are."

Our house stood on the corner of Silver and Garland. Worthy's brother, Oscar, waved from a small blue porch.

Flakes of paint fell with every footstep and littered the porch, the steps, and the small walkway leading up to the simple bungalow.

"We painted the porch for you," Oscar said, grinning. "Next we'll do the house." I tried to smile back. The house would never be painted, would always remain a dirty grey-white, at least in all the years I lived there.

Worthy dumped my suitcase in the front landing. "Be back in a minute," he said.

"Where are you going?"

"Have to return the car." Keys dangled from his fingers.

"It's not yours?" Part of me wanted him to stay; the other, sweatier part of me welcomed the chance to be alone, to sit in silence on my bed and breathe in and out.

"No, I borrowed it from one of the guys." He paused, wrinkling his brow. "You'll be okay?"

I nodded, watched him wrestle with the screen door (it stuck). The heel of his shoe had broken and flapped as he walked, making an odd sucking sound.

And then it was just me and Oscar. I rubbed my shoes on the mat, eyed the worn linoleum in the entryway. Oscar smiled on, his mouth crooked and hair dark and long and tucked behind his ears. He was too thin, all elbows and knees, as my mother would say. I waited for him to leave, but as he smiled and beckoned and waved me in, it dawned on me that he lived here too, and Worthy hadn't said a word about it.

"Well, come on in, then," he said. I reached for my suitcase and followed him, swallowing past my unease. And here was my palace: kitchen and dining room a long rectangle of linoleum, two small bedrooms separated by a washroom.

"My room," Oscar said, gesturing through the first door. He opened the second to reveal a dresser, tall wardrobe, and, over by the window, an impossibly small bed. "And yours." The air grew hotter and denser.

"That's about it," Oscar said. "Not too grand, is it? But not too bad, neither."

I let my suitcase drop, stood with my hands by my sides, palms sweating in the heat.

"Let's go to the kitchen, then," Oscar said. "We'll have us a drink."

I thought of the niceties, idle conversation, just killing time until Worthy came back. I shook my head. "I'd like to lie down," I said.

Maybe I should have said *please* or *thank you, no;* Oscar's smile slipped. "Sure," he said. "Whatever you'd like to do." He didn't move for a moment, then seemed to shake himself awake. "I'll leave you, then. If you need anything, just yell."

I waited for his footsteps to disappear, heard a creak as he settled on the sofa in front of the television in the living room. I had wanted to wash my face, rinse out my mouth with water, but I couldn't bear to move, couldn't bear to face Oscar and his pleasant face again. *No, no, everything's fine, just need to use the bathroom!* Desperate for cool air, I tried to raise the sash window, but too many layers of paint covered the swollen wood; it refused to budge.

Instead, I opened my suitcase. I hadn't brought much: jeans, overalls, my beloved sneakers, a nightgown; giant panties my mother bought me, matching bras. I stripped off my skirt and blouse, balled them up, and tucked them inside my suitcase. I never wanted to see them again. I threw on my jeans and a T-shirt, rolled the jeans up to my knees, and lay down on the bed, trying to get comfortable. After a while I sat up, unhooked my bra, and tossed it across the room. I pulled my knees to my chest, stared at the ceiling, traced the cracks and water stains until my eyes crossed. I fell asleep with my face under the pillow.

When I woke, a hand had crept up under my shirt, touching my bare skin, and I felt drowned in sweat. Beside me, Worthy huffed and puffed, his cheeks red and eyes glazed. He leaned forward and kissed me with wet, slippery lips.

"Belle." He pressed my back against the wall, wedged his leg between my knees. I kept my eyes closed the whole time. *I am a wife now.*

What I had felt with Worthy in Newfoundland, in my small cottage in Vermont, had disappeared. Now there was only lurching and grasping and hot, heavy breath against my neck, my ear. I closed my eyes and rewound myself, reversing the order of all that I'd done: got back out of bed, put my bra back on, closed my suitcase, and got back on the train. I blanked out Worthy's face and tried to imagine someone else. Since I didn't know many eligible bachelors (I kept focusing on my uncle Erik and Oscar), I settled on the train conductor, who was not bad-looking in an ordinary kind of way and wore a small blue cap and uniform. He was fine until Worthy broke my virginity; my eyes flew open and the conductor's face vanished. This, then, was the culmination of our grand passion, our first time together.

It didn't quite hurt, at least not as much as I expected, but it pulled and stretched, and I wondered why anyone would want to steam up car windows doing *this*. I remembered the way some of the girls at school—the experienced girls, the ones with reputations and slanted mouths—swayed their hips and looked at the boys with sideways eyes. They knew something I didn't, felt something that I missed.

I felt cheated and rolled onto my side. Beside me, Worthy lay on his back, his smooth chest covered in a layer of perspiration. There was no way to lie on this bed without touching; even bent, my legs brushed his, my knees pressed into thick thighs. He had put on weight over the last year and now seemed too soft and rounded. But there, that was me being mean. Worthy smiled at me, and I saw in his eyes all the things he hoped we could be together. I bit my tongue, said nothing about the heat, the tiny bed, and smiled back at him.

"We were meant to be together," he murmured. "We come from the same place. It was meant to be."

I pulled back to look at him, his face peaceful, satisfied, his eyes closed. Something clenched in my stomach, my chest, making my neck and head ache. *The wrong thing to do.*

WORTHY AND OSCAR went to work that night.

"Next week we're on day shift."

"What do you mean?" I asked.

"Shifts," Worthy said. "This week it's nights, next week it's days, week after that it's afternoons, then we go back to nights again."

It hadn't occurred to me that I'd be left alone my first night in the new house, but they both left and didn't return until after seven the next morning. I sat in the living room and watched television, filling the empty spaces of the house with the welcome noise of other voices, fiddling with the rabbit ears when the reception faded, the click of the dials satisfyingly loud in the empty room. I opened the refrigerator, found remnants of the crusty-edged meat loaf we'd had for dinner, a bowl of something unidentifiable, and three bottles of beer. I opened one, took cautious sips until I got used to the taste, the way it stung the back of my throat. Then I drank another, and another, and I could have drunk more, quenching a different kind of thirst, though my head wobbled on my neck, too big and heavy.

No one home. I turned off the television, half lurched to the bedroom, kept the light off. *Where are they? Here, or here?* Finally I found them, the rings, tucked into a pocket in the suitcase. Two shining gold symbols from my mother. I turned them over in my palm, watching them catch and hold the moonlight. She had pressed them into my hand with such hope for me. *Look at me now, Mother, drunk for the very first time, and all alone!* I closed my fist, felt the warmth of the bands digging into my skin, then carefully buried them in a drawer, nestled between underpants of soft cotton.

IF I HADN'T CARED what people thought of me in Vermont, I sure as hell didn't care in Silver Falls, here on the wrong side of the tracks or back in town where all the richies lived—mine managers, business owners, shop workers, and the like. Eliza Whittle's house backed onto ours on Silver Street. She lived with her husband, Dan, who'd been in the mines for over thirty years and consistently worked the coveted day shift. Two days after I arrived, Eliza showed up in the afternoon, knocking so hard the screen door bounced in its frame. In her left hand, she balanced a coffee cake.

"Yoo-hoo!" she called. I shuffled to the door in my bare feet, still wearing jeans and a T-shirt. Eliza took it all in: long hair that hadn't been combed yet, probably nipples poking through my shirt since I hadn't put on a bra.

"Welcome to Silver Falls," she said, her voice weak.

"Worthy and Oscar went to town," I said. "Groceries," I added, when she didn't move. She stood for a while on the porch, silent, until I realized she expected to come in. I held the door open, took the cake from her hand with a thank-you. She was much smaller than me, and as different as anyone could be, different from most of the miners' wives I'd seen so far. She wore a dress with a little collar, her hair was cut in a short bob with bangs slicing across her forehead, and she had pencilled thick black lines around each brown eye. She attempted to look modern, I suppose, and stylish, but small details had gone wrong: the dress was too tight, a layer of skin bulged above the collar, and the eyeliner only accentuated the puffy flesh beneath her eyes. Frosted lipstick made her lips appear thin, even as she pressed them together in a forced smile.

"You're different than I imagined," she said.

"How did you imagine me?" She didn't answer, only laughed nervously, so I filled in the blanks myself with all the things I wasn't: I would be blonde and delicate, innocent, with dainty wrists and sparkling eyes; I would have a southern, slightly lilting accent, a dress of small yellow flowers; I would become her best friend, maybe the daughter she never had, sharing recipes and advice about men over steaming cups of tea. I knew already that I wouldn't like her.

She followed me into the kitchen, tugging the back of her skirt.

"Would you like something to drink?" I asked and, before she could say no, opened the refrigerator and handed her a bottle of beer. She didn't seem to know what to do with it, stood with her hand around its neck until I handed her a bottle opener. Then she swallowed.

"Do you have any lemonade?" she asked. "Or iced tea?" I didn't, as a matter of fact. I liked the way the alcohol made me feel—or rather, the way it took away all my feelings, at least the bad ones. I liked the lightness of my step, the way my arms swung through the air as if to some private music. Anything seemed possible after a few beers, and everything was manageable.

She sat down at the Formica table in the kitchen, perched like a bird on the edge of the chair, her spine abnormally straight, head high. I leaned against the counter, my arms folded, and shook my head. The kitchen was cooler than any other room in the house, thanks to two windows on opposite walls.

"Won't feel cool soon enough," Worthy told me. "Wait until August."

Eliza kept smiling, small hopeful smiles, as if I could still change, could still become the girl she'd imagined would move in next door.

"So how do you like Silver Falls?" she asked.

I shrugged. "Haven't seen much of it yet," I said.

"I've lived here my whole life," she said. "I'm fifty-six. Married to Dan for over twenty-five years." She said it as if it was her only accomplishment in life, and I guess maybe it was.

I lifted my beer, began drinking, and didn't stop until I'd finished it in one go, overwhelmed by the thought of living in Silver Falls with Worthy for even five years. I belched, the beer burning my nostrils.

Twin blotches of pink coloured Eliza's cheeks. She looked again at her beer bottle, placed it back on the table, and stood, once again pulling down her skirt.

"Well, I should be going, then," she said, her voice too loud and bright. Out came the forced smile. "Welcome to Silver Falls. I'm sure you and Worthy will be happy here."

THROUGH ONE of the kitchen windows that looked out onto the street, I watched Worthy and Oscar on their way back from town, each carrying two brown bags. I saw Eliza call out to them, watched her animated arms and gestures as she spoke at length. I couldn't hear what she said, only the tone of her voice as it rose and fell. Oscar kept smiling, but Worthy glanced at our house, saw me framed by the window. He said something to Eliza, reached out and patted her arm. I stepped back, took another beer from the fridge, sat at the table, and waited for the army.

Neither of them said much when they came in. Oscar smiled, nodded, and headed into his room, and Worthy came over to kiss my cheek, sweating and stinking from the walk up the hill in the heat.

"I need a shower," he said, then waited expectantly, cheeks round and high. Hopeful cheeks. He wanted me to join him but would never come right out and ask.

"No thanks," I said instead, and his smile drooped.

"Be right back, then," he said.

By the time he reappeared, fresh and smelling of soap, his hair combed and parted, I had finished my beer and moved on to another. He seemed disappointed to see me like that. I wondered briefly how I looked—did I smell, look dingy and worn down?—but then decided that I didn't care.

"What are you doing?" he asked.

I shrugged. "Just having a drink."

"Have you even showered today?"

I touched my hair, smoothed and tucked it down behind my ears. He didn't know what to say to me, looked around the kitchen, sniffed.

"What's for dinner?" he asked. I put my head on the table. He sighed, took out a tin of corned beef and six potatoes, turned his back to me. "I talked to Eliza Whittle," he said.

"I saw." I made a game of moving my lips until they touched the top of the table.

"She said you were a little rude to her."

I sat up. "No one asked her to come over here," I said.

"She brought you a cake. She's been very nice to me and Oscar. Had us over for dinner a few times already. I told her all about you, and she was really looking forward to meeting you.

And now she tells me you were rude and acted like you didn't care to meet her at all."

"That's true," I said, "I didn't."

"You even burped in her face."

"That might have been on purpose," I admitted.

"Why?"

"She was already disappointed in me—I could see it in her eyes. She looked me up and down with a sour face. I'm not who she expected."

"You don't have to be mean to people, Belle. She was only trying to be friendly." He sounded too much like my mother: *you have to make an effort.*

"Well, if she's so nice, why did she have to go running to you and tattle?"

His shoulders tensed; he was too good, too gentle, for this, for me. And right then, I did feel a sudden self-consciousness and was ashamed. *Damn you, Eliza.* She'd made him see me in a new light, made all my flaws too apparent.

"I'm sorry," I said. "I'll try better next time." My apology seemed to work, and the worry lines in his face retreated.

"That would be nice," he said. Then he turned. "Where's the cake she brought?" he asked.

"I ate it."

"All of it?" He glanced down to my belly, its bulge hidden by my T-shirt.

I sat up, sucked it in. "I had nothing else to do."

He thought for a moment. "You'd better find a hobby," he said.

I MADE SURE Eliza knew how I felt about her and her meddling from that moment on. I didn't need anyone to point out my problems to Worthy, thank you very much. The next afternoon, I set out on a walk into town, and I could see her pale face with those pressed lips peeking out at me from behind her curtains. (It wouldn't be the last time I'd catch her spying; later, I caught a glimpse of her white face peering into our bedroom from one of her windows. After that, I liked to leave the lights on in our bedroom as I got dressed, taking perverse pleasure in knowing that should she dare to spy, she'd get more than an eyeful.) I knew she would catalogue my actions, take note of everything I did, and report anything suspicious to Worthy. And so that day I turned around and bent over, offering her a view of my wide behind, wishing I wore skirts so that I could moon her properly.

"Kiss my arse, you Nosy Parker!" I hollered, smacking my ass for emphasis. She pulled back from the window so fast her curtains fluttered.

Our cluster of company houses overlooked the town. From up here, it looked small, a tiny square of shops and signs. Downtown, it wasn't much better. Silver Falls was sad, washed up, though it didn't seem to know it yet. There wasn't much to write home about: Harold's Department Store (*They have everything you need*, Worthy said), a few smaller shops, one hotel and beer parlour blasting country and western music. Winos lurched on street corners with empty, lost expressions. Later, I would come across a group of nine-year-old boys, giggling and drunk on cheap wine, carrying makeshift torches of rags and hockey sticks, heading toward the abandoned mine shafts. Truth was, there wasn't much else to do in Silver Falls but play in the mines and hope not to die. I didn't see anyone my age.

When I returned home, I dragged a dining room chair onto the small porch and just sat. I felt like one of those old people you see in small towns who just sit on their porches and rock in their chairs, chewing ever so slowly on a piece of straw. I picked the lint from my clothes, I brushed and plaited, tied and retied my hair. I rolled up the hems of my jeans to my knees and wore my sneakers without socks. I sat on that tiny square porch and waited for something to happen.

I wandered around the house for the first few months, not really sure what to do with myself. *Get a hobby,* Worthy had said, but what? Oscar and Worthy together in the house was almost worse than being alone. Oh sure, we talked. We talked about how much colder the weather became, how bare the trees seemed as the summer gave way to the fall; we talked about Danny Bellows and his wife, what a shame it was, how *tragic,* when they lost a child to cancer; we talked about everything and nothing. We didn't talk about the great silences between us, didn't mention the quiet unravelling of our marriage. Worthy didn't have enough love for the both of us, and that was the problem.

One afternoon I dug through my suitcase and unearthed all my maps. I found some tape in the kitchen and spent the next hour papering the walls of our room, then sat cross-legged and traced the roads and rivers with my eyes.

Accused in Kidnapping Case an Oddity

Sources say that searches through suspected child molester Belle Dearing's trailer have revealed a number of curiosities, including a multitude of old maps gracing the walls, a pair of gold wedding bands in a small velvet box, and a jar of what Ms. Dearing originally told police were cremated human remains (later confirmed to be dirt). Stranger still, she appeared to have collected photographs of and articles about Pierre Elliott Trudeau in a type of scrapbook. In one photograph in the scrapbook, a much younger Ms. Dearing shares an intimate kiss with the former Prime Minister of Canada. When questioned by reporters about the meaning of the photograph, the police refused to comment, although one source said, "Well, Mr. Trudeau was a potent guy. It wouldn't surprise me if they had an affair."

EIGHT

I miss being at home with all of my memories. They went through it all, you know. The guard brought me a newspaper this morning; there it was, right on the front page, as if I was the single most important piece of news in this day and age of wars and famine and terror: *Accused in Kidnapping Case an Oddity.* They poked through everything in the house and in the trailer, and those local reporters of ours were quick to snap up the details of my life. Ludlow is a small town, really, with not much else going on. I should have moved to a big city, where I would have been left alone to do as I pleased, no one to point fingers and whisper. Now they're sorting through everything, making neat piles, trying to label it all, give it some kind of meaning. I picture them pausing, chins cupped in palms, before the maps that were taped to the walls, trying to piece together my journeys, wondering how they fit with the many pictures of Mr. Pierre Elliott Trudeau and the wooden carvings of pregnant women. My life in a nutshell. When I think of this, I start to laugh and can't stop for a long while, laugh until my voice rises into a harsh scream, bringing running footsteps down the hall.

I KNEW that Pierre Trudeau would never love me as I loved him, but a girl had to have one dream, after all. After a few years in

Silver Falls, there was nothing left for me, and the blankness of the days began to press, smothering me from all sides. I started collecting photographs of the Prime Minister a year after I arrived, when I realized that Silver Falls—no matter how romantic it sounded, how impossibly exotic—was nothing more than a miserable hole in the land.

"Is there an actual falls?" I asked Worthy once.

"What?"

"A falls? Like *Silver Falls*? Where is it?"

He seemed to think long and hard, but then simply shrugged. "Don't think so," he said.

I thought I was used to small towns, small minds, but the people in Silver Falls seemed set apart, close-knit and nosy but still adrift, somehow, suspicious of everyone around them. What I didn't know then was that everyone who stayed in the town had nowhere else to go, stayed even when their dreams of fortune went belly up. If ever asked, those who stayed beyond the silver rush, those who buried roots and kept standing when the veins dried up, could never come up with a reason for their loyalty. I don't think anyone truly loved the town; it had just never occurred to them to leave. Or at least this is what Gema would tell me later.

Though the town had boomed when the nickel mines began in the late fifties, I could tell that it wouldn't last long. There were signs of decay already by the time I arrived in 1968. There were few young people; most got the hell out as soon as they could, away from the prying eyes and mean mouths, away from limited opportunities and the stale sameness of everyday life.

With nothing else to do, the ones who stayed took an inordinate interest in the details of other lives: eyes followed us wherever we went, scrutinizing the items in our grocery baskets, counting the number of bottles we returned to the beer store, gauging the space between our bodies when we ventured into town. And the truth is, Worthy and I moved awkwardly around each other with the unbearable sense that we were intruding in the other's space.

It wasn't long before I hated everything about Worthy: the way he tapped his fork against the side of his plate at dinner, the whistling noises from his nose while he slept, the way his earlobe curved, big and fat, against his cheek. When he was in the house with me, I couldn't stop my mouth from opening, couldn't stop the sharp nagging as the complaints piled on top of one another and merged into a single unhappy whine.

It's no wonder he left almost every night, whether he was working or not; I would have too, if the town's one bar (in the lobby of the hotel) hadn't frowned on women drinking. When people ask me why my marriage to Worthy failed, I usually say that Worthy drank. That's not entirely true; I drank too. It started out of boredom, something to fill the time, but it didn't start right away. For a while—until the winter set in—I simply sat on the porch and waited, pulling my sweater ever tighter as the winds picked up and the leaves dried and shrivelled and fell to the sidewalks.

When the snow forced me inside, I tried to keep busy. I began knitting, using a set of instructions, needles, and a ball of wool I unearthed from a dresser drawer, left behind by previous tenants (purple wool shot with flecks of yellow; ugly even in the sixties, but remember, what did I care?). I knitted a scarf twelve feet long until I realized the page of instructions on casting off was missing and threw the whole lot in the trash.

I made a half-hearted attempt at becoming a success in the kitchen, a real Julia Child, but I wasn't any good. I would always forget to buy some crucial ingredient at the supermarket; my *chicken cordon bleu* would end up without the *cordon* or the *bleu*. I know it sounds funny now, but you should have seen Worthy and Oscar sampling each dinner with a bit of fear.

"Mmm," they'd say, trying for enthusiasm, their anxious smiles sliding into surprise or bewilderment, bite after bite.

In December, I had nothing else to do, so I started cleaning and didn't stop for three weeks solid. I cleaned under baseboards with a metal nail file, scraped grime from the edges of linoleum tiles, scrubbed fixtures with an old toothbrush and baking soda. And then one day I just stopped, wedged partially beneath the refrigerator, and pressed my forehead to the kitchen floor. There I stayed until the boys came home, stayed while Worthy, embarrassed, tried to haul me to my feet, his meaty hands tucked under my armpits, stayed while Oscar turned three shades of red and escaped into his room.

Meanwhile, I wrote cheery letters home describing the *landscape* of Silver Falls, the *awkward beauty* of a land destroyed by mining. I couldn't admit my defeat, imagining Gardie's smirk. *I told you so.* I christened the walls of our bedroom with more maps. My mother had sent the last—a map of Vermont—with her latest letter. *So you won't forget,* she wrote. She drew a smiling face next to the line to soften her words.

I let my failure swallow me whole. There was no money to visit my family at Christmas, so we stayed home and drank schnapps, staring at the scraggly tree the boys dragged home, decorated with popcorn and cranberries. As the alcohol burned down my throat and settled in my stomach, I felt all right for the first time, warm behind my eyes, a muffled buzzing in my ears. I saw the kindness in Worthy, sensed his own sadness. I sat down beside him on the couch and threaded my arm through his, my throat aching to see his surprise, his smile. The next morning I woke to grey winter light slanting through the window and Worthy's leg thrown heavily over mine, and the old emptiness came back in a rush.

Only alcoholics drank in the morning; I waited until noon. As soon as I had a few beers, the pleasant buzzing would return and reached in to fill the gaps inside me, inside our life in Silver Falls. Then I didn't mind Worthy so much, could even look at him with a sort of fondness, could say *there's my husband* without choking. I never drank a lot all at once; I spaced it out to keep a constant flow so that I was never outwardly drunk. I never slurred my words or swayed. You would hardly know it was happening at all if you couldn't smell it on me.

So I was mildly drunk whenever Worthy came home from his day or afternoon shifts, and Worthy was mildly drunk when he came home from the bar. We were never both sober when we were together, and I suppose this made it all bearable. When other people reminisce about 1969 and all that it meant to them, I remember it as a time before anything happened. I was so *unaware* back then. I didn't realize that boundaries had been cut, that people my age and younger were doing so many important things, following their hearts and living, breathing new ideas. There was no revolution—quiet or otherwise—in Silver Falls, and news trickled in slowly.

This was probably when I fell in love with Trudeau, though I can't say for sure. I just remember seeing his face on the front page of the newspaper and feeling drawn to that smile, a certain spark that caught my attention. Or maybe it was the flashy car, the dignified but flippant way his arm raised in a wave. He looked, to me, like a man who knew what he wanted and exactly how to get it, a man who lived his life as he pleased. I didn't pay any attention to politics at the time, but there was a photograph of Trudeau in the House of Commons wearing sandals on his feet; that made me like him even more. I began to take an interest in the newspaper, but only to flip through for mention or more pictures of the Prime Minister:

here with two long-haired hippies of some importance or other, here making some witty remark to a reporter, here signing autographs. I cut out all the photos I could find, leaving gaps and oddly shaped holes in the paper, and pasted them in a scrapbook I kept, a big wide cardboard-backed book with manila pages that I found in the gift wrap section of Harold's Department Store. We had a television but could only get two or three channels, and only after bending to fiddle this way and that with the antennas until the snow on the screen cleared to a more manageable fuzziness. I sat close to get a better look as crowds of women screamed and swooned, his voice perfectly rounding out elegant sentences with a cheeky wink or grin.

"You'll go blind if you sit that close," Oscar snapped, stretching his neck in exaggeration to prove that I was in his way, but I ignored him. I wouldn't swoon if I met Mr. Trudeau, I thought, but how wonderful it would be to get him into bed.

To say that I was disappointed in my sex life would be an understatement. Those first gropings with Worthy—first in Newfoundland, later in my cottage—were promising. I liked what he became, touching me like that, his eyes alight and his hands almost rough. When he fell asleep on our honeymoon, I should have known right then that it wasn't going to be as I'd imagined, and it all went downhill from there, frankly.

All that unfulfilled energy has to go somewhere, I suppose. I posted an advertisement down at the grocery store for house-cleaning services; it was the only thing I figured I could do to both keep me occupied and work off my increasing irritation and make money at the same time. I spent four mornings a week peering into other lives, scraping out dirt from corners and finding hidden stashes of secrets (pornographic magazines and books; love letters, tear-stained and crumpled; small bags of dope or enough prescription pill bottles to keep many a Silver Faller in a state of deep sleep).

I'd become obsessed with order, the way things had to be. Everything had its rightful place, and it was my job to make sure it stayed that way. It went beyond clean, you see. Chairs were placed just so along the edges of tiles so that the perfect amount of linoleum showed on each side of the legs; towels in the bathroom had to hang evenly, tags tucked down and in; socks were folded together and lined up in colour-coordinated rows in drawers; the bar of soap had to be rinsed free of any excess bubbles before it was returned to its plastic holder in the bathtub.

Worthy knew well enough not to throw his clothes in a heap on the closet floor, knew to brush any crumbs from the dinner table onto his plate at the end of the meal, but Oscar—Oscar was a different story. He had no sense of neatness, that boy, and no reason to. When he lived at home, his mother cleaned up after him; when he moved to Silver Falls, Worthy had done the housework. But now I refused.

"He can at least take his own plate from the table," I said to Worthy more than once. "He just leaves it there for me. His plate, his napkin." Everything smeared with food and saliva, waiting to rub against my skin. Even that I could live with, but Oscar had a habit of leaving small bits of toilet paper in a trail along the floor, the sink. What he did with all of it I didn't want to know, but those bits of paper, sticking to my bare feet, drove me to distraction.

But maybe we aggravated each other, I can admit that now. For example, people have a lot of words for alcohol. For some reason, I called it *pooch* for a while. I don't know what I was thinking, or if my mind was confused with some other word, but in any case, once I said it, I couldn't go back, and the word stuck. Worthy thought it was funny; he'd grab my midsection and jiggle it up and down. *Here's your pooch, missus.* But it drove Oscar crazy. The cords on his thin neck would thicken and bulge, his mouth pressed down.

"Pooch means dog," he'd say. "Not beer."

"It does now."

"You can't just use any old word you want, Belle."

"Why not?"

"You just can't!" And that's when his jaw would clench and seem to widen, his eyes blinking fast. So I'd smile like a sweet little nothing, nod my head as if he were right. And just as he relaxed, just as his shoulders dropped down again, I'd throw it at him.

"Before you go, grab me a pooch from the refrigerator, would you? There's a good boy."

MY THIRD SUMMER in Silver Falls, the summer of 1970, Prime Minister Trudeau came through the town on his way to Thunder Bay, and I was ready. He wasn't stopping for long, not like in the bigger cities, where he'd get out and walk around signing autographs or ride mini-motorcycles with glee, but still, it was something, wasn't it? The town newspaper (called *The Silver News*—how original, don't you think?) printed his name in block letters for weeks leading up to the visit, first in speculation (TRUDEAU COMING TO SILVER FALLS?), then with orgasmic glee (TRUDEAU HEADS FOR SILVER FALLS!). It was all anyone could talk about. According to Eliza Whittle (who herself attempted to look blasé and bored but had already bought a new lipstick and outfit for the occasion, or so she told Worthy), the town's one beauty salon was overbooked in the days leading up to his visit.

I considered it my one chance, braided my hair wet the night before, then unwound it in waves on the big day. Everyone dressed up; even the dowdiest of wives put on a collared shirt or the nicest dress. I knew that I'd stand out more in my overalls and sneakers, but I figured that Pierre (for that's what I called him now) preferred someone a little more refined and bought myself a new outfit at Harold's with some of my cleaning money. I couldn't bring myself to buy a dress—especially those short numbers they were parading down at Harold's—so settled on a nice aqua tunic belted over a pair of tan summer slacks. I still wore my sneakers.

There were too many people at the railway station, too many smells. It seemed that everyone wanted a glimpse of his brightness, a chance to touch him as he lowered his arm out the window. I fanned myself with my hand, looked over my shoulder, stepped on someone's foot. You think it's an exaggeration to say that the whole town showed up, but in this case it was true. There really wasn't anything else going on, and hadn't been for some time. Eliza smiled and waved, then pushed her way toward us, her pointy, bony little fingers tucked into her husband's elbow.

"We never get any excitement here," she said. "Imagine, the Prime Minister in Silver Falls."

"Not really *in* it," I said. "Just *passing through*. There's a big difference." Her mouth sucked in when she frowned at me, glanced at Worthy in reproach as if to say, *You see?*

"Still, it's something," she said. "Almost as good as having the Queen." I was about to tell Eliza what I thought of the Queen, just to see her face harden and crack wide open, but good Lord, *he was here*, the train chuffing slowly toward the station.

I pushed my way to the front of the crowd, leaving Worthy and the rest behind. *Pierre, here I am!* Bodies crushed and surged forward, arms raised, the stench of perfumed powder and the darker, rank smell of sweat. A great cheer swelled as the train came into sight, and his arm dropped down through the window in a wave. Hands clasped his briefly, then released, everyone straining to touch or be touched.

This was my moment. Here he was, in the flesh—full-blooming smile, his cuffed shirt and striped white suit pristine against the dark windowsill, the bright sun adding layers of sheen, the single red rose tucked in his lapel. I pressed my palms flat along the side of the train for an instant before the heat seared my skin, then looked up into a pair of piercing eyes that seemed to hold a promise of understanding. I believed he was here to rescue me, and that was all I needed.

He bent his head down and smiled at me—and only me. *Oh, Pierre!* Up, up went my arms, so quickly that no one reacted. I still can't believe I did it. I hoisted myself up on the window, legs hanging, and kissed him on the lips. That kiss seemed to go on forever, until strange hands pried my fingers loose from his neck and I tumbled to the ground.

I must have screamed as my arm bent backwards and broke in a snap, sending a shard of bone through my skin, because all of a sudden the crowd closed around me and faces peered down, concerned.

"Someone get a doctor!"

Blackness spread from the corners of my eyes and closed in on blurry faces. I smiled, I think, before I fainted, remembering the feel of the Prime Minister's lips against mine.

I WAS FAMOUS after the kiss, if only for a little while. A reporter managed to capture a photograph at the very moment our lips connected, and placed it on the front page of *The Silver News*.

"My cousin in Ottawa said it was in the papers there too," Eliza told Worthy. "Can you imagine?" Worthy smiled, but it didn't spread to his eyes. After I got home from the hospital, arm set in a thick white cast, I began to bleed. My fourth miscarriage.

He wouldn't come right out and say it was my fault, but I knew that my fall from the train couldn't have helped matters. Worthy desperately wanted a baby. I could see it in his eyes, could feel it in his heavy breath every time he approached me with that poking intrusion. He kept track of my monthlies so he knew right away if I was late.

The first time we were pregnant, his smile stayed on his face for two weeks, and his hands would reach out for me, my shoulders, my neck, my hands, whenever they could. He stood in Oscar's room, arms crossed, his eyes imagining all that it could be with a little paint, a little paper, a little baby in a crib by the window.

"What about me?" Oscar whined. "Where will I sleep?"

"You can go where all the bachelors go," I said. It's where he belonged, in any case, the boarding house outside the mine gates, instead of crushing in here with us, crowding our house, our *space*.

I thought I liked the idea of a baby. I knew for sure I would like the way it would send Oscar away and please Worthy. It was bad enough that I wasn't the kind of wife he needed; month after month I proved I couldn't be a mother either. After a while I stopped hoping, came to expect Worthy's long face and the disappointment in his eyes.

The summer of 1970 was different. The bleeding stopped after two days. Three weeks later, Worthy came home to find a half-cooked pan of ground beef left on the stove; the smell had suddenly driven me from the room and up to my bed, where I lived for the next six weeks. I couldn't keep anything down, threw up five to ten times a day. When I couldn't take it anymore, I visited the town's one family doctor, a bachelor Frenchman with a thick moustache and a bulging belly, who told me that morning sickness was all in my head. He sent me home with pamphlets on nutrition and detailed diagrams of what was happening to my body.

They were all thrilled, of course, my mother, my aunt—even Gardie signed her name to a card. My mother said she'd come out to help when the baby was born and sent me a list of questions that (she said) would help identify if it was a boy or a girl. But no one was so happy as Worthy. Out came his hands again, touching and patting until I wanted to scream. Hormones? My skin buzzed and crawled when he came near me in those early weeks; I wanted nothing to do with him.

I was miserable. I kept reminding myself why I'd ever wanted a baby in the first place, kept trying to picture the happiness Worthy would have, but my noble ambition became smaller and fainter with each day I spent hunched over the toilet bowl. And I was tired, so tired my legs felt filled with lead. My head and eyes ached, I sniffled with a cold, my nose bled, and my breasts jutted out, veiny and tender.

Worthy brought home thick obstetrical books from the library and pored over them in the evenings, making soft grunting noises from his chair in the living room as he read.

"By twelve weeks you'll feel a lot better," he said hopefully. He lined up various items representing the size of the baby over the weeks. They remained on the kitchen counter until I threw them out in a fit of cleaning in my fifth month: the tiny apple seed, lone cashew, the plum, the orange.

I only hoped for one thing: that this baby would make everything all right again. I was convinced I would feel more like a wife, Worthy would be happy, and we would all get on with our lives instead of wandering aimlessly in this void. As you might have guessed by now, I couldn't have been more wrong.

NINE

When I first met Theo Visser, I paid no attention to him, though he said he noticed me right away. And of course he would—I'd burst through the entrance of the bar in the Silver Inn downtown, where few women dared (or cared) to venture. I pushed my way through thick cigar fumes and grabbed Worthy by the collar.

"Enough!" Every man in the place set down his glass and looked me over. It was unusual, frowned upon, to see a woman in the bar, even a woman like me—hard around the edges, you might say, feet thrust into rubber boots, winter coat pulled around my flannel nightgown, pregnant belly just beginning to blossom. Never mess with a pregnant woman, I always say.

"You told us to go out," Oscar protested. This was true; I had driven Worthy and Oscar out of the house with my constant nagging and grumpiness. But that didn't mean I wanted them to have fun.

Oh, then they cursed me, they did, in drunken slurs all the way home, but I didn't care. I stopped to let Worthy vomit (meat loaf and peas and potatoes) onto a snowbank, stepping back at just the right time so that nothing could splash on my legs. I was tempted to kick him in the bum and send him flying face first, but held myself back to retain some of my dignity. And Oscar, laughing wildly at me, at Worthy, his gangly arms and legs pinwheeling in a comical stupor.

The next time I saw Theo, it was all Gema's doing. I'd met her at the supermarket, when she suddenly appeared behind a cash register wearing the store's red smock and silly bow ribbon around her neck. Her hair hung iron straight down to her elbows and was a strange orange-yellow (meant to be blond, she told me later, but obviously something had gone wrong). She stood out because there were no women or girls my age in town, none at all. She must have been surprised to see me as well, though her brown eyes beneath a thick fringe of bangs gave nothing away. Instead, she looked me up and down slowly—my chest straining against the bib of my largest pair of overalls, five-month belly pressing, uncomfortable and tight, against the waistband, the man's woollen overcoat covered with nubbly fuzzballs, the itchy red scarf twined twice around my neck—then looked away.

I never understood those movies about girlfriends, never felt the yearnings that others obviously did for whispered secrets shared and endless afternoons listening to records. But as I stood in Gema's line, I felt inadequate in my friendless state. Her easy dismissal of me made me determined to make her my first true friend.

"Nice bow." I gestured to my own scarved neck, wondered if the neckband of my T-shirt was clean, decided I didn't care, but then buttoned up my coat. When she looked at me, the light hit her eyes so that they glowed yellow around the edges. She raised her eyebrows and kept punching in my items: five apples, loaf of bread, carrots, mushrooms, butter, ground beef, and pork chops.

"A girl with your fashion sense must be able to help me." I said it with a straight face. She couldn't help it; her eyes flicked over me again, over my hair tied into one thick braid that fell to the middle of my back. I saw the exact moment she realized it was a joke, saw her lip twitch. She leaned forward on her arms. The sleeve of her white blouse rose to reveal an olive wrist and simple leather bracelet stamped with the peace symbol.

"Sure." She drew out the word so that it poured, thick as the molasses we used to slather on our bread back home. "We'll go to the shop."

WE MET the following day at three in the afternoon, after she finished her shift. She'd changed from the red smock and white blouse that made her look so wholesome, and now wore purple bell bottoms and a shirt with a scoop neck that was too small and dipped low under her open winter coat. She fussed with a beret and matching scarf and gloves, her breath pluming out in front of her.

"Do you think I look all right?" She looked better than all right to me; she matched and seemed practically cosmopolitan. She liked hearing that, smiled in a secretive way.

"I haven't seen any other people my age here," I said as we walked.

"That's because there aren't any. They all left." She had that northern Ontario accent I'd come to recognize and adopt as my own; almost lilting, but the edges left innocent, a tone that made everything hopeful and young and new.

"Why did they leave?"

"Because nothing ever changes in places like this," she said. "Nothing progresses. The only change would be backwards. Once the mines close down for good, this town will just kind of fade away. And that's why they leave." She herself was from Sudbury, used to have a job as a receptionist in a doctor's office and an apartment just blocks from her parents' house.

She was wrong about the town: years later, Silver Falls would explode in a single blaze. But I could see then the signs—the old getting older, the young children drunk in abandoned mines, the dry scrapings of leaves across deserted sidewalks as the cold set in each autumn.

"Why did you move here?"

She smiled, her face softening and pinking. We had arrived at the shop. She touched her palm briefly against the display window, leaving ghostly fingerprints that slowly disappeared. Our reflections caught us as we were then, and I can still see us, untouched by life's tragedies, faces smooth and perfect as the glass.

His name was Nathan, the reason she came. When she pushed through the doorway of the shop, she became someone new: brighter skin, wider eyes, hair that bounced jauntily rather than slid down her back. She lost the edge of sharpness that hardened her eyes and words. Nathan smiled absently from behind the cash register, tucked a piece of wheat-coloured hair behind his ear, and I could tell he didn't feel the same about Gema, could tell he thought she was great but *not in that way*. Later, in her apartment in town, she smoked a cigarette and told me how his hands felt.

"I was alive for the first time," she said. I wondered at that, envied her flushed cheeks and damp fingertips at the mention of his name.

The store carried anything and everything handmade or grown in Silver Falls. It had a name, but now I can't remember what it was; everyone simply referred to it as *the shop*. There were wooden carvings shining smooth and bald, crocheted pot holders, vegetables in wicker baskets at the front that gave off an earthy smell. And way at the back, there were clothes. I wrapped coloured beads around my neck and picked out a pair of red pants with an elastic waistband and a white peasant blouse.

Gema trailed behind me, murmuring about the pants, the beads, but her eyes slid sideways every few minutes, watching

Nathan. He sat in a chair behind the counter, legs crossed, a ratty paperback balanced in one hand, long slim fingers twisting his bottom lip as he read. He was good-looking in a gangly, light way, but there were too many sharp corners—all elbows and knees, the outline of his Adam's apple jutting beneath the skin of his neck. He looked up once or twice to find Gema staring, and smiled back before returning to his book.

"He does things to me I didn't even know existed," she would tell me later, describing them in such detail that even I would feel embarrassed, would have to turn my face away. And I would think back to that first meeting in the shop and wonder if she was making it all up.

The shop was owned by a Canadian but run by a group of draft dodgers who lived on a ramshackle farm on the outskirts of town, not quite out, not quite in. *War resisters*, they called themselves. *Them hippies in the country*, the older folks in Silver Falls called them. No one really knew what went on over there, and some people (Eliza Whittle whispered in Worthy's ear) believed there were drugs and orgies and other satanic American rituals. Still, no one interfered, and certainly no one called the Mounties; the wars had taken too many men from Silver Falls. More than that, it was hard for anyone in town to much care about the war or what a group of young men who didn't cause any trouble, at least not in town where respectable citizens could see it, did with their time.

I didn't look at Americans any differently in those days; I'd almost been an American once, before turning back into a Canadian, so I knew how it felt to be both and realized we were all the same, no matter what border you faced. And I didn't know or care much about the Vietnam War, though Uncle Erik had signed up in November. I didn't read the newspaper and rarely watched the news unless Pierre was on. And there were lots of people like me, you'd better believe it. We didn't want to see horrible pictures of burning villages, not here in Silver Falls.

"Can I try these on?" I asked Nathan, holding up the pants and blouse. He nodded, slowly made his way over, and showed me into a back room hidden by a curtain where I could change. He had pale blue eyes, dark eyelashes, thick lips. I would have said he was *pretty*. It smelled musty in the back room; along the shelves that lined the walls were yet more carvings, small gourds from the fall, canvas bags stuffed and bulging mysteriously, a half-eaten sandwich in waxed paper.

I removed my overalls and T-shirt and bundled them into a tight ball. As I stood naked except for my underwear, cold air brushed beneath my arms and against the back of my knees, bringing goosebumps. I wondered what would happen if Nathan walked in and saw me, pregnant mound of belly and breasts, imagined throwing open the curtain to looks of surprise and shock.

Instead, I wound the beads around my neck, first cool, then warm and solid against my skin, slipped on the new clothes with relief. I began to put on my boots, then stopped, wrapped them in the ball with my overalls, suddenly aching to feel the ground against my bare feet. I slid back the curtain.

Gema leaned forward on the counter, her cheek pressed against Nathan's as he whispered in her ear. When she turned to me, her eyes glowed yellow again.

"Better?" she asked. She noticed my bare feet, paused, then came around behind me and unbraided my hair, letting it out in waves that felt feather soft against the back of my neck. Nathan smiled his approval, and something inside me shifted there in the musty store, the smell of gourds and Gema's smoky hands. For the first time, I was aware of my skin against fabric, the sway of my hips, the weight of my breasts.

"Nathan's invited us up to his place tonight," Gema said. "Can you come?"

I thought of Worthy and Oscar, the closeness of the walls waiting for me at home. I nodded.

"Let's go now," I said.

I DIDN'T GO HOME that night but slept on the faded green couch in Gema's apartment, shifting and turning to make myself comfortable, my hips aching and neck twisted the wrong way. When I woke in the morning, deep guilt and shame pressed on my chest. I pictured poor Worthy, his face white and drawn and worried, waiting at the kitchen table all night with his hands in fists. How to explain my absence, how to explain that something extraordinary had happened when nothing really tangible had happened at all?

There was Theo. I noticed him, all right. He sprawled on the couch in the front room of the farmhouse, hair the colour of mocha fudge, shaggy and unkempt, thick sideburns curving over his cheekbones, black turtleneck and low-slung blue jeans. When I looked at him, it was like being sucked into the end of a vacuum cleaner; everything in my head tumbled about and rearranged itself so that nothing seemed right or real. I ran upstairs and was sick to my stomach.

"You're in love," Gema said later, when I told her what happened.

"No."

"Yes." She folded her hands in front of her as if she was praying. "Belle, that's your body telling you something."

"Maybe he makes me sick," I said.

"Maybe he's going to change your life."

Bodies moved in and out of the rooms in the old farmhouse. My senses overloaded: the smell of food baking in the kitchen, the echo of plates and bowls stacked in piles on a giant wooden table in the dining room, voices overlapping with muffled laughter and conversation and music that seemed as thick as syrup. I passed on a joint that suddenly materialized between my fingers. Theo took it from me, dimples flashing in his cheeks, the touch of his skin against mine nearly burning. He didn't talk to me at first, just watched with a small smile, as if he knew things that he shouldn't.

"I've seen you before," he said.

"I don't think so." Gema had disappeared into a room with Nathan. I felt a momentary sense of bewilderment at finding myself alone with this man in this place. My vision narrowed, all other sounds drowned out by the intensity in his eyes.

"At the tavern downtown one night. In your nightgown." His lips moved, twitched; he might have been laughing at me.

I tried for indignation but could only feel mortified. "That was me, all right," I admitted.

He smiled then, a lazy, slow smile that spread languidly from one corner of his mouth to the other. He leaned forward, placed his lips against my ear, his breath raising goosebumps along my arms. "You looked like a goddess," he said.

That's when I excused myself, lurched to the washroom up rickety old stairs, and threw up.

I stayed in the bathroom for a long time, peeling yellow flowered wallpaper from the corner behind the toilet, until someone pounded on the door. My wrists ached and shook; my knees felt bruised.

"Are you all right?" I looked at his hair, the way it fell over his ears, the blue jeans that weren't too tight but fit just right, hugging his thigh muscles and settling on his hips gently. They've done research now; they're called *pheromones*. I was afraid to get too close or I'd be pulled forever to his side.

"I think I need to lie down," I said.

Lines on his forehead crinkled. "You can sleep in my room." He grasped my elbow and led me forward, down the hall, and pushed open a door.

My word, the mess, the mess. Every surface covered by books, wooden carvings half completed, canvases and brushes upended and stiff with hardened, cracked paint. In one corner, dirty clothes toppled onto a row of empty beer bottles. Spare change and crumpled bits of paper littered his dresser. A lone grey sock peeked from a lumpy comforter bunched up on his bed, where clothes—presumably clean—were stacked and merely pushed aside when he slept. You may guess: it made my scalp itch, this mess, this disorder. But then his fingers brushed my arm, and I simply forgot about everything. He pushed aside the laundry, pulled the bedspread taut, patting the lumps until they disappeared.

"Sleep," he said, leaving me alone in the dark room that smelled musky and deep.

I awoke disoriented and stumbled downstairs. Gema touched my elbow. "I've been looking for you," she said.

I didn't see Theo again that night, left without saying goodbye.

I EXPECTED WORTHY to be at work when I crept back home like a guilty teenager, but I found him in our room, methodically tearing my maps from the walls.

"What are you doing?" He froze when he heard my voice, turned slowly to face me. He crumpled a map in his fists, bits of paper stuck beneath his fingernails. His mouth pulled down, opened, shut again. There was no colour to his face, no expression.

Without a word, he pushed past me. That was Worthy's problem: he needed to rant and rave, grab me, demand to know where I'd been. But instead there were only distant sounds of anger: heavy feet stamping down the hallway, the front door wrenched open and then slammed. From the living room window I watched him head north toward the mines, his hands shoved in the pockets of his winter jacket. He'd forgotten his toque; his shoulders rose as if to protect his ears from the cold. He looked back once, his face still and flat.

Almost all my maps were torn or squashed into tight balls. I flattened each one out carefully and hid them at the bottom of my suitcase before lying down on the bed, my hands resting on top of my belly. I wished for an upside-down world where everything was different. I wished I weren't pregnant, wished I weren't married, wished I weren't trapped in a box. I'd had my first taste of freedom, and I liked it too much.

When Worthy came home that night, he refused to look at me. We three ate silently at the kitchen table, Oscar darting narrow looks at me, curling his upper lip.

"Have fun last night?" he said finally.

"Oscar." Worthy's jaw clenched, bulging against the side of his cheek. Oscar pushed back his chair hard enough to gouge the linoleum. Carrying his plate over to the garbage, he began to scrape the remains of his dinner into the bin while I watched. I chewed faster, pressing my molars together with force, bit my lip accidentally. The taste of blood angered me.

"Didn't like your chicken?" I asked.

He stopped, narrowed his eyes again. In slow motion, he held up the plate for me to see, then dropped it into the trash, fork and knife clattering on top. I looked at Worthy, but he kept his head down.

I CLEANED THE KITCHEN after dinner, moving slowly to delay the inevitable. The sponge rubbed soapy and soft against my palm and drew wet lines along the countertop.

"He waited up for you all night." Oscar leaned against the kitchen wall, arms crossed in front of him.

"I know."

"He thought you left, did you know that? Thought you hopped on the train and went back to Vermont."

"He thought I left him?" This had never occurred to me.

"Thought he'd never see his baby."

I opened my mouth to say something, perhaps to tell Oscar that it was none of his business, but he didn't wait to hear it, slamming his bedroom door shut before I could say a word.

I turned off the lights, feeling the dark silence wrap around me like a blanket. Worthy was already in bed, curled up under the covers, his back to me. I could tell by his breathing that he wasn't asleep yet, though he pretended. I sat on the edge of the bed in my nightgown, hands folded in my lap. Just sat, trying to form the words to explain. Moonlight crept through the edges of the blinds, giving everything a faint blue-white glow.

"Yesterday, you know what I did?" He didn't move, but his shoulders rose and tensed, his breath caught for a moment. "I took off my shoes and went outside, stood in the snow with bare feet." Gema and Nathan had laughed, called me crazy. I stood for only a minute, maybe less, before the sensation changed from wet, cool liberty to something closer to pain.

Lying down, I pulled the comforter up to my neck, matched my breathing to Worthy's. It wasn't much of an explanation.

"Worthy, I'm sorry," I whispered, and touched his arm. And then, "I would never take this baby away from you."

He sighed, a long, noisy exhalation, and pulled his arm away so that no part of our bodies touched.

TEN

If you fast-forward a few years, what will you have? A fistful of tear-stained pages, Uncle Erik's disappearance (MIA: three little letters blotted and blurred as if dipped in water), Gardie's downward spiral as she overdosed, not once but twice, and then also disappeared. But if you skip past those years, what will you miss? A waiting period of sorts, and then all the events that tumbled forward, too fast.

The Christmas after I met Theo, I sat down to dinner with Worthy and Oscar and didn't think of anything at all. The turkey tasted flat, dust in my mouth, the potatoes lumpy, cold. But we ate in the kitchen with red candles lit in the centre of the table and patterned snow that came from a can sprayed on the windows in the shape of snowflakes. We had a tree, decorated with coloured lights and silver icicles, but our voices were too loud and bright, our laughs too hearty. We weren't very good at the game, not anymore.

On New Year's Eve, Worthy stayed home with his pregnant wife and pretended he didn't want to go downtown with Oscar instead. We ate canned creamed salmon poured over slices of buttered toast and clinked glasses of champagne at midnight to welcome in 1971. I was twenty-one, Worthy twenty-three, and it felt like we'd been married for all our lives. When I looked in the mirror, I imagined an old, worn-out face.

I stayed away from *them hippies in the country* for a long time. I saw Gema often; she would sometimes whisper *And Theo?*, but I'd just shrug as if none of it mattered at all. I didn't want it to matter. Instead, I busied myself cleaning homes, ate creamed salmon on toast, and let Worthy make love to me when the shades were pulled down and darkness covered my face.

And then, suddenly, there he was in the shop, planting himself in front of me as I ran my fingers over yet another carving.

"Do you like it?" he asked. I could barely look at him, my arms and legs tingling. I nodded.

"Those are my carvings," he said.

"They're wonderful." And they were—all birds and horses and dogs, fine details etched into dark or light wood.

"Wonderful," he repeated. He stood too close; his breath brushed my neck, raised goosebumps.

I turned my face away and pretended to examine the carvings more closely. "You only do animals?"

"I'd like to do you." He smiled at that. "I'd like to carve you. Do you mind?"

I didn't know what to say, felt my own heat spreading up from my legs to cover my chest and neck and face.

I borrowed gema's car and drove up to Theo's farm on a Thursday near the end of January while Worthy slept off his night shift, seven months pregnant and knowing full well I was playing with fire and setting myself onto a different path. Theo unfolded long legs from the couch, led me outside again toward a silver trailer parked behind a red Chevy wagon at the side of the house.

"What's this?"

"My trailer. Bought her in 1968 with the Chevy. She's beautiful, isn't she?" He ran his hand alongside the trailer, palm flat in a caress. I wondered what that hand would feel like on my thigh. I stepped inside.

"Toilet, shower, stove," he pointed out. "Bed." Grinning.

I poked through canvases leaning against the wall, wooden carvings arranged on smooth surfaces. He wasn't very good at drawing, I saw, though I didn't say so.

"You've had a lot of girlfriends," I said instead, examining covered canvases that were stacked against the walls and rescuing pages torn from his sketch pad that were tucked behind the seats or that peeked from beneath cushions and red-checked fabric. (He was never neat, he said, not even when his mother picked up after him, scolding and shaking her head in disgust. It was one of the reasons he'd left home; he just couldn't stand the disappointment anymore.) All showed women in various forms of undress.

"Hardly any," he said. "There just must be something about me that makes women want to take off their clothes." He ducked his chin and smiled, flicking his eyelashes.

I stood back and crossed my arms across my chest. "Is that how you do it?" I asked.

"Do what?"

"Get them into your bed? You do that little trick—" I copied his movement, bending my neck, then looked up at him and batted my own eyelashes, smiling coyly. "And they collapse at your feet?"

"Without any clothes," he said. "You must have been there one time. Seen it happen."

"I don't have to see anything," I said. "I have a good imagination." But then I blushed, and his words followed, involuntarily.

"What else have you imagined?"

He could have touched me then; it would have been the perfect, unguarded moment that I would have accepted. He waited too long, and I folded my arms across my chest again.

"Let's get something clear," I said. "I'm a married woman. I'm pregnant. I'm only twenty-one, but I'm all those other things too. So whatever you think is going on here, you're wrong. It wouldn't be right." It had to be said, that's what I thought then. Maybe I imagined the words would protect me from any wrong-doing—that I could be forgiven.

"What's right?"

The mild question threw me off balance. I just stared, thrusting my bottom lip in and out.

"So, like I said, we can just be friends," I said finally.

He shrugged, pushed his hair out of his eyes. "Whatever you want," he said.

"Good." I hoped my words, my face, were stronger than I felt, here in this small space, the towering length of him so close.

"I'd like to sketch you first," he said. "And then do the carving." He smiled, pressing his fingers against his lips. "And whenever you're ready, you can take off your clothes."

HE WORKED in the ruins of the barn, set farther back on the property.

"It was like this when we got here," Theo said. "I think part of the roof caved in during a storm." He opened the barn doors to let in what little January light spilled down from the skies, pointed to the farthest corner of the roof, where rotted beams sagged below a splintered hole.

"Aren't you scared the whole thing will collapse?" I asked.

He shrugged, a slow smile creasing his lips and the corners of his eyes. "Fear is good," he said.

A rusted ten-gallon drum leaned against a wall next to a

three-legged stool. He'd rigged up a makeshift partition, hanging sheets along a length of clothesline that stretched from one wall to the other. Pulling the sheets to the side, he sat me on a wooden platform covered in cushions and a wool blanket, the window above intact and cleaned of grime.

"How do you want me to sit?"

"I just want your face today," he said, reaching out and pulling my hair forward to fall over my shoulders. My spine curved forward, as if to hide from the rest of myself, my elbows bent and held stiffly against my sides. "Try to relax. Do I make you nervous?"

"Do you come here a lot?"

"All the time. It's quiet here."

There were six others in the house with him then, but most came and went, a rotation of faces and bodies. Some came with money, some with girlfriends or wives; none burned their draft notices, but kept them in their back pockets, a constant reminder.

"I found this place by accident," Theo said as he tore newspaper and tossed the shreds into the tin drum for kindling. "Came up from California, east across the country. Something in me just wanted to stop here, keep this place as my own. Falling down and crooked, but away from the town, out here in the country. And dirt cheap." And finding here in this town of misfits and drunks and miners a place to fit in.

"You own the farm?" I knew nothing about him, this Theo, only knew the way my stomach clenched and unclenched when he bent to look at me and flicked his hair from his forehead.

"It's mine," he said. "The others pay what they can. Sometimes beer, sometimes nothing. Nathan works in the shop, and I work at the high school at night. Janitor."

The fire in the drum flared, fell back, the smoke rising up and disappearing through the hole in the roof. I shifted on my platform, wondered briefly if I should take off my boots, but didn't.

He came from a small town in the southeast (*You wouldn't have heard of it*, he said). "I have three older brothers who call home on time, went to college, married nice girls, live in respectable houses with gardens out back and double-car garages, with plans for up to ten children each. They think I'm a lazy bum."

"Well, I don't," I said. "I think giving everyone a home here is—well, great." And damn it, I sounded then like a schoolgirl with a crush, my face hot.

"I've always done what I wanted with my life. After twenty-eight years, I'm not going to change for anyone." He pushed the sleeves of his sweater above his elbows. "I won't be tied down to anything or anyone. I won't be trapped like my brothers, with mortgages and boring jobs at a desk. Can you imagine?"

I envied him, the way he spoke, earnest and firm, his eyes staring at me steadily.

"I left my sketch pad in the trailer," he said. "Be right back."

With the barn doors closed, the fire swallowed most of the chill. Even rotting beams and musty corners smelled fresher than the house on Garland. I removed my coat, tossed it onto the dusty floor. I've always thought that if you listen for it, silence can be louder than a roomful of screaming children. There in the barn, waiting for Theo, my ears seemed to grow, widen on the sides of my head, until I heard every creak of wood shrinking in the cold, my breath rasping outward, blood pounding in great surges along my neck, all senses renewed, sharpened. It wasn't the first time I was alone in Silver Falls, but it was the first time I felt at peace. I closed my eyes, lay back against the cushions.

When I woke, Theo sat on the stool in front of me, his sketch pad balanced on his knees, fingers smeared with charcoal. I watched through half-opened eyes as he drew, slight scratchings of charcoal against paper the only sounds. Beyond the window, the sky stretched grey and white, bare branches of trees lonely against the blank canvas.

"You don't talk much," I said.

He looked up, charcoal suspended over the page. "You must have been tired," he said.

"Just comfortable." I began to rise, but he held out his hand.

"Don't move," he whispered. He tucked the charcoal behind his ear, came toward me, swept the hair away from my face, his fingers burning against my neck. "Belle." I wanted him to say my name over and over again.

I'll always remember the smell of the barn, the fire, the warmth of his mouth on mine (the taste of him) before I pushed him away.

WORTHY WAS AWAKE when I let myself into the house.

"Where were you?"

"The baby was restless. I went for a walk." I put my hand on my belly, the beginnings of a headache clamping down and inching toward my eyes. I wanted only to lie down, but sat at the table and ate with the men, trying not to notice the yellow sweat stains ringing the armholes of Worthy's undershirt, the pieces of spinach caught in his teeth. When I'd dropped off Gema's car, I'd said nothing about what happened. She saw through me anyway, pressed a spare set of keys in my hand.

"Take the car when you need it," she'd said. "I hardly use it around town."

Oscar wiped his mouth with the back of his hand, belched, and then grinned at me.

"When are you moving out?" I asked, not caring if it was too mean or direct, not caring if the timing wasn't right. I'd tried *subtle* before, and it hadn't worked. One day I moved all but two chairs from the dining room table, stashed them behind the house in the backyard. I laid the table with sets of two—a pair of plates and glasses, two knives and forks—and served up two helpings of pork chops and roasted potatoes and corn. Oscar didn't get it.

"Where're all the chairs?"

"Right here," I said, beaming and smoothing down an imaginary apron across my thighs.

"But there are only two."

I blinked, pretended to be confused. "Why should we need more than two?"

Oscar had shrugged, pulled out Worthy's chair, sat down, and picked up his fork, pressing his face forward to inhale, sniff the food I'd arranged carefully on the plate. *Worthy's* plate.

"Smells good," he said. *Useless.*

But now he just glanced across the table at Worthy, who kept his head down, suddenly fascinated by the patterned edging of his fork.

"You didn't tell her?" Oscar asked.

"Tell me what?"

Worthy coughed, cleared his throat, folded his hands, and rested his elbows on the table.

"I don't think Oscar's going to move out," he said, looking down again at his fork, pretending to rub an encrusted piece of food, then jabbing his tongue with one of the prongs.

"What do you mean? He's staying here? With the baby?" My dinner rose in my throat until I thought I'd choke or be sick all over them, and wouldn't *that* be something to watch?

"I'll help out," Oscar said, smug now and belly full.

"Just like you help out now?"

"Belle, he's going to try. If you have a problem with him then, he can move." If *you* have a problem, he said, not *we*. Only I shouldered the blame.

"I have a problem with him now," I said. "And where will the baby sleep?" My voice rose, tears threatened, though I hadn't cried since my father died. But this—this was too much.

"Calm down," Oscar said, the corners of his mouth lifting in a smirk, one eyebrow cocked as he glanced at Worthy. *Told you so.* And I saw that they'd already discussed it, expected my reaction. Worthy bent his head, shoulders hunched forward, resolute and solid. *He doesn't want to be alone with me in the house.*

I felt as if I might faint, gripped the edge of the table until my fingertips whitened. *To hell with them.* I stood, hefted my chair, and threw it onto the centre of the table, not caring as milk spilled across the plastic tablecloth from broken glasses and dripped onto the floor and pooled into chipped plates, not caring as Worthy and Oscar jumped back with shouts.

"Crazy bitch!"

Who said it? Not Worthy, surely. But maybe. His mouth hung open in disbelief, pink streaks of embarrassment, maybe shame, creeping up his neck and across his cheeks and forehead.

A normal pregnant woman would probably have burst into tears then, but not me. I felt better already, smiled, walked to the bedroom, and shut the door—quiet, measured. I lay on the bed, my hands resting on my belly, and cursed the movement within. For this was my dark, dirty secret: I wished with all my might that something would happen to the baby I just didn't want anymore. And that will be my curse forever, that I could wish something like that. If there were no baby, I could have reclaimed the years and said goodbye to Silver Falls and the dreary square box on Garland forever.

In the kitchen, Oscar laughed, and the sound cut through the darkness. I pushed the curtains open so that moonlight fell on the maps I'd re-pasted to the walls. When Worthy opened the bedroom door and hesitated, I curled onto my side and pretended to sleep, deepening my breathing so as to be more convincing.

The next morning, I made coffee and surveyed the mess on the kitchen table from the night before. Worthy and Oscar hadn't bothered to clean up before heading off to work, and I suppose that was fair. It seemed almost funny now: the plastic tablecloth bunched up around the legs of the chair, the broken dishes, dried food stuck to the plates, and congealed puddles of milk on the linoleum. I made up my mind.

I STOOD in the doorway of his trailer, scarf wrapped around my neck to my nose. When I lifted my face, the wool slipped down my chin.

"I've been thinking about you," he said.

"Worthy's my husband," I said. "I'm supposed to tell him everything. We're supposed to love each other. We're supposed to be in love."

"Are you?"

"No."

He held the door, stepped aside. Unbundled, I felt normal again, not so lost, my hair trailing against the tabletop in his tiny kitchen.

I looked around the trailer. "There's a lot I don't know about you, Theo."

"That's right," he said, "you don't." You can't call a man beautiful, but that day in the trailer the word felt right. He wasn't exactly perfect: his nose was a little crooked, his jaw too strong, shoulders wide but rounded forward in a slouch. Shaggy and lean, he walked with a swagger, the sure-footed confidence of an animal. (Maybe a predator. Later, I'd watch nature shows, you know, those documentaries that always play on certain channels, and I'd see a panther moving slowly, turning deadly green eyes on the cameraman, and I'd shiver, remembering how he looked to me in those early days.)

"I've come to take you up on your offer," I said.

"What offer is that?"

I smiled at him, stood. "To sketch your nude," I said, keeping my voice low, watching his eyes deepen.

I didn't begin with my boots, as expected, but pushed my bell bottoms down over the swollen belly, letting them gather around my ankles before kicking them off impatiently. I stood like that, in flannel shirt, work socks, boots, a hand on my hip, looking at him. Expecting. He wanted to put a cigarette in the corner of my mouth, he said, wanted to let it dangle, unlit, to complete the portrait. Later, he would carve that same image, his hands smoothing over a rounded belly and breasts by memory.

He sketched for an hour, until he could stand it no more, rose to unbutton my shirt and push it from my shoulders, catching the material in his hand, pressing the flannel against my back.

"Stop me," he whispered.

I shook my head, violent, shivering, my hair falling back as I brought his hands to my neck and bit down on his lips, his tongue.

A CRAMP woke me from sleep that night, blood streaking my thighs, soaking the sheets. Worthy called an ambulance.

ELEVEN

They've taken me out of my cell and put me in a hospital of sorts, or at least that's what I suppose. I try to sleep, but the ghosts come and line up in front of me, sit curled in a corner of the room, eyes blinking in pale faces and burning, burning while I sweat and shake and try to disappear. I think I must cry, because my hair sticks to my face.

I dream of children. A young girl in a yellow dress, a flower tucked behind her ear, smiling as she grows smaller, no matter how fast I run toward her, my arms stretching longer and longer, twisting. And then two boys blur into one—blue eye, brown eye, a tear sliding down a rounded cheek, and then a scream.

They come to check on me, footsteps down the corridor. My eyes are blind, my ears stuffed with too many memories. Lips move, but nothing comes out. A doctor leans down to listen to my heart, a band wraps around my arm and tightens until I rip it off and curse and then hunch forward to protect myself, rock back and forth. *Go away, go away.*

AFTER A WHILE, the dreams loosen their grip but leave me wasted, weak. I think about Polly a lot, not only because there's nothing else to do. I wonder at the woman she's become and the scars I left behind, I wonder what she must think of me. Soft baby-powdered skin, rosebud mouth, starfish fingers, and gently closed eyes: those memories must be here, somewhere.

I never meant for any of it to happen. Probably that sounds strange to some who can see what I did and point fingers easily, and it's not entirely true. Even though I fought it at first—I knew it was wrong—I knew what would happen, saw the inevitable arc and the downward slope. As soon as I took off my clothes for him, the path was set. And sometimes I lie, even to myself.

POLLY WAS BORN on March 5, 1971, after a month spent in the hospital on bedrest. You can't imagine how it felt to be kept in that white bed separated only by curtains from other mothers with tiny infants wheeled in from the nursery. But in truth, I'd been scared that my wishing had come true, that I'd managed to kill my unborn child with terrible thoughts.

The bleeding stopped after only a day, but still they kept me in. We need to monitor the situation, the doctor said. You don't want that baby coming out any sooner than it's meant to come out.

But I'd obviously disturbed Polly from her slumber in my belly. I thought about that a lot, wondered if Theo's intrusion could possibly have left a scar of some sort or altered the person she would become. She came out almost sideways a little more than a month later, as if she was splitting me in half, ready to fight. I looked at her red face, screwed up in fury, and silently apologized.

Crazy as it sounds, I'd expected Theo to visit, though I knew he wouldn't. I wanted our one time together to mean as much to him as it had meant to me. I'd think of him—his hands, his lips, the sharp weight of his hip bones against mine—and my belly would lurch, or Polly would twist and kick me from the inside. I'd remember the way he'd touched and tasted until my thighs shook and my toes curled under, the way I must have looked at him with a kind of wonder when it was all over. He had opened up a craving that needed to be filled. I knew I had to have more.

He didn't come. Gema brought me magazines and books from her apartment, piled them in a carton that she placed beside my bed. I'd never been a big reader. Even in high school, I barely skimmed the novels we were to read, or asked the smartest girl in our group to summarize for me. Reading was tedious work, for the most part. Here in the hospital, I had nothing else to do save shuffle my feet in bed and listen to the wails of newborns. So I read, mostly paperback romances with cardboard characters I despised for their wishy-washiness, women who waited for the telephone to ring and strove to keep house for their men.

"Trashy novels," Gema said. "But easy to read, and maybe they'll take your mind off things." They embarrassed her a little, I could tell by the way she hid them beneath magazines and a few other books, weightier classics.

But as much as I rolled my eyes, sometimes the endings caught me off guard. To live an orderly life like that—imagine. The heroes sweeping in to gather the heroines in their arms, smothering kisses on ample bosoms. I craved such simplicity, wished I could set everything right with a single wave of a magic wand. And sometimes I woke in the morning with eyes crusted from dried tears I never knew I'd shed.

AFTER POLLY WAS BORN, Worthy came to me earnestly in the hospital and said he would quit drinking for good to become the best father, the best husband. He spent hours just tucking his finger into Polly's small fist and stroking her tiny knuckles.

"I'm going to change, Belle," he said. "I know things haven't been so good between us, but that'll change starting from now."

Before he left, he turned back suddenly, threw the day's newspaper onto the foot of the bed.

"I forgot to tell you," he said, a slow smile flattening his lips. "Your lovely Pierre Trudeau got married yesterday. I guess you're stuck now, huh?"

Oh, Pierre. I studied her photograph, that twenty-two-year-old vixen who'd stolen my man, and wondered what it would be like to be in her shoes instead of here in this hospital, waiting to love my new daughter.

I had problems breastfeeding. The nurses at the hospital grabbed me roughly, forcing the nipple into her mouth, but she promptly spat it out. She had a way of flailing her arms and legs at the same time, spasmodic and alien. It seemed impossible to me that she came from my body or was in any way connected.

"Are you sure she's mine?" I asked the nurses once, searching for some reason, some excuse. Why did Polly hate me, and who rejected whom first? The nurses shook their heads at me, lectured me on the correct way to change a diaper without sticking her with the pins, then released me into the great unknown with a stack of diapers and blankets and giant pads belted between my legs.

Worthy couldn't get enough of her. One small noise from her pursed lips and he would jump up nervously, peer into her crib or bassinet. *I think she's hungry,* or *She needs her diaper changed,* or *She just needs to be held,* he would say. He would push me aside when I changed her—*Let me, let me*—grasping pins in his thick fingers, jabbing himself and drawing blood. He stayed home at night and took to sitting with me in the living room after Polly had gone to bed. I would catch him staring at me with a wishful, wistful expression on his face, disappointed by my failures as a mother. He expected more of me; so did I.

THE WEEK AFTER Polly was born, my mother and aunt drove up in George Dillard's old Buick, springing to life as they unfolded from the car. My aunt reached back to fluff her hair, thick turquoise beads encircling her right wrist. Behind her bright smile and eager kisses I sensed her fear; Uncle Erik was in Vietnam, still alive and not missing, not yet.

My mother was new: gone were the great circles under her eyes, gone the grey-streaked long hair. She'd had a makeover of sorts. Now she sported a shorter, jauntier haircut, and she was consistently brunette, a hint of blue shadow on her eyelids.

I waited on our porch, dimly wondering if they'd notice the peeling paint or the drab town spread out below us.

"You look wonderful," my mother said, hugging me. I certainly did not. She smelled fresh, like soap; at that moment I wanted to follow her back to the car, curl myself into a small ball in the back seat, and return to Vermont. Without Polly.

They have a fancy name for it now: postpartum depression. Back then we just called it the baby blues.

"You'll be a pro in no time," my aunt promised. And, as if she sensed my hesitation and detachment, "The bond will grow. You wait and see."

My mother made it look so easy, taming Polly's wild, frantic arms and legs in tight swaddling that I could never master. Polly didn't cry with her, sensed her expert touch, I suppose.

"The first is never easy," she said. "Don't worry. This, too, shall pass."

I resented her cheerfulness. She and my aunt washed the laundry and cleaned the house while I sulked at the kitchen table. My mother chattered as if she didn't notice, though I saw her flash secret glances at my aunt.

"Why don't you go to bed, Belle?" my mother asked. So I did, and slept for six hours straight. When I woke, the sky beyond the bedroom window was black. Hearing voices in the kitchen, I pulled on my housecoat and stumbled into the washroom. I splashed water on my face, combed and braided my hair, and tried to erase the long pull of my muscles that dragged my mouth downward.

They'd fallen silent at the kitchen table: my mother, aunt, Worthy, and Oscar.

"Feel better?" my mother asked.

I looked at their faces, so strained and falsely cheerful, and felt miserable. They were trying so hard. I forced a smile, nodded.

"Where's Polly?"

"Sleeping," my aunt said. "Your mother just fed her." She pointed to a drained bottle on the counter, as if to prove to me that what she said was true, as if I wouldn't believe her.

Worthy stared at me with hooded, disappointed eyes. "She's in the bedroom," he said. "Didn't you notice?" I hadn't.

I smiled again. "I'll just go check on her," I said. I couldn't stay in this room with their disapproval any longer.

She slept in a corner of our room, so I could never escape her. In the crib, she slept face down, her fists curled up by the side of her head, her breathing fast and shallow. I placed my hand on the back of her head, imagined my blood flowing under her skin, felt her warmth, and wanted to weep and wail at my failure as a mother. I sank to the floor and leaned my head sideways against the crib. I wanted to love her, wanted to feel what I was supposed to feel, instead of the urgent desire to flee, escape. It was then that I became convinced that something was wrong with me. I wasn't normal at all.

Even now it's hard to understand or explain or describe the darkness that strangled me and wouldn't let go. I resented Polly for the pain she'd caused my body—the ache between my legs that didn't go away for almost a month, the cracked and bleeding nipples before I finally gave up and used a bottle instead, and the constant torture of no sleep. I'd never been so tired in my life. I'd sink down after feeding and burping and changing Polly, fall into a harsh deep sleep, only to be woken by her cries a few hours later. This, then, was motherhood?

MY FAMILY STAYED for two weeks at the Silver Inn. Usually when they arrived at the house, I had tried to make an effort, showering or at least brushing my teeth, though I often stooped forward and pressed my forehead against the bathroom mirror for long moments.

"You look better today," my aunt would say.

"Yes, I feel better," I'd lie.

There they sat, the two sisters. My mother, in her long skirt and tucked-in blouse, her hair neatly combed and sprayed so that the sides flipped back, wearing only a hint of lipstick and some blush. And my aunt, in a man's green sweater and blue jeans, her legs crossed as she smoked a cigarette, her new habit. *Disgusting*, my mother said to me when they first arrived. *She and Gardie just sit around and puff all day.* My aunt's dark hair, streaked with white strands, hung loose and wavy past her shoulders. As I looked at her then, it struck me that she and I were most alike, more alike than my mother and I.

I poured myself a glass of orange juice. We three sat in silence at the kitchen table, our elbows in our laps, while Polly dozed in the bassinet my mother set up in a corner of the kitchen.

"Is that Uncle Erik's sweater?" I don't know why I asked. We all avoided his name as if he were poison, as if my aunt wouldn't remember whom she was missing if we didn't mention him anymore.

She blinked, looked down at herself, and briefly touched her palm to the thick wool. "It is," she said, and smiled. "It still smells like him."

"Just like I wore my dad's slippers after he died," I said.

My mother folded her hands around her mug of tea. "I did that too," she said.

"You wore his slippers?"

"No," she said with a laugh. "But I kept his shirt under my pillow, and when I went to bed at night I would curl it around my face and under my chin so that his smell was all around." I'd never thought of my mother grieving that way. I suppose I'd never thought of her beyond the face she showed in public, the one with hints of lipstick and carefully sprayed hair.

My aunt's lips had tightened, bloodless. "Except that Erik's not dead, of course. He's just away."

"Of course, Hannah. We know that."

My aunt nodded, her eyes heavy and full. I will always remember her look then of forced hope. Uncle Erik would disappear seven months later, leaving behind a stack of letters and wool sweaters for my aunt to tuck beneath her pillow.

She tried to smile. "Well, I think I'll go out for a walk," she said, pushing away from the table before either of us could offer to go with her.

When I heard the front door close and I was sure she was gone, I looked at my mother. "Do you think he'll come home?"

She lifted her eyebrows, tilted her head to the side. "I don't know."

Polly woke with a cry. My mother rose from the table, but I stopped her. "I can do it," I said. "I should do it."

I released Polly from her swaddling, brought her up to my shoulder, and held her tightly while I warmed a bottle on the stove.

"She looks so much like you already." My mother had twisted on her chair so that she could peer at Polly's small face.

I brought her back to the table and wrapped the lower half of her body so that only her arms were free. As I fed her, one tiny fist wrapped around my finger and she looked up at me with trust. I could feel my mother watching me.

"I'm better," I said, my voice soft and quiet. "You don't have to worry." I did feel at peace then, in that moment. Everything seemed right.

She released her breath in a long sigh. "Yes," she said.

Polly drank in great gulps.

"Belle, are you happy here?"

"Happy?"

"Yes."

"I'm all right. You don't have to worry."

"I'll always worry," she said. "That's my right as a mother." She smiled. "You'll see."

Maybe I was still caught in my sense of rightness, of ease. I needed to confide, to let her know that I wasn't just a silly girl who'd married on a whim.

"I thought I needed to escape," I said.

"Escape from what?"

"It's hard to explain," I said. "I thought I would be caught forever on the farm, with you and Aunt Hannah and Uncle Erik." That didn't sound right. I tried again. "I knew that Gardie would find her own way out, but I wasn't so sure about me."

"But why would you think that?"

"I don't know." Now none of it made sense, why I'd left. I wasn't sure there ever was a reason.

"And that's why you married Worthy? To escape?" I didn't answer, couldn't. "Oh, Belle." And now I was sorry I'd said anything in the first place.

"Father would have been happy for me," I said.

"Happy that you married someone you didn't love? I don't think so, Belle."

"But he tried to escape too. He almost did."

She put her mug down, frowned. "What do you mean?"

"The Bibles he sold. He almost escaped the mines. He almost lived another life."

"Oh, Belle," she said again. "He hated it—the driving from town to town, never stopping for long in one place. He needed to be in his cove, where he grew up, he needed roots. He was destined for the mines. As all his family was. And then his father died, and he had to go home in the end to take care of his mother. There weren't any other options for him." She leaned forward, stroked Polly's cheek. "But you had options," she whispered, looking at my daughter instead of me. "You always had endless options."

And where was gardie?

"Going through a phase," my aunt said.

"Nothing but trouble," my mother said.

My aunt wound a long scarf around and around her neck, frowned. "She just thinks she's outgrown us and wants nothing to do with us. Every teenager goes through it."

But I knew there was more to it than that. It wasn't just the way my mother's eyebrows pulled together and her forehead shrunk when Gardie's name came up.

"She would have come," my mother said, but I didn't mind. I didn't need her here, not with me like this, at the end of my rope and ragged. My mother sighed, set her cup down on the table so hard that weak tea spilled down over its lip. My aunt passed her a towel, but she just held it in her hands, twisted it this way and that.

"She's taking drugs," she blurted.

Tsk. My aunt's tongue tapped the roof of her mouth briskly. "We agreed we wouldn't talk about it," she said.

"I know, Hannah, but it just makes me sick with worry, and Belle should know. Maybe she can talk to her."

"What do you mean, drugs? What drugs?" I asked.

"Oh, I don't know—what are they again, Hannah?"

"Dope," my aunt said. "Probably other things as well."

"She's fallen in with the wrong crowd," my mother said. "She sleeps in that ratty chicken coop of yours and stays out for hours, sometimes all night. I just don't know what to do about it."

How the tables had turned. It was a relief to point the finger at someone else for once.

"I don't know why you think she'd listen to me," I said.

"You're her big sister. She looks up to you, despite what you may think. It's only natural."

THEY PILED INTO THE CAR, my mother and aunt sniffling and tears leaking down their cheeks as they smiled and waved goodbye.

"Remember Gardie," my mother said before she drove away. "Write to her, will you?"

I said I would, and I did at least try. I sat at the kitchen table for an hour, a blank sheet of paper in front of me, thinking of what to say. But nothing came out except long rambling lines that read like accusations and lectures. In the end, I made Worthy write a letter and signed my name to the bottom, along with his. *We can help if you're in trouble,* he wrote. That sounded good to me: supportive, but also vague enough to promise nothing.

WHEN POLLY WAS THREE WEEKS OLD and just settling into colic that lasted from seven at night until three in the morning, Worthy began working nights again. Nothing I did soothed her.

After bouncing, rocking, walking, singing, swaying for hour after hour, I finally just put her in her crib, shut the door against her cries, and sat outside, my hands covering my ears. Even here the sound carried, enough that Eliza Whittle stuck her head out her front door, then made tentative steps in my direction.

"Everything all right?" she called, holding her winter coat closed with one hand, men's rubber shoes slipped over what looked like hairy feet, there in the dark, but must have been shaggy slippers of some sort. Each breath heaved forward from my lungs. Eliza advanced, coming ever closer; if she placed a sympathetic hand on my arm or anywhere near me, I thought I'd pick up a rock from my stony front garden (where no flowers ever grew) and bash her in the skull. So instead, when she was only steps away, I stood on shaky legs, dragged my hand down my face roughly, and went back inside without a word. Polly was still crying, her body sweating and tightly wound. I picked her up and held her in my arms, praying that I wouldn't throw her against the wall. I cradled her against my chest and sat down on the couch. I wasn't aware that I was crying myself until she fell silent, soothed at last by the hitching of my chest and shoulders.

I WENT BACK to Theo when Polly was two months old, showed up at the trailer one Friday morning when Worthy and Oscar were working. I didn't know what to expect, and as I stood before the closed door I unconsciously ran my hand over my hair, pulling at snarls, and looked down at my unwashed pants and spit-stained shirt. I should have made more of an effort. The desire to see him had grown so that I didn't think I could bear it if he was polite and distant, or if his smile didn't travel any farther than his mouth.

What a relief when he opened the door and grinned, unkempt and wrinkled.

"About time you showed up," he said. He hooked an arm around my waist and pulled me close to press himself against me, tucking his thigh between my legs and unhooking my overalls to slide his hand along bare skin.

"Did you miss me?"

He grasped the back of my head, his fingers in my hair, blew on my neck. "I missed you," he said.

I PICKED POLLY UP from Gema's later, and when she raised her eyebrows questioningly, I just shook my head and then almost cried, my head on her kitchen table.

"I told you he would change your life," she said, settling me on her couch and tucking me in with a blanket thrown over my knees and a cup of tea.

"I thought you meant for the better," I said.

"Maybe it is," she said. "Or will be."

"What am I going to do?" I asked.

"What do you want to do?"

I wanted to be with Theo, and I wanted to be with him all the time, burying my face in his chest and breathing in his smell, tracing the curled hair that covered his chest from his neck to his belly button, where it trailed down to a point and then exploded again between his legs. I wanted to press myself against him and stay that way for days on end.

"Just take it day by day," Gema advised. "You never know when these things will just fizzle out. Or maybe Worthy will get tired of you."

"But he'll never get tired of Polly," I said. "I could never take her away from him. He loves her too much—it would break his heart."

Gema made a sound of understanding and nodded. "Day by day," she said.

Day by day. We met in his trailer on Friday mornings, and I came to live for our few hours together. In the morning, I'd shower and scrub every nook and cranny until my skin burned and the water ran cold, guilt and anticipation making me sick to my stomach and light-headed. I sat through breakfast with Worthy and Oscar and made up a fictitious woman whose house I would clean that day (adding more details over time: a tight blue perm, a yapping dog with pee stains down its back legs, plastic-covered furniture, and ashtrays overflowing with shredded bits of paper). I left the house around nine, dropped Polly off at Gema's, then drove up to the farm for a stolen three hours. Sometimes Theo was sleeping when I arrived; more often, he waited for me inside the trailer, pulled me to him to rub unshaven cheeks against my skin. And sometimes I waited before knocking, taking pleasure in the delay, feeling my chest expand and impatience tickle the back of my neck and ears until I couldn't stand it anymore.

Theo left behind a high that carried me back to Garland Street, that dull crowded space where Worthy suspected nothing, though there were certainly signs. For one thing, I'd avoided his physical touch for as long as I could. I told Worthy that Polly tore me inside out when she came into this world (Worthy turned away, cringing, not wanting to hear the details), but that excuse only worked for a while. Truth be told, I was too tired most of the time, and I'm surprised Worthy wasn't, what with Polly in our room making strange grunting noises and sighs, Oscar taking up more space and only a room away, the shifts at the mine, working long nights. But no, he was a man, after all, putting his hands on me like a sneak in the middle of the night, pitiful *I have needs*, like I should feel sorry for him. Well, I had needs too, and I was sorrier for myself as he huffed and puffed above me, sticky drops of his sweat falling into my hair. I'd tasted what Theo had to offer, and nothing else could compare.

And before you get to rolling your eyes and thinking it was all about sex with Theo, I want to tell you you're wrong. We did talk, Theo and I; we joked and took walks around the farm, his arm slung across my shoulder or his big hand swallowing mine. He made me feel dainty, despite my height and extra padding. I loved everything about him, and he, in turn, took my ferocious appetite with a mixture of surprise and appreciation.

"The way you move, woman," he would say as I lay on top of him, spent and inordinately pleased with myself.

And then there was the music. Inside the trailer, he'd play me album after album on the little portable record player he kept under the table or stashed in a corner. I'd never paid attention to music before, not the way Theo wanted.

"Music is life, Belle. Until you've really listened to music, you haven't heard anything."

I began to pay attention. We played records until the batteries wore out and he scrambled to replace them. Sometimes we'd move to the farmhouse to listen to a particular song on the real stereo. He'd wrap giant padded earphones around my head so I'd get the full experience and hold my hand as I listened, watching my face, waiting for the crest of emotions that came naturally. Because it was true what he'd said; that music opened up something in me I didn't know existed. We made love to Jefferson Airplane and Quicksilver Messenger Service on the little bed in the trailer throughout the summer and fall and into the winter and new year, the songs becoming as familiar to me as the lines and creases of his body. When we lay together, sheets damp and crumpled, he would run his fingers through my hair, spreading it out on his chest to mesh with his own, laughing to compare the bristly, coiled hairs bravely pressing through the longer strands.

Sometimes the music rose and my chest felt close to bursting, Theo's eyes intense and shining as if fevered, the soft pleasure of vinyl grooves against my fingers as I pulled another album from its sleeve. Brief moments of clarity and a sense of fullness, as if I'd devoured a feast and then fallen back, satisfied at last. Other times, the music would crest and wash over me, and I'd think of the way you could almost feel the ocean breathing and sighing, and a crippling homesickness tumbled me sideways and backwards.

THE ANNIVERSARY of my father's death in February fell on a Friday that first year with Theo. Silver Falls disappeared beneath a layer of patchy grey-brown snow in the winter, leaving the streets deserted, desolate. Outside the trailer, I pressed my forehead against the cold silver shell, the chill reaching my bones and my eyelashes stiff.

"Why are you crying?"

I lay on the unmade bed, my toes tucked under the bunched-up comforter. When I told Theo about my father and the great ache deep inside my chest, he listened without a word, his arm curved around my body, his hand resting on my hip. I talked through the losses—my father, my brothers, our old wooden house battered and beaten by the winds—and felt lighter as the words layered and built and came pouring out of my mouth.

"Maybe you should go back," he said when I'd finished.

"But there's nothing there for me anymore," I said.

"Maybe I'll go with you one day. I'd like to see your beloved ocean."

I didn't answer but pressed my cheek against his chest and felt his heart, my own swelling in response.

TWELVE

ardie showed up in the summer of 1972, her legs bruised and pale beneath her gypsy skirt and a shirt that was too big and dropped tent-like from her arms. She didn't say anything, just stood as if she had all the time in the world to spend waiting. At first she didn't even seem to focus on me, but swayed slightly, dancing to a private song.

I opened my door, stood back to let her pass. I was afraid to speak until she was safely inside, afraid that my words would make her bolt. She followed me to the kitchen, where I sat her down and gave her a cold glass of lemonade. She drank greedily, not stopping until the glass was empty and ice cubes crunched beneath her teeth. She wiped her mouth on her sleeve, licked her lips, and studied me.

"You never answered my last letter," she said. I hadn't wanted her to visit, not as messed up as I'd heard she was. And I didn't trust her plea for money; I had no way of knowing how she would spend it.

"No." I should have apologized, I suppose, but the words refused to come out. Instead, I just looked at her.

"Are you wearing a *dress*?" she asked.

It wasn't an old woman's dress, or at least I didn't think it was. It was modern, flowing down from my hips in bright vertical stripes of green and gold. I thought it made me look slender and tall, *like a willow tree*, Theo had said.

"What's wrong with that?" I asked.

She shrugged, twirled a piece of hair around her finger, made a face. "I haven't washed my hair in eighteen days," she said.

"Where have you been?"

She shrugged again. "Around."

"Everyone's worried sick about you," I said. My mother's letters were stacked upstairs, chronicling Gardie's slide: *I'm telling you, Belle, there's something funny going on and I pray to God it's not drugs again.* And Gardie had written to me, asking to come visit, but I hadn't found the time to respond, not knowing what to say, how to tell her that there just wasn't room for her here. And then that March, she'd just disappeared.

"Hmm." She didn't seem to care, just flattened her hands on the table. I noticed her nails, oddly perfect and polished. "I was wondering if I could crash here for a while."

"Crash?"

"Stay for a while. You don't know what it's like, living with them."

"It can't be that bad."

"It is. Aunt Hannah is crazy now, with Uncle Erik gone. Keeps staring out the window, waiting for him to come home. Sets his place at the dinner table, just in case. And Mother! She and Mr. Dillard are like lovebirds—it's sickening. And I can't do anything without going under their microscope."

"They're worried about you. Because of the drugs." There were two overdoses. After the first, they found her on the sidewalk clawing at her face and screaming about spiders. The second almost killed her, left her in an alleyway behind a row of shops, her body curled between garbage bins.

She blinked, seemed to shudder. "I know." She sighed, rolled her eyes. "Mistakes," she said. "The first time, I thought it was Aspirin. They didn't believe me." I didn't believe her either—she was just too thin, too twitchy, as if unseen hands pulled tiny strings under her skin at random. "What else do you take?" I asked, but she just shrugged and pulled her knees up to her chest, avoiding my eyes.

"I have nowhere else to go," she said. "You said you'd help if I needed it. Well, I do."

Curled up like that, she seemed so small, fragile, a broken version of what she had been. But I didn't want her here in this house, not now, not ever.

By the time Worthy and Oscar came home, Gardie had taken a long shower, scrubbing off layers of God knows what, and brushed her teeth with my toothbrush (after sterilizing it with a kettle of boiled water). Oscar sauntered in first, stopping so fast at the sight of Gardie, combing out her long hair, that Worthy almost plowed right into him. His eyes lingered over every stroke of the brush, taking in the details: the almost-blue skin, slender neck bent at an angle, delicate wrists and long fingers.

"Gardie." He smiled slowly. "I knew you would come back to me," he said.

The shower had helped. No longer jittery, she relaxed, placing the brush on the armchair, resting her hands, limp, on her thighs. She even laughed.

"Oh, Oscar. I just couldn't get you out of my mind." But she turned from him quickly, said hello to Worthy, then looked back at me.

"Gardie's staying with us for a few days," I said. "But just for a few days. Just until she figures out what she wants to do with her life."

"She'll marry me, of course. How old are you now?" Oscar asked.

"Nineteen."

"Perfect." He beamed. "I'm twenty-two. We'll have three children a year after we're married, one each year in a row. Then we can sit back and watch them grow up."

"Will we live here as well?"

"Of course. All four of us together, a nice family."

"Five," Worthy said. "Don't forget about Polly."

"Oh, that'd be perfect, just *perfect!*" I forced a laugh to blunt the edge of my words, but my fist slipped and crashed onto the table.

Worthy stiffened, his face rigid, lips pressed together. "Don't start," he said.

We never mentioned the night I threw the chair on the table, but it was always there, an unspoken rebuke. It was unbearable, Oscar's presence in the house, especially when Polly was first born and up all night, but I refused to ask him to leave again. It was Worthy's turn.

I wondered briefly if Gardie would be interested in Oscar, who was good-looking, after all, with dark hair and blue eyes. A little too angular for my liking, but maybe Gardie would find him attractive. It was hard to tell; she had a way of laughing with her mouth while her eyes stayed blank.

"SHE CAN'T STAY." I lay flat on my back in bed, my hands linked and resting on my belly.

Beside me, Worthy shifted and rolled. "Belle, she's sick. And she doesn't have anywhere to go."

"She does," I said. "She can go home." I'd already written to my mother to tell her the news, lessen the worry. *I'll send her home as soon as I can,* I'd said.

"Just leave it," Worthy said. "We'll talk about it later."

My mother wrote back to Gardie with a flurry of letters. She read none of them in front of me, tucked them instead in the back pocket of her jeans. She'd already come down from the drugs, whatever it was she'd taken, already been through the worst of it on someone's couch out west, or so she said. But still she twitched and sweated and sometimes threw up what little dinner she managed to eat, and she shivered on the couch where she slept, a giant comforter wrapped around her thin body, hair stringy and smelling rank and dark. Some days she never moved from the couch.

Polly—by then a year and a half, thin and smart, with tufts of dark hair and big eyes that followed you everywhere—made her smile.

"She looks just like you," Gardie said. On good days, she would crouch down, run her fingers up Polly's leg to just under her chin in a long tickle, or sit her on her lap, tucking in the edges of the comforter, to read books or simply sit, Polly's head nestled under her chin in a way I never wanted. They were good for each other.

You couldn't really talk to her in those first few days, not that I made much of an effort. She always seemed poised for battle, her eyes glinting with hostility, anger, and she retreated if you asked too many questions. Maybe she had been telling the truth about my mother and aunt; maybe living under their scrutiny had taken its toll. Instead, she moped around the house and appeared in sudden places to startle me. I'd look up from feeding Polly to see her hidden in the shadows of a corner, not moving, just watching me, intent and serious. Her silence irritated me.

"Why did you come, if you're not going to talk to any of us?" I asked. She seemed surprised, opened and closed her mouth, a fish gasping for air. There was something in the way she stood then—a piece of hair twisted in her mouth, the sharp elbows jutting out by her sides, like stick figures come to life—that made her seem so much younger than she was. And the wariness in her eyes, as if waiting for an attack, saddened me. Something had happened to her, and suddenly I did feel sorry for her.

"Were you taking care of my cottage?" I asked.

She pulled out a chair, sat down, and wrapped her arms around her legs. "Yes." She rested her chin on her arms.

"Then what else?"

She shrugged.

"You're too thin," I said. "And pale. You need to get outside more." She looked like some of the girls I'd seen at Theo's farm, with her bell bottoms and embroidered shirt, her belt buckle and peace sign.

"Now you sound like them." She frowned, pulled a new piece of her hair forward and stuck it in her mouth, chewing.

"They're just worried about you."

"Nothing to worry about now," she said. I wondered if there'd been some man she kept hidden, someone older maybe, or married even. I looked closer. Yes, she had that look.

"Who was he?" I asked.

Her eyelids fluttered. "Also not something to worry about," she said, barking out a sort of harsh laugh and rolling her eyes. She pushed herself up, wiped her palms against her pants, paused. "I came because you offered," she said. "Or Worthy did, in that letter you sent. And I came because I wanted to see Polly. She makes everything real. You probably don't understand."

But I did: Polly made everything too real.

I never pressed her for more details about what she'd done since she ran away from home, and this seemed to work. She relaxed her guard around me, lowered her shoulders and stopped fighting.

I'd started cleaning homes again when Polly was three
months old, not because I needed the money (though I had some
vague idea that it could come in handy at some point) but
because Gema offered to watch her in between shifts at the
grocery store so that I could get out of the house. And this I
desperately needed. I kept my earnings in a tight bundle under
the far corner of our mattress. Worthy asked about it only once;
I told him I was saving it for a rainy day and that it was none of
his business what I did with the money I earned. You might think
that would have caused a fight, but Worthy never really fought,
not outright, and so he shut up about the money and never
mentioned it again.

When Gardie arrived and seemed determined to stay for a
while, despite my sour face and obvious attitude, I figured I'd
make it as hard as possible and assigned her a job: she would
mind Polly the mornings I worked, in exchange for her room
and board. I also made it clear that I wouldn't tolerate any funny
stuff, not in front of Polly.

"I don't care what you do any other time," I warned her. "But
if I find out about any drugs when you're watching her, then
you'll be on the next train out of here." If my remark bothered
her, she didn't show it, just smiled and nodded as if to say, *Yes, I'll
behave*. And then she winked at Polly, who hunched her small
shoulders, covered her mouth with both hands, and giggled
wildly.

In the first months, she tried hard. In return, I ignored the
little things that bothered me (her plate never scraped clean and
left for me in the sink; crumpled tissues left in her pockets and
put in the wash; her fascination with her hair, the way she always
stroked and pulled and brushed it). I also ignored the obvious:
she still had a crush on Worthy. She blushed when he looked at
her, fell speechless when he spoke, twisted her hands in front of

her in nervousness or pulled on her hair. I wondered at this, looked at Worthy from a new angle, trying to see what it was that Gardie liked about him. Worthy himself noticed nothing out of the ordinary; he might have been as surprised as I had he known.

And I didn't care. Gardie was just another burden thrust on me, another person to make the walls of our house smaller, more pressing. I didn't care if she was necessarily better, didn't care if she hadn't figured out what to do with her life from here on out; I just wanted her to go back home to Vermont without sniffing out what I'd managed to hide for the last year. I worried that she would find her way up to the farm and into Theo's main house, where some of the people were closer to her age and more alike in philosophy. But she didn't try to make friends with anyone— at least not that first summer.

"Why bother?" she would say. "It's not like I'm staying here for long." Instead, she'd set up a lawn chair in the backyard, put on a halter top and cut-off jean shorts, and sit smoking in silence under the hot sun in her spare time.

"Planning my future," she'd say if I asked what she was doing. But beneath her half-closed eyes, she sleepily noticed everything I did.

And that was the biggest problem with Gardie. She had a way of sneaking into a room without you noticing, as if her bones were made of rubber, her skin so translucent she faded into the background when she pleased.

True to her word, Gardie stayed home that summer of 1972. *My summer of nothing*, she would say, smiling in just such a way that I knew she enjoyed herself. And why shouldn't she? She suntanned while Polly splashed in a small plastic pool Worthy had ordered from the Eaton's catalogue, flipped through magazines and ate Popsicles that stained her mouth purple while Polly napped.

But as each day passed, the pressure grew so strong I was sure I couldn't bear it for much longer. I worried about the smallest things: the way my neck smelled when I came home from an afternoon with Theo, my fingertips rough with the memory of the bristly stubble that crept down his jaw; a swollen burst of colour on the corner of my mouth (he didn't mean to bite); a sunburn along the edges of my scoop-necked blouse and on the inside of my arms after long drives in the Chevy and picnics in fields, the sun warming us both into complacency. I worried that she'd smell the heat in my hair, let loose on those drives from its long braid and left to whip about this way and that, tickling my ears and blinding me in great lashes. On Friday mornings I slipped into my nicest underwear, massaged rich scented lotion on my legs all the way up to the very top of my fleshier thighs, and worried that she'd see through my casual wave as I slumped in Gema's car, drove up Main Street, and headed east toward the farm. I was careful in everything I did—the way I quickly washed my laundry and took showers, the way I would smile when Worthy dared put his arm around me or touch my hand under the dinner table—counting down the days until I would see Theo again.

One Friday afternoon, Theo pushed me back on the bed in the trailer and pressed fistfuls of wildflowers into my hair and down my shoulders and breasts, petals in my mouth and his. That night, Gardie and I washed up after dinner, soapy water dripping down on our toes, fingers brushing as plates and knives and glasses changed hands. Her hair had lightened in the sun, her cheeks had rounded and curved back out; she'd lost her sickly glow and seemed content, a smile curving up the corners of her mouth. Polly ran from the end of the hall, pulling a wooden duck with wheels on a string, her hair tucked up in a single pigtail, like a fountain of feathers, shrieking at us until

Gardie scooped bubbles from the sink and blew on her hand, froth floating gently, gently, onto Polly's cheeks. Gardie picked her up and kissed her neck, turning her face toward me and blinking once. As she carried Polly from the kitchen, a single wildflower stuck to the back of her heel. I tucked my hands in my pockets, touched the soft velvet of crushed and wilted petals.

THIRTEEN

I should have seen it coming, I suppose. In the months leading up to it, something shifted. Summers have a way of relaxing people. We sat down as a family once a day for a hot meal, sometimes lunch, sometimes dinner, depending on Worthy and Oscar's work schedule. And there, passing plates of food, wiping Polly's chin, all of us tanned and easy, we were on our best behaviour. *A family*. But as fall led into winter and our skin paled in patches, as layers of wool replaced loose cotton and bare feet, the novelty of a new person wore off, and the reality of too many bodies in such a small space set in. By November, mouths opened only to shovel in food, heads turned in stiff, jerky movements. No one had much to say.

"Well?" I asked one night when it all became too much. I stood in the kitchen, balancing plates in my hands, stopping forks from sliding onto the floor with my thumbs. Three sullen faces turned toward me, then looked away.

"Well, what?" Oscar asked.

"When are you moving out, Oscar? It's time."

"Too many extra people here now," Worthy said, mumbling so that I almost couldn't understand him properly.

Gardie snorted, tucked her hair behind her ear. Oscar shifted his eyes from her to look at Worthy. I waited, but nothing else happened; no one spoke or even moved, save Polly, who shrieked, slapped her palms against the tray of her high chair. I brought the plates to the kitchen counter, my fingers aching to pinch or twist or slam. Instead, I ran water in the sink and went on with it.

By New Year's Eve, we were all miserable and tense, waiting for something to happen that would throw everything else into chaos. Worthy and I went to a mining party held at the Hall, a brick building smack dab in the middle of our neighbourhood. There was always something going on at the Hall—bowling, dances, plays, even movies—but I'd only been once before. We'd taken Polly to a children's party the Saturday before Christmas, forced her, screaming, to sit on Santa's lap for a picture. She'd reached up and scratched a long bleeding line from his eye down to his lip. The hundred or so other children stared dumbfounded as Santa let loose with a string of curses, blood staining the white, pristine curls of his elastic beard, while the parents glared at us for ruining the party.

In the basement dance hall on New Year's Eve, a bounty of polyester flowed down the concrete steps. Gone were the regular acrylic housedresses (*Repels stains! Easy wear!*) bought in bulk from the Eaton's catalogue; in their place, floor-length halter dresses or shiny blouses with balloon-like sleeves and long scarves mistakenly tied in giant bows. A few men wore suits, but most, like Worthy, wore various shades of slacks and vests (Worthy's best set was brown polyester, the vest a lighter shade of tan, the matching shirt in a swirled paisley pattern). Worthy surprised me with a dress he'd picked out down at Harold's all on his own: an orange-and-brown number with wide, swooping sleeves and a neckline that wrapped across my chest.

"What's wrong with my other clothes?" I asked.

"I thought you liked dresses," he said, confused. "You wear a lot of them now."

It's true that I wore dresses, but I wore them for Theo, not as an invitation for Worthy's eyes to probe and peer.

"Don't you like it?" he asked. "Why don't you try it on?"

"Not now, Worthy."

He looked down, then away, and I suddenly ached for him and for what I was doing to him. On the couch in the living room, Gardie smirked. I watched her gaze shift from the dress to me to Worthy, then back to the dress, staring as if she wanted to reach out and stroke the fabric and hold it up against her body, the way I'd stared at her velvet dress in the church that day, while I wore that horrible wool. *This is my velvet!*

"I think I'll try it on after all," I said. Worthy perked right up, his cheeks pinking in pleasure.

That dress did the damnedest things to my body, hugging the right curves and hiding the bumps. I could barely keep Worthy's paws off me when I came out of the room. I'd pulled my hair back into a shiny knot, added gold hoop earrings, and makeup Gema had given me for Christmas, telling me to give it a try: purple eyeshadow, great gobs of mascara that felt like spiders crawling across my face when I blinked.

They nearly fell over, especially Gardie, who stared with her mouth wide open. There was something in her expression that I didn't quite trust, a calculated glance from me to Worthy.

"Watch it, Gardie, you'll catch flies," I said.

At the party, Worthy wrapped his arm around my waist, pressed his nose against my neck, drank too much, and ground his pelvis into me during the slow dances. I wished I were at home, like Gardie and Oscar, drinking champagne straight from the bottle, my feet wrapped in the fuzzy pink slippers Worthy had given me one year for my birthday. If I closed my eyes and didn't breathe in too much Old Spice cologne, I could almost pretend that Worthy's arm belonged to Theo, that the thick fingers poking my dress into my ass were slender and more adept.

When Eliza Whittle came up to us sporting a new bouffant wig, her husband, Dan, trailing behind with two drinks in his hand, I'd already had enough.

"We were just leaving," I said.

The music stopped. A man mounted the stage and grabbed a microphone.

"It's time," he said. "Let's count down to 1973!" The crowd cheered. Eliza linked her arm through Worthy's, smiled up at him, her cheeks shiny. *Ten, nine, eight.* Dan Whittle watched his wife and Worthy, reached out to grab her arm and pull her toward him. *Seven, six, five.*

I licked my thumb, cupped Eliza's chin in my other hand, and wiped the corner of her lip, pressing hard. "Lipstick accident!" *Four, three, two.* She grimaced and pulled away from me, swiping at her mouth. Worthy stared at the makeup smeared down her chin, the way her wig puffed out at the sides, making her head twice as big as it should have been. *Happy New Year!*

I woke the next morning to Polly's chattering, lifted her from the crib and let her body warm me, her arms wrapped around my neck. Worthy rolled out of bed and lurched down the hall to the bathroom, began to retch behind the closed door. He'd manhandled me all the way home from the party, his hand down the front of my dress on our front porch, then passed out after a shuddering kiss, his lips open and hot on my shoulder. I used my feet to turn him over onto his side, where he snored and mumbled the rest of the night, my eyes wide and staring dry into the darkness.

Gardie was up when I made my way into the kitchen, had already made a pot of coffee and was on her second cup, her arms folded on the kitchen table, three cigarettes stubbed out in the ashtray. "Good party?" she asked.

"It was okay. How was last night?"

"Polly? She was great." She didn't look at me as she spoke, but lit another cigarette.

"Something wrong?"

She shrugged, picked at her fingernails. I rolled my eyes, made Polly some cereal, and sat her down in her high chair with a glass of milk. *Moody girl.*

Gardie waited until Worthy slouched into the kitchen, his hair sticking up in places like an overgrown lawn and toothpaste dotting the corner of his mouth.

"Morning," he said.

"Good morning!" she chirped. "Worthy, I wanted to tell you, Oscar is going to move out into the boarding house."

Worthy didn't seem to know what to say, and coffee dribbled out of my nose from a sudden coughing fit.

"Well, that's good, I guess," he finally said.

"How on earth did you get him to agree to that?" I asked.

She shrugged. "I have my ways," she said. But then smiled coyly.

Oscar moved into the rooming house near the mines the following week, and he did it without complaint, a single duffle bag of his possessions slung over his shoulder.

"Don't worry about me," he said. "I'll be around." He grinned, winked at Gardie, who waved and waved until he was out of sight.

"I don't know how you got him to leave," I said, "and I'm not sure I want to know."

"Oh, Belle, don't be so naive. Men are such simpletons. It's so easy—give a little bit, then promise a little bit more, and you'll have them eating out of your hand."

What do you say when you find out your sister is a little bit of a tramp? I didn't say anything, but secretly I *did* admire her.

"I suppose I should thank you," I said.

"I didn't do it for you," she said.

Gardie moved into Oscar's old room and became too comfortable, too fast. She had very little with her in Silver Falls but managed to spread it out along every surface—clothes hanging out of drawers, a hairy brush sticking to the wet sink in the bathroom, pieces of her here and there. I even found her hair elastic on the dresser in our bedroom.

Oscar showed up for dinner that first Sunday, hopeful and combed and shining, sharing meaningful smiles and deep glances with Gardie. I suppose she had a talk with him, because he didn't appear again for a few weeks. When he did, he was curt and dismissive of her, and held his knife and fork so tightly he left indentations in his fingers.

Over the next few months, she became freer around us, casually slinging an arm around Worthy's neck and kissing him on the cheek when she said good-night, her tight men's long johns clinging to her legs. It didn't bother me in the least, but Worthy seemed uncomfortable, stiffening and pulling away slightly when she leaned in. When she stopped wearing a bra around the house, he pleaded with me to say something. Now, Gardie never had the kind of breasts I did; she was more delicate, like our mother. But her nipples poked out of the thin shirts she wore, and they bounced around an awful lot.

"What do you want me to say to her?" I asked him. "Can't you just look away from them? It's not like she mashes them against your face or anything."

By the spring, she was venturing outside more and more, heading down the hill with Polly in her stroller. She told me that she'd buy all the groceries now; we ate too much garbage, she said, too much fatty food and red meat. She dug a little patch in the backyard and planted beans and tomatoes, tended that garden every chance she got, a floppy hat on her head, Polly on her knees beside her, digging with a plastic shovel.

One day she came home and announced that we'd no longer be buying most of our groceries from the supermarket. *Too commercial*, she said. Instead, she'd found the perfect store.

"It's called the shop," she said. "Imagine that? No name, just *the shop*."

"It has another name," I said automatically.

"Not anymore. They used to, they told me, but now they've taken down the original name and put up a piece of cardboard with just *the shop* written down. Handwritten, no capital letters." She smiled at me, as if this were the greatest idea in the world. And me? My throat grew tight; she'd taken the first step toward the farmhouse and my other world, and I didn't want her anywhere near it.

I became paranoid. I thought I felt her eyes following me, studying me closely, as if she knew, a secret smirking smile on her lips. But as the months passed and nothing happened, I began to relax. She seemed to skirt around the edge of that community, visiting the shop once a week. Gema had seen her down there and reported back that although she was friendly and chatty with the girls and guys behind the counter, she shied away from personal questions or invitations. Gardie herself told me that someone had asked her out on a date but she'd said no.

"Why not?" I asked.

She studied me for a minute, as if debating what to say. "I have my reasons," she said. "I'd like to stay clean."

BY THE SUMMER of 1973, I had tired of the charade and wanted out. Theo and I had been together for almost three years, no one even suspected, and I decided that Gardie could kiss my big sweet ass. I didn't care anymore if someone found out, began to consider moving out of the house on Garland and permanently into the trailer, convinced myself that Worthy might even be *relieved* to see me go. As unbelievable as it probably sounds, it didn't occur to me that my leaving would cause any kind of problem. If I thought about it at all back then, I'm sure I imagined a kind of neighbourly relationship, where I'd run into Gardie at the grocery store with Polly or go over for dinner once in a while. Easy chatter, civil, friendly almost, as if we'd once been roommates but then had moved on into different parts of our lives. But really, I didn't have to think about it that much, because the decision was made for me.

I suppose I felt reckless, invincible. In July, we went to the lake together just outside of Silver Falls. I can still remember the way the warm water lapped against my calves that day, my thighs. We swam side by side, not touching, treading water and grinning. Theo kept flicking his head, sending droplets of water to land in soft patters on the surface of the lake. On the shore, a few teenage couples sat on checkered blankets with sandwiches, bottles of beer stuck sideways in the sand.

Our own personal stillness swallowed us. We moved into shallow water, so that our toes pressed into softness. Theo's eyes that day seemed remarkably large and clear and truthful.

"I don't think I can do this much longer," I said. Beneath the surface, his thigh brushed mine, my words hanging over us. The moment was too full, too knowing and rich, there with the sun bearing down and making us squint, drops of water dripping from the tips of our ears and the ends of our eyelashes. Fridays weren't enough anymore, not for me; I wanted *this* always, not the drab company house perched on the hill or the sweaty nights when I let Worthy climb on top of me. I leaned into Theo, inhaled the smell of his warm, wet skin, slid my bathing suit down my shoulders, my knees.

ONE MORNING before I set out for work, I gave Polly her oatmeal, watched as she gouged a spoon into the bowl with enough energy and enthusiasm to send the mush flying into her hair, onto the wall. Gardie sat across from me at the kitchen table, drawing deeply on a cigarette and blowing smoke in my face with a stare.

"What?" I asked.

She didn't answer, narrowed her eyes. "Everyone left, you know."

"Left where? What are you talking about?" The smoke irritated me.

She smiled. "Left Vermont. Well, everyone who wanted to *be* someone. The girls who just wanted to get married stayed. Everyone else went west, all the young people. That's where I went for a while."

"So?"

She shrugged. "You should have just stuck around a bit longer," she said. "You would have found your escape all on your own." She looked at me steadily until she saw my recognition, the awareness that I didn't need Worthy or anyone else to carry me away on his shoulders.

She took something from her pocket, placed it on the table. I could feel everything about to come crashing down: the first carving Theo had done for me—a carving of a naked woman, seven, almost eight, months' pregnant, a rounded, ripe belly—wobbled in front of me, began to roll, then stopped. He had pressed it into my hand after Polly was born, and I carried it in my pocket for a long time so that I could reach down and feel its smooth edges whenever I wanted, a constant reminder of what we had together. I don't know where Gardie had found it; I had hidden the piece in my underwear drawer next to the rings my mother had given me. Or so I thought.

"You went through my drawers?"

"That's not the point," she said, her face flushing.

"I think it is. It's none of your business."

"Really? I think Worthy would think differently."

"You're not Worthy, and I'm not sure what you're getting at."

"This." She lifted the carving, thrust it in front of my face. "This is what I'm getting at."

"It's a carving, so? So what? I got it down at the shop—there are a lot of them down there."

"That's not what they say at the shop," she said, searching my face, watching for my reaction. I wouldn't give her the satisfaction.

"If you have something to say, come out with it. I'm late for work."

"Oh yes, work," she said. "Your job on Fridays. Your cleaning job, right?"

I rolled my eyes, wiped Polly's face with a napkin, willed my hand to stop shaking.

Gardie drew her feet up onto the chair, leaned forward to stub out her cigarette, and wrapped her arms around her knees. "I know what's going on," she said.

"What do you want?"

"You've never loved Worthy."

"That's none of your business at all," I snapped.

"I think it is."

"Yes, you seem to think it is."

She smiled, said nothing. I took Polly from her high chair, settled her on my lap so I could press my chin into the top of her head, needing to feel her skin, smell her hair, but she squirmed

(*No, Mama, down!*), throwing her arms up so that she slid to the floor. I let her go, watched her run to the living room to play with the dials on the television.

"What do you want?" I repeated, my words clipped and harsh.

"If you don't tell him, I will." Gardie spoke slowly, as if to make sure I understood what she said. I looked across the table at her, stared hard. She didn't look away but tilted her chin up in defiance.

I shrugged. "Go ahead," I said. "Tell him anything you want. See if he believes you. Or maybe see if he thinks what *I think*. You've been parading yourself around here for months, showing off your body, flaunting yourself. You think you've been so sneaky, but even Worthy thinks you're a bit of a tramp." I laughed. "Actually, I *dare* you to tell him. Let's see how fast it lands your skinny ass out on the sidewalk." And with that, I stood, ignoring the blotches of pink that spotted her stunned face, and gathered up my bag, kissed Polly on the forehead.

Gardie found her voice as I reached the front door. "I will tell," she nearly shrieked. "You watch! And you know why, Belle? You've treated Worthy like garbage for *years*. You don't know how to love someone, but I do. And I'll show you!"

"You can pack up your bags," I told her. "You're going home."

I closed the door behind me gently, feeling sick to my stomach. Everything that happened was linked to everything that had come before, and as it all piled up, I could only cover my head and wait for it all to crumble.

"I'm thinking of leaving Worthy," I told Theo. He stiffened, said nothing. "Well, what do you think of that?" I asked.

"I think if that's what you want to do, you should do it."

"But what about you?"

"What about me?"

"Would that make you happy?"

"It would make me happy to see you happy."

"Stop being so cryptic!" I threw my dress on, tugged and pulled as it caught on my head.

"I don't think you should rush into something like that," he said, catching my wrist and running his thumb over my skin. I pulled away, opened the door of the trailer, braiding my hair hurriedly, the top button of my dress undone, and almost stumbled over Worthy, pale and twitchy and nervous.

I think the blood stopped moving in my veins, but I braced myself. Here it was, then. Time for anger, accusation, maybe tears. *We're not happy,* I imagined myself saying. *Let's just admit it.*

"So it's true," he said simply. My throat closed up so that none of the rehearsed lines could squeak out. Behind me, Theo hung back, silent. "After everything I've done to try and make you happy." *This isn't the way it should happen.* I couldn't bear his disappointment, the flatness in his eyes.

"Worthy, I'm sorry." I licked my lips. "You knew we weren't happy—" I tried, but he cut me off.

"Don't bother. Just go home and pack your stuff. He can have you." Something in Worthy's eyes I'd never seen before—a hardness, even hatred—took hold of my throat. I nearly gagged on my unexpected feelings of guilt.

"And don't even think about taking Polly," he said. "She's mine, and you never really loved her anyway."

"That's not true."

"Of course it is, Belle." How pale his face was, blotched with pink streaks high up on his cheeks, marks of my betrayal showing on his skin.

I loved Polly, didn't I? Had I really ever thought of her, or had I just seen through her chatter, ignored the chubby fists grabbing at my pants, hanging on to my skirts, cheeks stained with oatmeal or smeared with jam as I lifted her into the bath, going through the motions? In all my sketchy plans for the future, she stayed on Garland Street with Worthy and Gardie, unaffected, unchanged.

Worthy looked at Theo for the first time, simply looked for a long moment without saying a word, his eyes hooded and dark. Theo broke the gaze, looked away, allowed him that small, meaningless victory.

Sometimes you can tell the thoughts of a man by the slant of his shoulders as he walks away. Worthy's rounded forward, dipping toward the ground in defeat.

How naive I was, *laughable* even, to think it would be easy. I went home to the house on Garland and packed my bag, alone. I packed quickly, afraid that if I slowed down, the guilt would sneak back in. I had no time for it. And anyway, it wasn't like I was leaving the country; I wouldn't be far at all. Worthy would calm down—I felt sure of it. In the back of my drawer, I found the wedding bands my mother had given me and, thrown in a corner, the lighter, tawdrier version Worthy gave me when I arrived. His had never fit properly; I'd removed it when I was pregnant and never put it back on again. I hesitated, then placed Worthy's band gently on the top of the dresser.

I put my nose to Polly's mattress in her crib, breathed in her scent, trying to memorize all that she was, as if I knew, somehow. (She was two years old. By the time I saw her again, she would be six, and it would be too late to stop anything.) I wonder now if things would have been different if Polly had been home when I went back to the house. It eats at me these days, churning and chewing away like worms. Would I have changed my mind if I had had the chance to touch her face, look into those dark eyes so like mine? I'll never know, but I'd like to think so.

I lugged my suitcase onto the porch, watched the blue paint flaking around my shoes for the last time.

"Was it worth it?"

And wouldn't you know it, there stood Eliza Whittle, always ready to butt in where she wasn't wanted or needed. She'd crossed her arms and widened her legs to look sturdy, maybe forbidding.

"Oh, for God's sake," I said. I slammed my suitcase down on the porch but misjudged; it teetered, then tumbled down the steps and burst open, snaps broken. "Fuck."

Eliza shrank from the word, her outraged lips pressed together hard in disapproval.

"I always knew you'd leave him," she said. "The moment I met you, I knew you wouldn't fit in around here. I even said as much to Dan. *Thinks she's better than us,* I said."

"It's really none of your business," I said, stuffing giant panties and bras back in my suitcase and carrying it to the car. In the trunk, I found a roll of twine, began winding it around the suitcase over and over again. "You've always stuck your nose in where it doesn't belong, and now you've gone too far." I made a double knot, finished with a bow.

"You made it my business," she said. "Did you think that no one has eyes? A lot of people saw you down at the lake, not that you made much effort to hide it." Her mouth twisted; I remembered sliding off my bathing suit, Theo's hands between my legs.

All this time I'd assumed Gardie had somehow managed to find Worthy while he was working and dragged him back with the news, Polly in tow. Of course, it was Eliza. *Of course.* I closed the trunk, got into the front seat, and started the car. Still she stood staring at me, her face drawn and looking somehow oddly lost as I drove down the hill into town.

GEMA DROVE ME up to the farmhouse but didn't come in with me, muttering about Nathan and the problems they were having. "We're not exactly speaking," she said.

"Why didn't you tell me?" I asked. Selfish me, for not noticing the whiteness of her skin and the way it stretched, taut and hollow, under her eyes.

She shrugged. "It's nothing," she said.

We sat together in the car, the windows rolled down, her arm resting on the door frame.

"What's going to happen next?" she asked.

I didn't know for sure. "I guess I'll stay here for a while," I said. "Maybe I'll get an apartment downtown."

She hugged me then. "Come see me soon," she said.

I FOUND THEO hitching his trailer to the Chevy around the back of the house, a few bags on the ground by his feet. I watched him while his back was turned, the way his T-shirt rode up to expose the curve of his spine as he knelt.

"What are you doing?"

He spun around, a look of surprise sliding into one of guilt before he managed to smile. "I didn't expect you for hours," he said.

I looked again at the bags on the ground, the way he stuffed his hands in his pockets, removed them, then stuck them back in again. *I wasn't expecting you for hours.*

"You were leaving?"

He puffed out his lips in dismissal, made a face, shook his head too vigorously. "No."

What a crock of shit. My own bag slipped from my hand and toppled onto its side on the patchy grass. I sank down to the ground, lay back, and spread my arms, face turned up to the sun, closed my eyes, fists digging into pebbles, weeds beneath my

fingernails. Small stones dug into my skin. That bastard, Theo—
he was leaving without me.

"Open your eyes," he said. I kept them shut, the glare of the
sun bright against my lids, red spidery lines climbing across my
eyes. "Belle."

"Just go, then," I said. "What do I care?"

"I'm not leaving, I already said that."

"And I'm the Queen of England."

Feet shuffled in gravel, crunching steps in my direction, then
shade as his face hovered over mine. "Hysterical lady collapses in
a faint," he said.

"I didn't faint," I said. "I'm dead."

"Well, that's no good at all."

I didn't move, but opened my eyes. He sat down beside me.

"I'm not good for drama," he said, "and I'm not going to stick
around waiting for people to throw shit at me."

"Where are you going?"

"California," he said. "Not for good. Just for a while, a few
months maybe. Let things settle down here." Yes, let them settle
back into place, a new order.

And you tell me, what were my options then? I had my house-
cleaning money stashed away in my suitcases, enough to last a
while, to get me settled. A few months without Theo on my own
in Silver Falls, I could do it. An apartment, a new job at the
supermarket or cleaning more houses to pay the rent. For a
moment I thought it wouldn't be so bad, felt a brief spark of
something like interest, even excitement. *Starting over.* I didn't
need Worthy or Theo to make it all better.

"I miss the ocean," Theo said, and suddenly the longing and
need hit me so that nothing else mattered. The ocean, just like
home. *Yes.* Something inside my chest loosened.

"I'm coming with you," I said, just like that.

He touched me then, ran his fingers through my hair, tugging through snags, then curved his hand over my forehead—gentle, smooth. I focused on the clouds, imagined stuffing their softness in my mouth, avoided looking at his face, his green panther eyes. Felt his hand on the nape of my neck, his fingers twisting in my hair as he pressed my head against his shoulder.

FOURTEEN

By my third day in the infirmary, I'm feeling better enough to notice what's going on around me. The nurse comes in to give me my medication, a bunch of drugs and vitamins in different sizes—*Librium, iron, and Zantac, oh my!* She's the most familiar face around, coming to check on me a few times a day. She's round and looks stern, but when she smiles, her face nearly splits in half, and the corners of her eyes crinkle into tiny lines, so that you can't help smiling back at her, no matter how wrecked you feel inside. Most of all, she doesn't ask any personal questions or bother me, which I tend to like in a person. I almost think she might be my friend. She brings me newspapers, which I scan for mention of my name, and paperback novels.

"You're just like a friend I had once," I tell her.

"Oh, yeah? How's that?"

"One time I was in the hospital, and she kept bringing me these romance books to read."

"Sounds like a good friend."

"She was." I pick at the white sheet, suddenly sad.

The nurse touches my wrist. "What happened to her?"

I jerk my arm away from her fingers. "I don't know," I say. Gema's part of the lost years.

THROUGHOUT THE DRIVE WEST, I focused on the ocean, imagined my toes dipped in frigid water, the wind pummelling my body as I closed my eyes and just drank it all in. We stopped at night in heavily wooded campsites, the smell of burning wood soaking into our hair and clothes, the fire warming my cheeks and making me drowsy. I let Theo put his arm around me, let him burrow his nose against my neck. We slept in the trailer, the curtains on the small window above the bed parted so that the moonlight fell on the sheets, tangled and bunched up between my legs, my skin pale, glowing.

On the road, we left the windows open so that our hair whipped about our faces, Zeppelin or the Stones playing on the eight-track. When he drove, I studied his profile, relaxed and easy, his skin painted brown by the summer sun, the hair on his arms turned golden. Impossible to tell what he was thinking, and worse than that, would I believe him if he did tell me? Something shifted inside me, but I managed to shrug it off when he looked over at me and smiled, when he touched the back of my neck, dropped his hand to my knee and slid it up my thigh. The music formed a soothing, rumbling wash, filling my ears and forcing my eyes closed, my head angled to press against the window. I was twenty-four years old. The lost years in Silver Falls disappeared, eaten and digested and then simply erased.

I would say that California was good for a while, but *good* is such a pasty, pale word, bland and lifeless. In California I had everything I imagined I wanted, at least for a while: the ocean and the breathing, shifting sky, tracing the swollen veins on the back of Theo's tanned hand as it wrapped around my waist, the freedom to leave my footprints in the morning sand, washed clean and smooth. I imagined long days spent watching Theo sketch and carve, or posing as his muse, taking breaks to swim naked in the ocean, covering our wet bodies with sugary-soft sand, stepping on broken shells. I suppose now it was all part of the picture I'd painted of Theo and what our life would be like together.

We drove down the coast and stopped in Bay Point, where Theo's friend Sam and his wife, Hamiko, lived with their two daughters. Sam managed the Ardmore, a once-posh resort that had lost most of its charm back in the fifties and was just beginning to climb out of what it had become: a staggering hole for permanent drunks and sad-sack poets who composed sonnets while lying soaked on the black rocks slowly eroded by crashing waves.

Our first night in Bay Point, we stayed in their apartment on the top floor of the hotel. Sam and Theo spent quiet time apart from us, chairs pulled together so close that the legs almost touched, wine sliding down their throats as easily as water, while Hamiko and I sat in the living room on pillows thrown onto the floor. She fascinated me: her long hair parted in the middle, four necklaces of multicoloured beads draped around her neck and dipping between her breasts, long tapered fingers and toes. She had smooth almond skin and shining hair, the whites of her eyes stark against the black pupils. Hamiko's daughters, six and four, watched me from the doorway, fingers hooked in mouths or noses, their limbs round and soft and pleasing. Hamiko slid a glass of wine across the coffee table toward me, silent but studious, her eyes as probing as her children's.

"So someone's finally tamed our Theo?"

"I suppose," I said, forcing a smile.

"Next thing you know, he'll be dragging you back to Canada to meet his parents," she said, tossing the comment over her shoulder toward Theo and Sam, her lips twisting and eyebrows raised. Theo laughed, shook his head, and I didn't know what that meant at all.

"Canada?" I asked. "I thought you were from the States."
Hamiko turned to face me then, her mouth smiling, patronizing,
and I saw that she knew more about Theo than I ever would.

So Theo wasn't American, wasn't a war resister as I'd thought
all along. Instead, he came from a small town in Ontario called
Bressler. I laughed it off there in the living room, shrugging as if
it made no difference, but I gathered this discrepancy and hid it
on a shelf up high along with his other faults. I could hear the
waves through the sliding balcony doors.

Theo took me down to the beach the next morning, watched
as I kicked off my shoes and waded in up to my knees. I stood
there waiting, my eyes closed and face tilted to the sky. Theo
cupped his hands around his mouth.

"Are you happy?"

I spread my arms wide and smiled my answer, but inside I
shrank and nearly cried. Such a sad attempt at my sea, no cliffs
and rocks carved in smooth crescents by the tide, secret shelters
from the wind, wild raspberry bushes and thistle and rounded
stones, tall grasses, clumps of seaweed. No red river or rickety
wooden bridges, no wildness at heart, no hills covered in pine
trees and dotted with small houses in primary colours. *Not like
home at all.*

"I knew you would like it," Theo said.

By the next day, we both had jobs at the hotel and had moved
into an apartment across the hall from Hamiko and Sam. Theo
raked the sand in front of the hotel, clearing out garbage and
dead fish, bits of wood caught on the ends of the rake. He went
in the early mornings, before anyone else awoke, his collared
shirt unbuttoned at the top, one end hanging loosely over the
white pants he was given to wear, the other side tucked in neatly.
He hated the uniform but liked the solitude, the sun beating
down on the back of his neck, seashells stuffed in his pockets to

sell later at the tourist shops. When he came home, he tasted like salt.

I worked first in the restaurant as a waitress, then as a maid. Waitressing didn't suit me well; I wasn't used to serving other people. The first time a customer snapped at me for being too slow. I *accidentally* dropped a bowl of chunky seafood chowder into her lap, and that was the end of that.

I was better as a maid, used to cleaning from my days in Silver Falls, and could easily disappear into other worlds, the cleaners burning the inside of my nostrils with their harsh smells and sticking at the back of my throat so that I could almost taste them. I became an expert at folding down the sharpest corners on bedsheets, kicking piles of towels and used linens out the door, emptying and rinsing ashtrays, moving my body aside at the right moment to avoid the dark splash on my uniform.

Our apartment on the tenth floor had seen better days. We had one bedroom, a living room with a television, and a small kitchenette. One of the legs on the wooden coffee table was cracked, and of the four dining room chairs, three wobbled and one was broken. The oven worked only if you switched the dial on and off twice; two burners worked but not on low settings. And the olive green carpet throughout the place smelled of smoke and sweat. But the patio doors opened to reveal the ocean, the beautiful ocean. How I had missed living by the water.

WHEN WE FIRST ARRIVED in Bay Point, when our visit was only meant to be brief, I sent Worthy a letter, trying to explain myself. I wrote that I was sorry and was giving him the space he needed, but that I would come home soon, that I missed Polly. I'd like to think that I meant it, but a part of me knows I did it to ease the guilt that still clung. I did miss Polly, in a roundabout way, but my memories were remote and distant, as if I didn't want to remember. Worthy wrote back shortly, a single phrase on an otherwise pristine sheet of white paper: *Fuck you*. The palpable hatred sucked the moisture from my lips and made me dizzy.

The months stretched out flat, uncontested, and I knew we wouldn't return to Silver Falls anytime soon. Did I think of Polly then, her small face and wondering eyes? I would like to say that I did, but it wouldn't be true. I pushed her away, far back where I couldn't reach her, because it was easier that way. Since I couldn't erase my past, I just didn't think about it, and it was easy enough to do there, so far from the closed minds and stifling boxes lining the streets of Silver Falls.

Theo and I fell into a rhythm of work, fucking on hot after-noons between starched white sheets, and late candlelit nights of music and food and people. There were always people around, other dreamers who worked at the hotel but had no ambition except to suck as much pleasure from life as they could: Nelson, an eighteen-year-old busboy, and his fifteen-year-old girlfriend, whose real name was Elizabeth but who insisted we call her Raindrop; Alejandro from Mexico, who came up to California with his four brothers and stayed when they left to work in the vineyards up north; and Denis, an aging, once-famous writer who'd taken too much acid and one drunken night ate an entire manuscript, dipping the pages in mustard for flavour. There were others, but I can't remember their names; they drifted in and out of the apartment, or we into theirs, with copious amounts of wine and dope, pots of organic brown rice and vegetables, curries, and steamed kale.

I tried my best. We'd been there a few months when, half drunk with my bare feet tucked into a crumbling sandcastle on the beach late one night, watching the tide creep ever closer, salty licks on my toes, I took Theo's hand in mine, serious. It was the right moment, I thought.

"I love you," I said for the first time. Even as the words left my mouth, I doubted they were true, but I felt that after all this time (after all I'd left behind) *someone* should say them. And maybe I thought that, once spoken, they'd become true, that the growing sense of emptiness would shrink and fill with something more like content, like happiness.

His mouth creased. He took me in his arms and slid his hands under my dress, along my thighs. "Please."

Back in our room, I unearthed the rings from my suitcase, slipped my father's wedding band onto Theo's finger. He clenched his fist, took my hand, with its slimmer, matching band, and held it to his chest.

I don't know how long it took for the starched sheets to lose their crispness and fade into limp grey-white. Theo stopped working to focus on his carvings and sketches about a year after we'd arrived.

"We can live on your salary," he said, watching me from bed as I struggled into my polyester uniform that was too tight under my armpits and left a rash around my neck. "Work is draining my creative energies," he said.

I'd come home at the end of the day to find Theo naked, still in bed, cigarette ash all over the sheets as he read book after book and watched TV. And he was a pig, no doubt about it: dishes piled up in the sink, dirty, stinking clothes left in heaps on the floor, abandoned sketches crumpled but not thrown out, bits of wood from his carvings. Worse, he'd now embarked on a long epic poem about life.

"Denis inspired me," he said. And there was Denis, his legs slung over a chair in our living room, his hair growing straight up from his head and uncombed for days, his fingers stained from nicotine and the bags of Cheetos he devoured for dinner every day.

Now, maybe I'm just not artistic or deep enough to appreciate the creative impulse, as Theo accused; I thought he was just lazy. And I'm no art critic, I barely read anything these days, but—well, you be the judge. I can't remember his poem, but he worked on that damn thing for over a year. A year! He showed me bits of it but mostly shielded his drafts with his arm when I came into the room, annoyed and petulant like a child who refused to share. After the first few bits he did show me, I didn't want to read any more.

> *rip the wings from butterflies*
> *sliced throats*
> *lambs wailing*
> *(oh happiness, she breathes)*
> *awake! for the slaughter, the rape.*

Everything in lower-case letters, arranged so artfully on the page. I can still picture Theo hunched over the typewriter, his hair grown long and dripping into the corners of his mouth as he punched the space bar in concentration, counting, moving backwards again so that the words would look *just right*. And then crumpling it all up later. A poet? Maybe he was, but all I could wonder after a while was whether he'd brushed his teeth that day.

We never spent time alone anymore. There were always people, people, people, sometimes in our apartment, sometimes in another—all doors were left open so that you could just wander in wherever you pleased. We were too close; boundaries shifted, blurred, then disappeared altogether.

This was the life I'd chosen: a revolving group of men and women, a few bare-bottomed children running in and out of rooms wearing only undershirts, the same baked bean casseroles,

AND YOU KNOW, it went on like that for a while; I won't bore you with more details. I will tell you how it all ended, though, and how fast, in March of 1976. There was a party at Hamiko and Sam's, wax dripping down the sides of lit candles, velvet wine licking deeply scooped glasses, Bob Dylan in the background. I don't remember who was there or how many of us there were, but we were all slightly drunk, all warm and flushed and at ease. Sam pushed open the patio doors; a rush of warm wind rustled the drapes. Theo sat next to Hamiko, whose long straight hair hung down over her breasts, iron smooth and glossy. He leaned in close, whispered something in her ear that made her laugh and arch her neck. Sam stood by the balcony doors, his back to us, arms outstretched, taking in deep breaths as if meditating. Theo's hand rested on Hamiko's knee. She arched her neck once more, angled her head toward his, and murmured something. I read her lips: *Not here, Theo.* He looked right at me, smiled.

That's all it took. Across from me, Theo smiled. I remembered the curve of his spine as he bent over the trailer, the surprise and guilt on his face when I appeared that day in Silver Falls, thought of the months and years, the vomit and phlegm in bathroom sinks that I cleaned every single day while he sat on his ass with barefoot macramé hippies, crumpling pages of so-called art and letting them drop to the floor. I thought of the day a few months ago when I climbed the rocks around the curve of shore, tucked my knees under my chin, and thought of my father, desperate to sense something but feeling nothing but a great ache of loneliness. Remembered going back to an unclean apartment and keeping my eyes open when Theo made love to me, biting into his shoulder when he came, then walking naked into the kitchen to find the wine, drinking directly from the bottle. And knew in an instant that it was gone, all of the reasons for leaving my old life, gone.

I picked up a lamp beside the sofa—some crazy thing with pink, dangling beads—and threw it at his head, watched it shatter against the wall, glass shards raining down. No one spoke or moved. *You're nothing but a drunk, Belle.*

No one followed me as I left the apartment and wandered across the hall into ours. I think I was calm, though there must have been a great sense of disappointment. In our apartment, I surveyed the mess he'd left behind: dirty laundry thrown onto the floor of the closet, towels slung haphazardly over the rails in the bathroom, used plates and pots crusted with the remains of a spaghetti dinner. I fought an urge to sweep everything up in the bedsheets and throw it out the window.

Instead, I sat in the living room and pulled his records onto the floor, listening to each one, mouthing the words I remembered so that I would never forget. I pulled a small box from the top shelf of the closet in the bedroom, poked through maps and letters and pulled out one of the first from my aunt. Unlike my mother, who filled her notes with pleas to return to Silver Falls, anger and indignation seeping through the lines, my aunt was kinder, more understanding. *You must follow your heart*, she wrote, *but don't forget the ones you left behind.*

I knew he wouldn't come back to the apartment that night, but still I worked quickly. In the bathroom, I found my father's wedding band lying in its usual place on the soap dish. Theo never wore it, claimed he was afraid it would slip off his finger while swimming. Down to the parking lot with big garbage bags I went, and packed up all his things from the trailer. It only took one trip. Again in the apartment, I dumped it all in the middle of the living room and added whatever else of his I could find, so that clothes, toiletries, and books mingled with his carvings, paintings, sketches, and album after album. I considered lighting a fire to the pile, but changed my mind. I took only three things

to remind me of him: the original carving of me and my pregnant belly, my father's wedding band, and that small portable
record player that meant so much to him. Well, four actually—
at the last minute, I plucked his sketchbook from the pile and
tucked it in my suitcase, along with my maps and scrapbook of
Trudeau.

Silly Theo, he left his keys just sitting there. How easy it was
to slip out of the hotel with my bags and the things that meant
so much to him, how easy to drive away in the dead of night. I
drove north into British Columbia, hours and hours of half-
awareness before stopping to think and sleep. I pulled into a
campground, made up the bed in the trailer, opened my suitcase,
and found his sketchbook. I didn't recognize all of the women,
but there were some I thought I knew. That one there, she
worked in the restaurant, and that little one with tiny nipples,
she was someone's girlfriend. And there's Hamiko, so thin you
can count her ribs, her pubic hair dark but sparse. That *bastard*.

In my dreams that night, a small child brought me a bouquet
of hand-picked forget-me-nots, pressed them in my hands, and
watched as the tiny blue flowers began to bubble and melt,
leaving burning welts in my flesh before turning into ashes that
rained down on my bare feet.

When I woke, I imagined taking out my map of the world and
dropping a random finger down to pinpoint my direction, but a
sense of hopelessness gripped me like a tight fist and wouldn't let
go. It would be nice for me to say that I decided to go back to
Silver Falls because it was the right thing to do, nice to pretend
that I'd face my mistakes head-on. But really, I thought Worthy
would just take me back after all this time, imagined him pining
away for me and waiting patiently. After all, I was the mother of
his child. How could he say no? And where else could I go?

FIFTEEN

I've been moved again, this time back to a regular cell. I'm no longer a danger to myself, or at least that's what they say, and I'm through the worst of the withdrawal. My cell is small but adequate; most importantly, I'm alone. I sit on the edge of my bed in my blue uniform, my hair combed and braided and neat, my hands crossed in my lap for a while, just absorbing all the details. So much noise: people talking, always someone moving down the corridor, screams, shouts, hard laughter. When I'm tired of sitting, I lie on my bed and close my eyes against the glare of fluorescent lighting above. I don't want to feel things right now, and that's the plain truth. I'd rather just turn my face to the wall and have it all be over.

AFTER BREAKFAST, everyone goes to court or sits down to analyze their life with psychiatrists outside the unit. Me, I head to the common room to poke through the rows of used library books on a shelf or flick through the television channels listlessly, trying to look as mean as I can so that no one will bother me. I've heard stories about what goes on in women's prisons, and I don't like the sound of any of them.

A mousy, thin woman slinks into the room and stands against the wall, smoking a cigarette and watching me out of the corner of her eye. I notice old, faded bruises wrapping around both wrists, a scratch running from her left ear down the length of her neck. When I ask her what happened, she touches the scratch fleetingly.

"Killed my husband," she says, her voice flat, dead. "My lawyer will get me off on self-defence. I'm going to court today." She shifts her glance over me, holds out her pack of cigarettes. I take one gladly, stuff it in my mouth to shut myself up. I don't want to ask any more questions.

But see? Like I said, everyone's got secrets. That woman, you'd never know it to look at her, couldn't imagine her even killing a weed on her nice manicured lawn at her suburban home, never mind taking a serrated kitchen knife and using it like a saw on her husband's throat.

She asks what I'm in for, and I don't answer her for a while, focusing on my unlit cigarette and the drone of a show about ghost towns on television.

"It's all a mistake," I finally say.

She snorts, nods as if she's heard it before. "I guess you'll be out of here soon, then," she says. "If your lawyer's worth anything."

"I don't have a lawyer," I say.

"Why not? No money? You can get one through legal aid, you know. It's your right." I shrug, but her eyes burn into me. "Don't be an idiot," she says. "Get a lawyer."

I lean forward as the scene on the television changes to something familiar.

"Oh my God," I say.

"Silver Falls was named by the prospectors who arrived in 1904 and found the first vein while blasting through the thick Canadian Shield for the railway," the narrator intones. "After the discovery, a gritty town of makeshift, temporary houses was born." Images flash: dirt roads, clapboard houses, old Fords, and men in suspenders and hats linking arms and flashing smiles, delighted. "In the thirties, Silver Falls swelled to over twenty thousand. But only ten years later, the town shrugged off prosperity and limped back to a population of just under three hundred—mostly women, children, and old men who carved out a space for themselves in the absences left by the healthy young who went to the war." The scene shifts to an interview, a woman with permed white hair, large thick-lensed glasses on a small, creased face. "Times were hard," she says, her voice quavering. "I was only ten back then. My father died in the war. My mother and I nearly starved, but we didn't think of leaving. We had nowhere to go."

"I used to live there," I tell the woman on the screen. I drag my chair up close to the set. "Maybe we knew each other." I watch her rheumy eyes for recognition.

On the other side of the room, the husband-killer coughs. "Hey, cuckoo, you're blocking my view."

"And then another shift," the narrator says in his buttery voice. "In 1958, the nickel operations began, and people with dreams and nowhere else to plant their feet landed in Silver Falls again."

"Me," I say, but I whisper it so that only I can hear. I look over my shoulder to see the thin woman lighting yet another cigarette. She's moved into a chair at least, and sits with her legs pressed together, spreading and smoothing an imaginary skirt over her knees.

"It blew up sometime in the eighties," I tell her.

She shrugs, looks away.

"I went back in 1976," I say to no one.

PULLING INTO SILVER FALLS, I sensed it immediately, the change, the ruin. Everything stood still, waiting. The smaller stores were all boarded up, windows darkened by layers of grime. I rolled down my window, heard the silence of hollow streets. A single dog, curled sleeping in front of the hotel, raised his head as I passed, watched me with disinterest. It was as if a nuclear bomb had dropped in the middle of the town and seared everyone into ashes.

I crossed over the train tracks, turned left and then right onto our street. Empty windows, yellow-brown grass, weeds poking through the cracks of the sidewalks. And there, our house, same dingy clapboard siding, the painted porch now only speckled with blue. I turned off the engine, listened for a moment, trying to beat down the rising panic.

"Well, look who's come home." Eliza Whittle stood beside the car, arms folded across her chest.

"Why is it always you, Eliza?" They weren't all dead, after all.

The door creaked when I opened it, but Eliza held out her hand as if to stop me. She'd put on weight, thickened under her chin. Her blue pantsuit stretched shiny across her bloated midsection. *Look what only three years can do to a person*, I thought. She wasn't going to age well.

"No point," she said, and began to laugh, not kindly. "They're gone. Almost everyone's gone now. The mines closed a year ago."

"But you're here." I couldn't think of anything else to say, unwilling to believe what I knew must be true: the silent, still streets, the signs of abandonment.

"Dan's retired." She shrugged. "Don't know how long we'll stay. Nothing left for anyone."

I'm too late. Now what would I do? "Tell me where they are," I said.

"I wouldn't think that would be any of your business," she said, hands on her hips, her chin lifted in an effort to look superior. I considered telling her to kiss my ass again, like the old Belle, but I'd lost my fight and hadn't the energy. I closed the door, started the engine.

She placed her hands on the frame of the open passenger window, smirked. "They moved about eight months ago, Worthy and your sister." She watched with an expression that could only have been glee, waiting for my reaction. "I think Oscar moved back to Newfoundland." I kept my expression blank, fought the sudden flash of anger and something more, something unexpected.

"Well, I suppose you can't stop true love," she said. "They went to Toronto. With your daughter." She smiled tightly again; I imagined she couldn't wait for me to leave now so that she could spread the news among her friends. How much pleasure do you think she got telling me that?

I gave her my best smile. "What's it like?" I asked, leaning forward earnestly.

She frowned, not sure what I meant. "What's what like?"

"What's it like to be the biggest bitch in town?" Her mouth opened in an indignant oval of shock. I frowned, shook my head. "You have lipstick on your teeth," I said. "You always do."

I drove away before she could respond so that I would always remember her that way: shamed, outraged, and speechless. But as I drove down the hill, my jaw tightened and my fingers dug into the steering wheel. *How dare they?*

Gema looked just the same, bless her, but her eyes were darker than I remembered, bruised and hurt.

"You never answered any of my letters," she said. I'd written to her only once, shortly after we'd arrived in California—a letter of self-absorbed fury, railing against Worthy and that single *Fuck you* he handed out. Her reply came weeks later.

You can hardly blame him, Belle. Just think about it. He came to see me after you left, showed up at the supermarket and waited in line, his face turning almost purple the longer he waited. And when it was finally his turn, he could barely speak. You knew, he said. I know you knew. He told me you'd destroyed the family and that Polly cried for days. I don't think he'll ever forgive you. I'm sorry I have to write these things to you, but I think you should know the truth. You can go on and on about how hard it was for you to leave, but deep down you know you had it easy compared with what they went through. I thought you were staying in Silver Falls, didn't imagine you'd actually leave for good. You never even said goodbye to me. So much for being best friends, I suppose.

My fingers tore at my lips as I read, peeling bits of skin, the sharp taste of blood on the tip of my tongue. I never wrote to her again and tossed the other letters she sent, crumpled and unread, into the garbage.

"They ran away together," I said. "Worthy and Gardie. My *sister*." My legs shook. I sat down on her battered sofa, pressed my hands to my cheeks.

"I wouldn't say they were in love," Gema said. "Or maybe your sister was. Worthy—I think he never got over your leaving." She stood before me, arms crossed over her chest, her expression unreadable.

"Do you hate me?" I asked.

"No, but it makes me wonder."

"What makes you wonder?"

She uncrossed her arms, sat down next to me, and looked so serious that I almost laughed to break the tension. "You left, Belle." She was trying to be gentle, but I could see anger in the way she narrowed her eyes and the stiffness of shoulders slightly raised, defensive. "And you left for a long, long time. Did you think that Worthy would just wait for you?"

"Yes."

"And what about Polly?"

I shut my mouth and looked away. I didn't want to think about Polly, but after long minutes of my silence Gema put her hand on my arm, and the weight of that warmth sank down deep, urging me to think and remember and realize; and when I did, I tilted my head back and closed my eyes.

"What am I going to do now?"

I GOT A JOB at the supermarket with Gema, restocking nearly empty shelves and mopping the floors in my red-and-white uniform. I worked for two days before I found myself face to face with an older miner's wife, struggled to remember her name even as she leaned in and blew sour onion breath up my nose.

"You're Worthy McCargo's wife," she said. *Donna Scrawley.*

"Mrs. Scrawley," I said, nodding.

"You ought to be ashamed," she said. "How can you show your face in this town?"

"Pardon me?" I pulled back.

"What kind of a monster leaves her child?" Her voice was thick with disgust, derision, the lines on her face deeply carved and set. She didn't wait for an answer, merely turned and walked away. I never went back to work.

"You know how it is," Gema said later. "The ones who stayed are probably the ones who'll remember who you are. You were the talk of the town for a while."

I stayed in Silver Falls for two more weeks, sleeping on Gema's couch, watching television for hours at a time. My skin broke out, my hair hung oily and flat, and my face felt puffy, stiff.

One afternoon, the early May sunlight pouring through the basement window made me overly optimistic, and I decided it was time to put my past behind me. I drove past *the shop*, boarded up now and deserted, toward the outskirts of town, to the crumbling farmhouse. It seemed to slant and shift even as I walked around it, cautious and quiet, focusing on the thick grime settled in the grooves of the windows, the weeds poking up through patches of gravel and grass. It too had been abandoned. I wondered when Theo would return to reclaim it. I stood for only a moment, letting the sun warm the top of my head, my eyelids, before a certain recognition seemed to punch me in the chest.

Gema waited for me back at the apartment. "We need to talk," she said.

"I think I'm pregnant," I told her.

Her skin turned ashen. "I just got fired," she said.

We both waited, testing each other's news.

"There's nowhere left for me to go," she said. "I'm moving back to Sudbury."

Sixteen

Vermont was my last option. I made it home to the farm and for a solid week fell into a blackness that wouldn't go away. My arms and legs felt heavy, useless; moving took too much energy and thought. I barely remember anything of those days, except the concerned faces of my mother and aunt, hovering at the door of my bedroom with bowls of soup. All that I had done fell down on my shoulders and pressed me back against the bed, holding my arms and legs and neck and belly with wide steel bands.

When I woke, my whole body ached and shook, as if my skin and muscles surrounded rubber instead of bone. I sat in the kitchen with my mother, both of us silent, staring at my plate of toast and eggs, uneaten and cold.

"Do you want to talk about it?" she finally asked. I didn't, as a matter of fact, but I knew I'd have to say something sooner or later. I couldn't admit to my failure, not like it had really happened, not now, with Gardie and Worthy living happily ever after, with Polly unreachable, abandoned. The lie surfaced, popped out before I could stop it.

"Theo died," I said, then covered my face with my hands to make it true. It was the only thing I imagined I could say to make my mother forgive me, to make it more bearable.

Even in her kindness, my mother wore a layer of frostiness that she couldn't dispel. And when she thought I was strong enough, she made it clear that she could forgive anything except leaving Polly behind.

"She was everything to Worthy," I said. "I couldn't take her away from him. He wouldn't let me."

"But you're her mother," she said, her voice rising. "And she'll never forgive you for leaving. Worse, you'll never forgive yourself."

"Don't tell me what I will or won't do," I said.

"Belle." She paused, considering her words carefully. "You've always done what you want, regardless of everyone else. I would never hate you for that—it's who you are. But you can't do things and then only think about the consequences when things go wrong for you." I didn't want to hear it, turned away. It felt unfair, her attack; Worthy had driven me away. Of course he had.

"I didn't have a choice," I said.

"We all have choices. And when you have a family, you have to think of them too."

"Oh, for heaven's sake, Ava, leave her alone. Don't make her feel worse." My aunt stood behind me, rubbing my neck.

My mother tensed. "Hannah, I think you should stay out of this."

"Why? She's here, it's my farm. And someone she loved has died. You know what that feels like just as much as she does. As I do." My mother looked at her oddly; I suppose it was the first time my aunt had acknowledged that my uncle was now more than just *away*. She looked the same as the last time I'd seen her, but grief had given her an air of quiet solemnity. She patted my back. "You stay here as long as you want. It's good to have you home. We need more voices in this place."

"I may stay awhile," I said.

"Good."

I looked back at my mother, trying to force the words that needed to come. "I'm pregnant."

I watched their faces slide into disappointment.

I MOVED through the farmhouse quietly, trying to make myself invisible, three months pregnant. I was certain it would be a boy, even named him (Jonah) in my mind, whispered it to him months later at night when he began to move around inside me.

"How can you be sure?" my mother asked.

"I can feel it."

She gave me a small smile. "That's what I thought too." Like me, my mother had been convinced Gardie would be a boy.

"Feels just like all my other boys," she would say. And everyone told her she looked the same: glowing, belly sticking out in front of her like a giant basketball. (With me it was different. *You sucked the life right out of me*, she always said. I made her break out in pimples, I made her fat all over.)

Maybe she convinced herself. Maybe she secretly hoped Gardie was a boy, to replace the baby she'd only just lost the year before. She consulted my father, who said he had always hoped one of their boys would take his middle name: Gordon.

They whispered the name to my mother's belly for months, stitched the name onto bibs and nightgowns. *Gordon*. To fill the gap left by a dead baby boy.

And then out popped Gardie, bald and fair and delicate, and no one knew what to do. By then they'd gotten used to the name, and any other didn't feel right. Ever practical, my mother pointed out the waste (all those embroidered bibs and nightgowns) should the name not be used. My father reluctantly agreed. And with the change of a single vowel, Gordon's nickname became more feminine somehow. Still, there it was on her birth certificate in bold black type, forever reminding her of what our parents had hoped for and what she could never be: Gordon Dearing.

I smiled back at my mother now, anxious for us to close the gap between us, but she had already turned away.

And so we lived, the three of us. My mother and Mr. Dillard went out often, and she would come back from these dates looking the way she did a long time ago, before the deaths of her men.

"Will you get married again?" I asked her once.

"No, never." She shook her head hard. "Your father was my one and only husband." And she shot me a look that said, *You see?*

And Aunt Hannah—my aunt was caught between obsession and reality. Though she seemed to understand that Uncle Erik was never coming home, collected her survivor's pay, and went about her days, she held on to a slim strand of hope that he would emerge from the jungles of Vietnam, unscathed and smiling. She no longer set the table for four—by the time I arrived, the fourth plate had been banished back into the cupboard—but the lines around her eyes and the slight tremble of her folded hands betrayed her. She still sometimes came to the breakfast table wearing his sweater or a scratchy scarf around her neck, letting her nose dip into its folds to smell any traces that remained.

Letters came now and then from Gardie. My mother left these lying open on the kitchen table, where the writing, flowery and hurried, mocked me. The envelopes, with their return address, were always missing—my mother just tucked them into her apron and transferred them to some secret location—but I knew she lived in Toronto. I read the letters when I was sure no one would catch me, dipping crusts of toast into lukewarm tea and chewing absent-mindedly. Polly was in kindergarten, had learned the alphabet, sang "O Canada" in clear high tones with only the barest trace of a lisp that lingered, and recited her entire address, including postal code and telephone number, if you asked her where she lived. *She's one smart cookie,* Gardie wrote, a mother's pride visible in the exclamation marks she tacked onto the end of every sentence: *Counts to one hundred! Knows all the nursery rhymes by heart!* Once she enclosed a photograph, showing a small child with her head tilted to the side, dark hair framing her face. She looked like me, all right, but it was those blue flashing eyes that caught my attention: a knowing, mocking expression, as if she knew something that no one else did and she wasn't going to share. I like that kind of attitude.

Before I left Silver Falls, Gema gave me one last piece of advice.

"Don't go barging in the way I know you want to," she said. "Just think about it. You left when Polly was two, and Gardie's been with her ever since. And if I know anything, I know she's a good mother to her, loves her more than she probably loves Worthy. Don't take them away from each other."

Was that my first instinct? Take back what was mine, make Gardie and Worthy suffer, no matter what the cost? Possibly. No—*probably.*

"Does she ever ask about me?"

My mother looked up from her knitting, swirls of yellow wool caught between her practised fingers. A cap for Jonah, she said, but yellow, just in case.

"Who?"

"Gardie." I knew that she didn't, at least not in the letters I'd read. But I also knew that there were long phone calls every Sunday night.

My mother shrugged, pausing to place a finger on the printed pattern she'd placed next to the lamp, her lips pursed and a frown creasing the skin between her eyebrows, before returning to her knitting.

"She's doing well," she said. "Trying to break into acting, you know. You remember how she was when she was little—always dressing up and acting out those plays for all you kids."

"I saw the picture of Polly," I said. She nodded but didn't look up at me. "She looks like me." She nodded again, but slowly.

I stood to open the window, letting the early June air, still cool but carrying a sense of the summer to come, brush my face. I leaned my arms against the sill, gazing past the porch down the long gravel driveway that vanished into the edges of dusk. We'd rarely used this front room before, but now, in the new quiet, it seemed the perfect place for our solitude at night—reading or knitting or just staring out into space with our thoughts.

On the mantel over the fireplace, my mother had placed the glass bottle from Newfoundland, the heavy stopper in place; she'd cleaned it on the outside to remove fingerprints and dust, and the light caught in the curve of the handle.

"You kept it," I said now, rising to cradle it in my hands.

"Of course," she said. "You gave it to me."

"And you never asked why." She smiled, shook her head, and I did tell her then, how Worthy had dug it up at the mine, how I'd filled it with earth from my father's grave.

"Oh, Belle," she said, and I think she might have been crying, though I couldn't see properly in the dim light.

I twisted the wedding band, still on my finger; she noticed, glanced up at my face.

"How did he die?" she asked. And at first I thought she was talking about my father, looked at her in confusion, then realized she meant *Theo*. And I knew that sooner or later I'd need to say something or admit to my lie, and now wasn't the time for that.

"He fell from the balcony of our apartment," I said. "We lived on the top floor of the hotel. One night he was leaning on the railing, and it just broke away, took him all the way down. They told me he died right away." She made a sound in the back of her throat, and the *awfulness* of what I'd done hit me. But I have to admit I was rather proud of myself for coming up with something so original. I could easily have said car crash or heart attack, couldn't I?

"I'm sorry," she said.

I turned from the window, noticed my mother's small hands and thin fingers, the way her knuckles bunched up as she brought the needles through each loop.

"You could send them a letter," she said quietly, without looking up.

"Sure, Gardie wouldn't answer it."

"Maybe not," she said. "And maybe you're not ready yet. But when you are, you need to take the first step. Don't wait for them to do it for you."

I hated the tightness in my throat. I went to bed early that night, slow steps up to my room. From my bedroom window I looked out at my little cottage. I hadn't been inside since I returned, hadn't wanted to face the memories again. In the darkness I thought of Theo, wondered if I'd ever really loved him or had only imagined I did because he offered everything but expected nothing. Or no, that wasn't quite right; Theo expected the same in return—*no expectations*, nothing to tie him down. And I'd thought I'd wanted the same, blamed my suffocating responsibilities for my unhappiness, when really it was just me. For the first time, I wondered if I'd ever be happy, would ever stop pasting up my maps and imagining myself in different places.

The next morning, I listened to a tree branch tapping against the front window downstairs, a clock ticking in the hallway.

Down the hall in her room, my mother shifted, turned over in her sleep, the old bedsprings creaking. Too much heated silence. I pulled on my robe and walked downstairs, stuffed my feet into a pair of rubber boots, and went out the door into the back. The red paint had begun to peel from the upper corners by the roof. I thought of Uncle Erik, his forehead beaded with sweat that summer as he cut lumber and painted, all for me. Inside, I smelled remnants of Gardie, saw an ashtray filled to the brim tucked away on the shelf. Remembered Worthy appearing on that bicycle, the way he'd leaned forward and grasped me with emotion and lust and love all rolled into one. I pressed my forehead into the rough boards, hoping to feel a sliver pierce my skin, to make me feel the pain, see the blood. I expected to feel nostalgia, a sense of the forgotten, but I felt nothing. Whatever I had there in that small space was gone, whisked away by years of wind and rain and snow. I kissed my palms, pressed them against the weathered boards, closed the door for the last time.

I walked to the field where Gardie and I went on the anniversary of my father's death so many years before, kicked at the same fallen tree trunk where we'd sat to clear dried clumps of leaves and dirt. I sat down, closed my eyes, and turned up my face to the early morning sun, letting it warm my skin until my eyelids tingled and pinpricks of stars burst in my eyes. I tried to remember how we were back then, the future stretching before us in great uncertainty. But what I remembered most were the sense of aching loss, Gardie's eyes darkened with pain, and the way I'd fought against an instinct to put my arms around her and pull her head onto my shoulder.

SEVENTEEN

It was my aunt who suggested moving up to a small town in Ontario called Ludlow when my mother started worrying about money and what we'd do once the baby arrived. Aunt Hannah had an old friend whose husband was the foreman of a candy factory, and she thought she could get both of us jobs. After a few phone calls, we'd landed not only jobs but also a rented house located near the construction site of a new university.

About six hundred people worked at the candy factory, making candy canes and other peppermint candies, the sweet smell rising and hanging like a cloud over the town. You might think it's a nice smell, but after a while it seeps under your skin and takes over every part of you, like an alien creature. That smell gets in your hair, clings to your eyelashes so that you almost smell it when you blink. Or at least I could.

Until Jonah was born, I worked in the wrap-pack room for candy canes, steadying the sticks as they came down the conveyor belt and dropped into the bender, where they were bent and shaped. My mother worked in the same room but at the other end, snapping finished canes into trays, before she was snatched up for a better position. It didn't surprise me; my mother just didn't seem like she should be there with the rest of us, looked strange in her cap and gloves, her spine too straight somehow, the angle of her chin too regal. It was like one of those questions on an IQ test: *Which one of these is not like the others?* Organized and smart, she was brought up into the glass offices as an office assistant, then assistant manager, and never came back down.

My head itched from the cap I had to wear, my back ached, and my ears rang by the end of each day, muffling all sounds. Still, I didn't mind the work, not really. It was easy, if boring. And, like the job in California, I didn't have to think of anything if I didn't want to. I mostly shut down inside myself and talked to Jonah or ran my hands over my belly as he squirmed inside me.

My mother and I weren't speaking to each other much anyway in those first weeks—hadn't since the move from Vermont. We drove up together in Theo's red Chevy in early September, the silver trailer lumbering behind us, a burst of golden leaves on either side of the road leaving us speechless. I wouldn't let her drive until we reached Quebec, though I still had no licence, and you could tell it made her crazy to lose control in that way. She sat next to me in the passenger seat looking the same as she always did in a car when she wasn't driving: one hand gripping the door, the other on her thigh, concentrated, eyes barely blinking. For the most part the driving was clear, the roads fine. When it started to rain, the squeaking windshield wipers and the silence in the car lulled her to sleep. She woke at a rest stop in Quebec, startled, hair falling from her careful chignon.

"You can drive if you want." We'd broken free of the rain. I pushed open the car door and released my legs, stretching them out in front of me with a sigh.

Back behind the wheel, my mother seemed more relaxed, happier. The memory of driving Uncle Erik's truck home from the school that day when she had pounded the wheel and stood up for me struck. I was suddenly angry, not at my mother but at myself. Hadn't we proved those men right? I *was* stupid, and look, I'd messed up and changed everyone's lives. And here was my mother, relaxed and at peace, even humming along to the radio a little. So you could say I was looking for a fight on that long drive, a way to pass the time and take the focus in my brain off me and put it onto someone else. My mother, as always, was an easy target.

"I don't know why we had to leave," I complained.

"Yes, you do," she said.

"So you could be closer to Gardie?" I knew where to push, wanted her to feel the tension and discomfort that stretched from my neck to my aching hips and legs.

"That's right, Belle, it's all for Gardie." She almost laughed then, as if she knew what I was up to and refused to play along. I pushed harder.

"And what about George?" I asked. "I thought you loved him. I saw the way he looked when we left. I would never leave someone I loved."

My mother glanced sideways at me. Her fists, loosely wrapped around the steering wheel, suddenly tightened until her knuckles turned white. I pictured poor George Dillard standing bereft by the road, waving as we drove away.

"He must have been *heartbroken*."

She sighed, shook her head a little, probably wishing I would just shut up so she could enjoy the drive.

"Sometimes you have two paths in life, Belle, and you have to make a decision which one to follow. It can be an easy decision, but usually it's not." *And I had chosen the wrong path.* She didn't say it out loud. "In Vermont you had no health insurance, no way of paying for the hospital, nothing. And I couldn't work, not without a green card. I knew that I would never marry George. I had a husband. I was only ever meant to have one."

I wouldn't let it go, not without a fight. "Didn't you love him?"

She didn't answer, merely pressed her lips together, hard.

I tilted my head so that I leaned against the window glass, watching a raindrop drip down its face and slide into oblivion when it met the door. My mother coughed, nose burbling; she raised a shaky hand to wipe savagely at her eyes. I can't say I felt better to see my mother cry, exactly, but some of the tension drained from my neck.

VIOLA PERKINS was our landlady, seventy-five or so—a stooped woman wearing long skirts up under her armpits at a point where her body seemed to double over, flowered blouses buttoned tightly around her neck, thick beige nylons, and brown shoes with spongy soles. She carried a certain odour with her, as if something inside were slowly rotting away. Although she no longer lived in our house—she'd moved into a one-bedroom apartment needing much less care—she came to call on us regularly. Her visits themselves—I mean, the timing—were anything but regular; she would appear on Saturday at eight in the morning, or on Thursday just after dinner, or even two nights in a row, both at eleven o'clock when we were tucking ourselves into our beds. I wondered why this would be. Did she wander confusedly until she wound up in front of the old house? Or did she do it on purpose, trying to catch us in the act of something sinful or immoral?

No matter what time she appeared, she would wait on the front porch, hands trembling, until we invited her inside. Even then she spoke little. Her eyes would scan the rooms quickly, as if to reassure herself that all was just as she'd left it. But you could tell that she took notice of the little things we'd done to make it our home: a great quilt thrown over the back of the stuffed chair in the living room, the glass bottle that Worthy had given me and I'd filled with soil from Newfoundland placed carefully on the mantel, the vase of fresh flowers my mother always kept in the hallway just inside the door (to greet people, she said). And always, as she took notice of these changes, there would be the smallest sign of disapproval in Viola's eyes, dismay that her own decorations hadn't been enough for us.

At first I felt sorry for her, a lonely old woman, it seemed to me, whose husband had died only three years before. Mostly I felt sad for the way her eyes suddenly hooded with long-ago remembrance, the patches of pink scalp showing through her white permanent, the fragile cords in her neck that stood out when she spoke.

Viola loved my mother, whom—with her own out-of-date dresses and polyester skirts, seamed nylons, and sensible shoes— she perceived as a kindred sort, a sister or daughter. My mother was more patient with her, kinder; I was more apt to invite her in abruptly, with a hint of annoyance. Often when Viola appeared, I would answer the door in my nightgown, something my mother would never do (such humiliation!), bad breath blowing out through my nostrils and over her frail body. She would flinch, blinking once or twice, and pause, uncertain, looking at the cushions my mother had made in light green cotton and thrown onto the benches flanking the porch. The cushions, in particular, confused Viola. *Those aren't mine.* You could see the instant alarm building, every time she climbed our stairs, until awareness snapped back. With me, her eyes would narrow and, after her customary glance around the front rooms, she would wonder (innocently) where the scratch in the hallway had come from or if that crack in the window had always been there? She never had these questions for my mother. But with me, there was a trace of disgust, disdain, as she looked me over from head to toe, taking in my rumpled nightgown, hair pulled back into a long braid (or loose and uncombed).

"You really should take better care of yourself," she would say, her voice rusted and creaking. And then, leaning in, about to impart a great secret: "If you let yourself go like that, you'll never catch a man." I never told her that I had no intention, no desire, to catch any kind of man. When we first moved in, we didn't mention my pregnancy.

"She wouldn't approve," my mother told me.

"She's going to find out anyway," I said.

"Belle, you don't understand her generation. Better to just leave some things unsaid. Of course she'll notice that you're pregnant. She'll especially notice when the baby comes. But it's better to just pretend that you're not, to never say it out loud."

And so we pretended, both of us, that I wasn't becoming bigger by the week, that I didn't gasp for breath in the middle of a sentence or sometimes have difficulties getting up. But when Jonah arrived, Viola fell in love.

The first time they laid eyes on each other, Jonah was only a week old. Viola followed my mother into the living room, where I sat with the baby, half asleep, the front of my shirt soaked with milk. These details could be ignored by Viola; she swooped in with a sound of surprise, leaned down so that her nose was only inches from his. He didn't cry, didn't move, but stared up into her face with a sort of stunned recognition that couldn't really have been possible. My mother, later, said she couldn't believe it; Jonah at that time was still cross-eyed and blurry from his rather rushed journey into our world.

Viola smiled, smitten. The very next day she showed up with a stuffed teddy bear she said had belonged to her as a child—its ear nearly torn from its head (chewed, she said), one eye missing. She presented the bear to Jonah, her eyes misting as she talked to him, voice high and giggly, almost girlish again.

Now when she arrived at the house, she no longer looked around, preserving her memories, but pushed both my mother and me aside, eager to see him, hold him, take him for walks in the ancient pram that she rescued from the secret corners of the basement (after much dusting and cleaning away the cobwebs and a small nest of mice). She called him the sweetest baby ever, looked at him as if he alone held all the secrets of the world, was forever smelling his head and closing her eyes in joy.

She told Jonah things she'd probably never confided in anyone else before, though we were often in the same room, ignored and almost unseen. For instance, she once whispered to him that she'd never been able to have children, that heartache had followed, crouched on her back, all her life because of this. That no matter how happy her marriage, how full her life of friends and other joys, there had always been the one empty space in her arms.

As she handed him back to me, I would smile at her in sympathy, trying to tell her with my eyes that I understood her pain. I almost felt friendly toward her then; I saw through the elderly shuffle, the narrowed eyes. But she had no patience or time for me at all, and her smile always faded.

A month after Jonah was born, Viola fell down the steps of our porch and broke her hip in three places. By March she was walking again, but everything was much slower than it had been. She too had changed: she looked thinner, frailer, a thick scarf wrapped around her neck emphasizing the smallness of her head, her shoulders. My mother wanted her to move back into the house with us. I hated the idea.

"Easy for you to say," I told her. "You go to work every day. I'm the one who'd be stuck at home taking care of her."

"Don't be so selfish, Belle. I just want her to be safe. You wouldn't have to look after her much."

I fumed and argued and slammed doors, but in the end my mother won. Viola, though, was horrified by the suggestion, when she realized what we meant.

"She likes her apartment," my mother said. "Can you believe it? She doesn't want to leave, doesn't want to live with us." I could easily believe it.

She made her last trip to see Jonah at the end of March, when the snow still clung to the sides of lawns and curbs, dotted with gravel and sand, burnt and yellowed and unclean. We slept as she arrived and knocked too softly on our door, slept still as she peered through the darkened windows and, after much indecision, stepped carefully away. Three o'clock in the morning, when time always stood still in the silence of the late winter streets.

As her foot came down from the last step, she stumbled. It was too dark; her hands fell forward into sharp crusts of snow, her head hit the edge of the walkway. She rolled to one side and lay still, her legs bare—unclad even in the stockings she usually wore—and splayed immodestly.

We didn't find her, for that I was thankful. They say she felt no pain after the knock on her head. They say there would have been no time for confusion or sorrow, a remembrance of what had been lost, before unconsciousness grabbed.

My mother couldn't shake the image of poor Viola knocking on our door in the middle of the night. She imagined her hands shaking from the cold. "Why didn't we hear her?" It disturbed her more than anything else could.

A few months later, we learned that Viola had left the house to us. To Jonah, specifically; in the event of his death, to my mother. When we asked, we were told that she changed her will in February. It took my mother only a few minutes to work out the dates.

"After she broke her hip," I said.

She nodded. "The day we asked her to move in with us."

I drove us home, Jonah cradled in my mother's arms. She tilted her head to one side to watch the houses flash past the window.

"She didn't die alone," I said. "She thought we were like family."

"No, Belle. She didn't have anyone else. She didn't even know us a full year, but we were all she had. I just find that so sad."

It began to rain. I switched on the wipers, listened to them scrape against the windshield of the car, and didn't say anything else. It seemed to me that I could be just the kind of person to wind up like Viola—all alone and slightly off-kilter, the messages telling me what time of day it was (and wasn't) somehow getting mixed up and leading me down a road of memory instead of letting me live in the present—but I didn't think I'd mind at all.

EIGHTEEN

I saw Gardie first by chance in an Eaton's catalogue from 1976, modelling patchwork drawstring jeans and an orange-and-brown poncho. The catalogue was nearly a year old, but I'd never seen it in our house before. I flipped through the pages without much interest, pausing at the baby section showing playpens with flip-down sides, booster seats, a great dresser decorated in clowns on vinyl with a built-in baby bathtub for only $61.99 (*You'd expect to pay more!* the good people at Eaton's proclaimed). A few more pages and I hit little girls in plaid jumpers, turtlenecks, and pantsuits (*Great style, a care-free fabric and a super low price!*). I studied each little girl, wondering which one would be most like Polly, then flipped forward. Men were always at the back, with their airbrushed crotches to hide any potential bulge even in the tightest, whitest briefs or the most form-fitting plaid pants. I had no interest in them either; the last thing I felt like doing these days was having any kind of sex, not even the kind I had with myself. I tossed the catalogue on the table, where it flipped open to the women's section at the front, and there she was, staring out at me.

People would later say she was a natural, but her absurd pose—chin raised, lip-glossed mouth slightly open, her left arm bent at an angle and pointing off the page—embarrassed me.

198

I left the page open (with the top corner folded down so as not to be lost) on the kitchen table for my mother and took Jonah for a walk to watch the construction of the new university around the corner.

I still remember the way his head pressed against my shoulder that April, a few weeks after Viola's death, his head mostly firm, strong, but still unsteady, wobbly at times, eyes wide and almost crossed. It was too early to see whom he resembled most, but already I knew that what I felt for him was different from what I felt with Polly.

Polly. I had stuffed her and the memory of what I had done to her so far back in my head that I rarely thought of her as a whole anymore. I thought of *them* often, Polly and Gardie and Worthy, a unit. *Them.* I knew they lived in Toronto; my mother visited them every weekend, never offering to take me with her. *You must take the first step.* Gardie had started to work in the theatre, appearing in small roles in plays, mostly working behind the scenes at whatever she could do. I had meant to write a letter, but I didn't know what to say to make it all better. The more I thought about what to write, the worse it all sounded in my head, and eventually, between my pregnancy and the move to Ludlow, I forgot about it.

Now there was time to think, and I developed elaborate scenarios in my mind, pictured our reunion, the great ache in my chest opening up once again. Now that I had Jonah and felt the first rush of protective love, I was ashamed of Polly's abandonment and felt a sense of urgency to make it right. *What kind of monster leaves her child?* I imagined her rushing into my arms, the instinct that would surely flood my being, her upturned face smiling, smiling. *Forgive me,* I would whisper. *I love you.* My reunion with Gardie was less certain. Scenes unfolded raggedly. I could feel her shoulder blades (thin, too thin) against my palm.

We would become a family again, we'd move in together, away from the factory and this small town. I never knew what to do with Worthy in those scenarios, always had him tucked to the side, looking on with sympathy perhaps. (And sometimes, I admit, he wasn't included in the scenarios; sometimes I moved him back to Newfoundland to stay with his brother.)

Every day, the guilt weighed heavier on my shoulders, the pressure to do something, to make it all better, building. I wanted to confide in my mother, wanted to describe the new feelings that were surfacing slowly and steadily. I couldn't put my finger on it, couldn't explain what had changed inside me— something more fragile, something motherly. But there were too many gaps between us, the biggest lie of all holding me back. *Theo died*, I'd said, to make them more sympathetic, more understanding. Before I could admit anything, I had to confess my failure, and that I couldn't do, not yet.

MR. DILLARD wrote my mother long letters throughout the summer that made her nose redden and her eyes tear up. She wouldn't say anything to me after reading one, but I could tell by her sideways glances that she was wondering if leaving had been worth it. She was tired, bone-tired, by the end of each day, and her skin looked dragged down. There were long calls with Aunt Hannah on Sunday evenings after returning from her visit to Toronto; I would listen in without seeming to and catch up on the gossip. This is also how I first heard about the hot dog commercial that caused such a fuss. According to my mother, the camera zoomed in closely as Gardie took a big bite.

"In slow motion," she whispered to Aunt Hannah. "Really, can you imagine?" She listened for a moment. "No, no. She licks the wiener, Hannah. *Licks it*." My aunt's laughter burst through the telephone receiver.

I watched TV religiously until I saw it. I didn't care about the whole tongue thing—that was just silly. But I couldn't believe what I was seeing on the screen. Gardie was a stranger to me, someone I'd never seen before. She was twenty-four now and had grown into herself. Still thin, she no longer looked sickly; her blond hair shone as she flicked it back over her shoulder, and her eyes—her eyes seemed to jump from her face, big blue marbles that pretended innocence and sweetness. The commercial ran only for a week before outraged feminist and religious groups declared it both immoral and insulting to women in a flurry of letters to the editor and local news interviews. My mother was relieved.

Gardie called one night in November. The sound of my voice answering the phone must have shocked her; a long silence stretched for miles through the lines.

"Hello? Hello?" I almost hung up.

But then, in a frozen, halting voice: "Is Mother there?"

Hello, Gardie, how are you? I just want to say that I'm sorry. I'm finally sorry for everything I've done, for all the hurt I've caused. Are you sorry too?

"Just a minute, please."

It would have been so easy but seemed so difficult at the time. I couldn't even swallow past the great ridge of pride pressed against the back of my throat. But her obvious fury hurt.

I bundled Jonah, almost a year old, in a snowsuit, went for a long walk. If I'd been normal, I would have cried then, cried not for Theo and all I had lost with him, but for Gardie and Polly and even Worthy, for what I had done to them. The sky black and starless above me, my tears would have turned to ice on my cheeks and chilled my neck, where they would have dripped down into my scarf. Jonah stared up at me with tenderness and love in hazel eyes so like Theo's, a little mittened hand figuratively wrapping itself tighter around my heart.

It seemed impossible to believe there was a time when Jonah did not exist. In sleep, his hands were tightly fisted; if he was awake, they splayed like starfish beside his head. I was at first afraid to leave him sleeping, worried that he would stop breathing or somehow wedge himself under the crib mattress. When I picked him up, the back of his head was heavy and slightly damp, his breath hot against my ear.

Polly was practice; with Jonah, I was a mother at last. Pregnant with Polly, my body scared me. Its very blossoming, in every way, was proof of what Worthy had done to me and how separate we had become. Polly was an alien, a separate entity; every jab, every twist, felt like angry, pummelling fists. I couldn't wait to get her out of there.

With Jonah, pregnancy didn't bother me, made me softer. I touched my belly constantly, crooned to him in quiet tones, feeling him bump against my palm. Sometimes I sat in our rocking chair cradling my belly and rocking back and forth, as if he were already in my arms. But I wanted him to stay inside as long as possible, felt a strange sensation, a warning prickle on the back of my neck, when I thought of him released, flailing, into this world.

I was a good mother. I felt every cry before he made a sound, sensed his need for me when he was out of my sight. When my mother cradled him in her arms, I wanted to fix her posture, position his head more comfortably. No one could take care of him as I could, no one knew the perfect touch against his back after a feeding or the proper way to fold his diaper under his jagged stump of umbilical cord. For the first time, I had that mothering instinct, the understanding that he grew from me, a joint creation of two of us. More than that, Jonah made me vulnerable in his innocence. He depended on me for everything; studying his tiny, helpless face, I knew I would die for him.

I thought of his father a lot in those first few months. Around the corner, a cluster of shops sold books and pastries and flowers. One afternoon, I'd put Jonah in his stroller sleeping, found a small record shop tucked in beside a movie theatre. A strange urge sucked me inside; that distinctive, slightly musty paper smell brought me back to Silver Falls in those first months with Theo. And somehow a resolution emerged: if Jonah couldn't know his father, at least I could surround him with the music that had helped bring him into this world.

A pimply boy behind the cash register had eyed me suspiciously, peering into the stroller to see what I'd stolen. I bought eight albums and new batteries. I hadn't been in the trailer much. My maps were scattered about, my scrapbook had slid under the seats by the table, and a stale stench permeated the small space. I opened the two side windows to air everything out, sniffed the cushions with wrinkled nose. I cleaned and oiled the stained mahogany interior, working my way methodically around the trailer until the wood glowed. After dusting off the record player and replacing its batteries, I was ready, brought Jonah in and set him on the table in his infant seat so that he could watch. One by one, I played the albums, sometimes explaining the lyrics to him or just singing aloud, swaying my hips and raising my arms above my head until he kicked his legs in spasmodic glee.

After a few months, I'd sent Theo a letter in Bay Point, finally, enclosing Jonah's picture. I don't really know why I did it; I suppose it was my last hope that things would turn around, that Theo would come home—not for me, but for his son. Time and my overwhelming love for Jonah had blurred the edges of my memory so that the past wasn't so bad. The letter never came back to me, but no one ever answered. I did it once more, when Jonah was nine months old, and again, only silence came back.

I wished I could talk about it, but my mother still believed that Theo was dead. Sometimes I'd forget about my lie, almost let bitter words spill from my mouth before sucking them back in again. My mother interpreted my silence, my moods, to mean that I was still in mourning. She'd sat me down in the kitchen one morning before she left for work, poured me a cup of coffee.

"Your life is your life," she'd said. "I'd never try to tell you girls what you should do unless you asked, would never interfere. So I'll only stick my nose in this once, and I'll tell you what I told your aunt: the past is done. You can't change what has happened. But you can make the future do anything you want it to do. Maybe it's time to start thinking forward."

Now, after hearing Gardie's voice on the telephone, I thought maybe my mother was right. *It's time.* The cold air brushed my bare neck. Jonah yawned, tiny mouth opening wide, his tongue pink and curling back against his throat. I couldn't justify myself anymore, couldn't point my finger at someone else and say *you did it.*

My mother was still on the phone when I got back, but quickly said goodbye and hung up when she saw me. She sat for a moment at the kitchen table, her hands held still in her lap, almost defeated.

She didn't expect anything from me at all; this in itself was the great disappointment, this lack of expectation. She neither believed in me nor didn't. She was simply my mother. And in the lines that crept across her forehead and shadowed the corners of her eyes, I read the simple plea for her family to be whole again.

"I'm ready," I said.

WE DROVE UP to Toronto that weekend. I had a licence by then, but let my mother drive; the people in other cars scared me—white-knuckled and mean, cutting us off as often as they could with quick swerves of the wheel. I looked back at Jonah, strapped in his car seat, watched his head jolt from side to side as my mother tried and then failed again to change lanes.

"Crazy fuckers," I muttered.

"Belle!"

"Sorry, Mother."

As the new and impressive CN Tower loomed up, my palms and neck began to sweat until I felt sick, had to lean forward with my head pressed between my knees, my mother's hand hovering. *Everything will be all right*, she said. I wished she would touch me, just lay her palm on my arm or shoulder and give me the warmth I needed, but she pulled her hand away before it made contact.

Gardie and Worthy lived on a small tree-lined street near Queen and Dufferin in a two-bedroom-apartment duplex. I found it difficult to open the car door, harder still to step out, move my legs forward. Jonah wrapped his arms around me, batted my face with cold hands, his eyes looking up to the grey November sky. Most of the snow from the night before had melted into dirty slush in the gutters, but the tips of tree branches were white.

Gardie answered the door, and there, peeking behind her knees with a grin, was Polly, six years old. My chest expanded, then squeezed tightly. She looked so much like me, the way she moved her head, the slant of her blue eyes as they stared, curious and bright.

"You're my mother," she said matter-of-factly, her tongue curling up to touch her top teeth, braided hair darker than mine and gleaming.

"That's right." My dry throat threatened to choke me. I wondered if the accusations, the questions, would come. But Polly's face remained smooth, trusting—childhood's honesty.

"You're not going to take me away, are you?" A small hand

curved around Gardie's leg, as if for protection. Gardie looked at me. *You see?* she seemed to say. *You see what marks you've left on her?*

I touched Polly's cheek with the back of my hand. Contact made.

"I've just come for a visit," I said. "It's about time, don't you think?"

She considered for a long moment, finally nodded. "Would you like to play with me?" she asked.

"I'd like that more than anything in the world," I said.

THE APARTMENT smelled of cigarettes and lemon-scented cleaner. An unshaven Worthy sat in a turquoise chair by a window that had been left open an inch, and made it clear he wished he could jump through that small space. Wearing a brown shirt and a pair of dirty beige corduroy pants with shredded hems, his sideburns long and overgrown, he seemed not to have moved in the last four years.

"Well, look who's here at long last, Worthy," Gardie sang.

Worthy didn't look up, just stuck a cigarette in his mouth and clamped down.

Polly tugged my pants. "That's my dad," she said.

"I know."

"He doesn't have a job."

"Oh."

"No, no job," Gardie said. "I mean, why bother?"

Worthy turned his face away, lit the cigarette, hiding his face in a cloud of blue smoke. Gardie sighed, stared at him for a moment, her hands hanging uselessly by her sides. She gave a half shrug, an apology in her smile to us then.

We didn't stay long. Jonah crawled after a shrieking Polly, who darted in and out of the living room, bringing me pictures she'd drawn at school, stuffed animals, her favourite book. My mother made an effort to chat lightly, as if unaware of the tensions drawn in a triangle (me, Worthy, Gardie, back to me again). Gardie never really looked at me, but what she said—about her jobs, the parts she'd been offered, her many friends—was meant for my ears. I saw then why Gardie had agreed to my visit. She didn't care about putting the family back together; she wanted me to see that she hadn't just been handed my leftovers. *I'm really doing something with my life now*. It was sad, in a way. She prattled on, every once in a while casting glances at Worthy, who had shrunk down farther into his chair, his eyes fixed on a point beyond the window.

Nineteen

I think I'm getting bored here in my unit, and besides, everyone's pissing me off, and the food is crappy. The least they could do is add some spices, if you're not allowed to have beer or wine to wash it down with. Nobody tries to molest me in the showers, and there are no gangs to fight out in the courtyard. There's not much to do at all. I've read a few books and watched a lot of TV. We're allowed to go to the gymnasium, but the thought of huffing and puffing and playing some b-ball, as the young men call it these days, makes my eyeballs ache. My court date's next week, but I don't think I can wait that long. I call legal aid.

We meet in a private room with a desk and chairs and nothing else. My lawyer's impossibly green and overconfident in his designer suit and fashionable shiny tie with diagonal stripes, his hair slicked back with that hardened, wet look. He carries a briefcase unmarred by scuff marks. (At first he can't open it, admits, embarrassed, that he has forgotten the combination to the locked clasps. Then, halfway through the visit, he suddenly recalls the numbers, as if they've appeared on the wall behind me. Now you tell me: what kind of confidence would someone like this inspire in you?)

He places a yellow pad on the table in front of us, poises a silver pen, just waiting for my story to pour out and spill all over the virgin paper. He wants to know my life, the events leading up to the charges. He leans in, face intense. He has studied psychology in school, I can tell. He thinks that by making his eyes sympathetic and trying to pat my hand, I will sink into his (rather thin) shoulders and unburden myself. His fingertips are smooth, his nails gentle crescents, clean and possibly manicured. His sleeve rides up when he leans forward with hands folded on the table, exposing a flash of pale skin and a watch that seems too large.

You can tell a lot by looking at a man's hands. Lawyer Liam is fresh and unsullied; in an instant, I picture private schools, late dinners with ties artfully angled askew, fine china, cloth napkins, and silent rooms, the ticking of grandfather clocks muffled by deep carpet. Worthy's hands were wide and meaty; a working man's hands. Theo's were large, his fingers long and tapered, with rough tips. A different kind of work.

He asks me how I am, is the prison okay? I say it is. He says he can bring me books, magazines—anything I want. And then he wants to talk about the boy.

"Trust me," Lawyer Liam says. "I can't help you if you don't."

"Do you spend a lot of time in front of the mirror?" I ask.

My question unbalances him. "Pardon?"

"You seem like one of those men who spends more time primping and preening than any woman."

That hurts his feelings, though he tries not to show it. He frowns, studying his pad of paper, running his finger across the top edge, giving himself small paper cuts and wincing. Under the table, his bony knees poke his creased pants as he crosses and uncrosses his legs. Maybe I do feel a little sorry for him.

"I'm innocent," I say.

He brightens and smiles, relieved. He riffles through papers pulled from his briefcase, reads through them, then clears his throat. "Let's talk about what happened the day you were arrested."

That little boy: frightened eyes in those last moments before he fled, thin shoulders shaking under my hands.

"You know who his father is?" I ask.

My lawyer nods. "The mayor," he says.

Their house across the street was custom-built five years ago, when they tore down their older, less-than-magazine-perfect two-storey century home. Construction took over a year. I don't have much of an opinion about the mayor; I suppose he's nice enough, if a bit bland, not that I ever paid much attention. Men in Canadian politics these days are either crazy or boring, with personalities of bologna sandwiches on white bread, no mustard. Crusts cut off, even. Not like in Trudeau's day, as everyone likes to say. Mayor Allister is my age, or thereabouts, somewhere around the fifty mark.

But his wife, Trina, now she's a piece of work. She's certainly made a name for herself in Ludlow. *Ice Princess* they call her on the sly (and sometimes in print in the free weekly paper for the younger crowd). At least fifteen years younger, she's the kind of woman who probably planned her wedding to someone rich, someone *going places*, down to the last detail, when she was ten years old. She's also the type of woman to look you over once and freeze your blood.

Let me give you an example so you can see what I'm talking about. Her greatest claim to fame happened in a restaurant when she noticed a young mother breastfeeding a baby a few tables away. Although the woman had made an attempt to cover up, the blanket had slipped and revealed some of her breast. After a nod from her husband, Trina slipped from her seat and placed a hand on the woman's shoulder.

Excuse me, she said. *I don't mean to be rude, but would you consider feeding your child elsewhere? People are eating here.* When the woman, embarrassed, mumbled something about breastfeeding being a perfectly natural function, Trina smiled. *So is vomiting, dear, but we don't want to watch you do that either. Particularly while dining in a nice restaurant.*

Lawyer Liam coughs. "We're not here to talk about her," he says.

"I didn't always live like I do now," I say. "I used to be normal, I had a child. Two children."

He nods, waiting. "Tell me."

CHRISTMAS CAME to Ludlow in 1977. Aunt Hannah came up by bus with a suitcase full of presents. My mother had sent regular letters and photographs of Jonah, but it was the first time she saw him in person. She held him against her chest and breathed in, tears filling her eyes. "Precious, just precious," she whispered over and over.

My mother rubbed her back, murmured in her ear as they hugged. And then when Gardie arrived with Polly, my aunt squeezed them both tightly, as if she wouldn't—couldn't—let go.

"I've missed you all so much," she said, swiping at her eyes. For once she wore no jewellery around her wrists, no beads or charms. She'd wrapped her characteristic scarf around her head, gypsy-like, and wore hoop earrings.

Polly clung to Gardie's leg at first, unwilling even to say hello. Gardie reached down to stroke the hair from her face.

"Misses her dad," she said, but offered no more. None of us could ask where Worthy was or why he would be apart from Polly at Christmas, but we all wondered.

On Christmas Day, we threw kindling and newspaper into the fireplace we so seldom used, struck matches until a blaze held. My mother and aunt outdid themselves with a grand turkey, stuffing, the works. Make no mistake: it wasn't as if we were whole, healed again. Gardie and I barely spoke in those first few days, my aunt still carried my uncle's ghost on her shoulders, drawing down the skin of her cheeks and making her seem older, more tired, and my mother looked lost at times, her hands playing with the strings on her apron, her gaze blank, distant (though he'd been invited up, George Dillard had refused to come, told my mother it was best to move on). But it was a start.

THE DAY AFTER CHRISTMAS, Gardie and I found ourselves alone, drinks firmly in hand and a few down the hatch already, after everyone had gone to bed. The fire had died down so that only embers glowed and occasionally sparked. I reached down to scratch my leg, dry crocodile winter skin, while Gardie lit a cigarette and smoked.

"How come you haven't asked me about Worthy?" she asked.

I shrugged, eyed the cigarettes. I didn't smoke but suddenly wanted to try, now, after all these years. Gardie passed one over. I let the acrid smoke slide down my throat, into my lungs, choking in a little cough and then dizzy as the nicotine hit.

"He just couldn't figure out what to do with himself there in Toronto," she said. "Couldn't find a job, hated the city, the smells, the rushing about. He's not the city type."

I wondered what that meant, exactly, though I could imagine. Worthy, with his solid, plodding ways, just wouldn't have fit in with Gardie's new life in the theatre.

"He wore the same sweater eight days in a row," she said. "Just sat in that chair every day." Her voice had changed, ridicule falling into a sadness of sorts. I didn't say anything.

"He never really got over you, Belle." She let her words sit between us.

"So now where is he?" I asked.

"Back in Newfoundland. St. John's, I guess." She stubbed out her cigarette, lit another immediately. "He's getting settled, and then Polly will go to him." The words cut, hot, sharp, just below my ribs. "She's having a bit of trouble with the news."

I thought of the day before Christmas when they'd first arrived, how Polly had lined up her dolls in a row on the edge of the bed then kicked them off one by one, over and over again, silent and concentrated.

"What about me?" I asked.

"What about you?"

"I'm her mother."

"So?"

How could I answer that? *So?* Such venom. And even though I deserved it, I struck back.

"Fuck you, Gardie."

We smoked silently, the ice in her glass clinking as she drained her whisky, stood for a refill. When she sat back down on the couch, she crossed her legs.

"You know, in all the books for kids, sometimes people don't have daddies, but everyone always has a mama. I've been her mother for all these years, and now I'm sending her away." She swallowed, her hand reaching up to smooth the skin of her throat, touching the corners of her eyes and pressing. "She can't stay with me. I'm never home and have to work in the evenings a lot. She needs more stability than that." And then, "She's so much like you, Belle. Can't you see that?"

I'd watched Polly closely the last few days, more and more surprised. She was just like me, and yet different. When she was happy, her personality was more like Gardie's had been when she was younger, always bursting with emotion, wearing a cape or hat or a pair of someone else's boots.

"She came to me yesterday with these shiny beads. God knows where she found them—probably Aunt Hannah's suitcase. She had them wrapped around her neck and wanted me to say how pretty they were. Then she preened in the mirror for a half-hour," I said.

Gardie laughed, her neck a glowing white column. With her head thrown back like that, she resembled her child self. I felt the release of all things hidden in that laugh; there was so much to say, so much time to recover.

"How did it happen?" I asked. I meant: how did we get here, how did we become who we are?

Gardie shifted in her chair. She smoked into a silence that stretched long. When she finally spoke, her voice had shrunk.

"You never talked to me when I was little, never played with me. You were always so wrapped up in your own world. You never had time for me at all. Even when Father died—remember when I tried to crawl into your bed that night?"

I didn't at first, but then remembered Gardie's feet, cold, pressing against the back of my legs.

"I just wanted to be alone," I said. "I never meant anything by it."

"All I ever wanted was your attention."

"You had Mother."

"Yes, but you were always first in line." I wasn't sure what she meant by that; the invisible line between Gardie and my mother and me and my father still existed, still shaped the way I remembered our home in Newfoundland.

"There's something I never told you," Gardie said, a new tone—hard, sharp—in her voice warning against what was to come. "I don't even know why I'm going to tell you." Maybe it was the alcohol, or the quiet warmth of the dying fire that carried a sense of nostalgia for times past, an affected closeness that we rarely shared. And now Gardie seemed to be struggling with her words, weighing them carefully as she lit another cigarette.

"Remember when Worthy came down to Vermont and stayed in that little chicken coop of yours? I was so jealous of that little house, jealous of everything you had back then. And now look at me, look where I am and where you are." She made a snuffling sound, a quick exhalation to put me in my place, remind me of the old challenge: *Who's better?*

"What was worse was that you didn't seem to even care. Here you had Worthy coming all the way down to see you, you had your own little place, and you acted like it was nothing, like you didn't even want him there. You never knew, never suspected anything." She laughed. "Worthy was ashamed, I think. He should have stopped it. I was just a kid, wasn't I? But he was older, he knew better. And he could never say he didn't know it was me. Though I think that's what he did to make himself feel better—believed that it was too dark to tell the difference, that it was really you."

It took me a moment to digest the words, the implications, but when I did, the blood rushed to my face. I put my head on the table to stop the slow spinning and pinched the skin behind my knees.

"How many times?" I finally asked, raising my head.

Gardie at least had the sense to look down as she shrugged. "Every night," she confessed.

I let the silence carry. This was more than wounded pride, more than petty jealousy or hurt.

"My God." I didn't say anything else for a long while, watched the fire sputter and heard the ice in Gardie's glass, the clicking in the back of her throat when she swallowed.

"I was just a kid, only fourteen," Gardie said. "You never did love him, but I thought I did." The night air seemed suddenly frozen, in permanent pause. "And then when you left, I drove myself crazy with jealousy. There was even an affair with a married man—did you know that?" She laughed. "I was so stupid, I thought that was love too." She looked at me as if expecting a smile in return, an understanding. "I always wanted Worthy, and I don't know why. Maybe he was home to me. Maybe he was home to you, and that's why *you* married him."

And there in the dim light, her face shifted and changed, her skin sucking in against her cheekbones, her eyes retreating into shadowed hollows.

"Why are you telling me this?" I whispered.

"I don't know," she said. "I thought you should know."

"Why? *Why?*" I slammed my glass onto the side table. "Do you feel better now? Your conscience cleared?"

Gardie's face puckered in something like fear. "He took advantage of me," she whined.

"That's bullshit, Gardie, and you know it."

"I'm not proud of it, if that's what you're saying."

"That's not what I'm saying, but you should have kept it to yourself. What good is it to me, now that I know? How do you think you've made me feel?"

"It's not like you were blameless, Belle. I was messed up. I didn't know what I wanted. I was just a kid."

"*I was just a kid,*" I mimicked. "Some excuse."

"Well, maybe if you paid more attention to him, it wouldn't have happened. Or maybe if you ever thought about anyone but yourself, you would have *seen* what was going on."

"You know what I think?" I asked, my hands twisted and claw-like on the arms of my chair. "I think you knew what you were doing. I think you wanted Worthy only because he wanted me, and you were determined to have him. And you went down to that cottage with every intention of doing what you did."

She shook her head violently. "No, no, Belle, you're wrong."

"And then you came to Silver Falls with every intention of doing it again."

"Well, what about you?" Her face was flushed, her eyes too bright. "I knew what was going on for a long time. That first day I went into the shop down the hill, I told them I was your sister, and they said, *Oh, Theo's girlfriend?* I waited for you to stop, but you didn't, not for a whole year, Belle. And there I was, thinking I was in love with Worthy, and you were jerking him around like garbage and not paying any attention to your kid, who was the most adorable thing in the world and who loved you like no one else ever would. And you tossed it all away, just like that." She shrugged. "What goes around comes around, Belle." She looked down into her drink, shoulders pulled forward. "I never stole him from you. You made your choice long before anything else happened between us."

I felt sick, pressure gripping my skull and sending throbbing pulses down the back of my neck. I wanted to grab Gardie by the throat and slam her head against the wall, wanted to sink down and weep or just cover my face and curl up into a ball. *Why didn't I know? Why couldn't I see?* But Gardie was right: I hadn't cared about Worthy. Maybe it was true, what she said: *maybe he was home.*

"I'm sorry, Belle," she said, her voice small and fragile. "I'm sorry."

I set down my drink and stood over her. For a moment she cringed, as if expecting a blow, but the anger had drained, leaving me spent.

"Stick your sorry up your arse," I said instead, then turned away and left her in the dark.

THE NEXT DAY, my mother piled everyone in the Chevy wagon to take Aunt Hannah, Gardie, and Polly to Toronto.

"I want to see their apartment," Aunt Hannah said to me, "and then I'm taking the train from there." I knew she wanted me to come with them so that she could spend every last moment with Jonah, but I couldn't. I didn't want Gardie anywhere near me, hadn't sorted it all out in my head.

"Belle, why don't we take Jonah while you stay here?" my mother said. "Be a nice break for you, in any case. You're looking a little pale."

My aunt's eyes lit up; I couldn't say no. I kissed Jonah on the forehead, his skin warm against my lips. He kicked his legs, twisted to be free. I handed him to Aunt Hannah, who buckled him in his seat.

I took Polly's hand in mine before she left, knelt down so that she could look directly at me.

"It was good to see you again," I said. I struggled for my words, but my throat closed up. She threw her arms around my neck, pressed her head under my chin, and I smelled in her hair the memory of a two-year-old child's innocence. Pain crept across my chest. I watched her climb into the car, wave and smile, and wanted to run after her, reclaim what was mine, rebuild the lost years.

I thought about her as I climbed the stairs in the empty house and crawled onto my bed. St. John's, Gardie had said. I could find work in St. John's. I turned the plan over in my mind to see it from all angles, working out the details of child care for Jonah, a job for me, a place to stay. I fell asleep, dreamed of wind thick with salt against my face. Home, finally.

I woke to the sound of the telephone. I blinked, rubbed my eyes, tried to see in the darkness of the room. *What time is it?* Again the ringing. I almost tripped on the way downstairs, tying my hair back in a loose braid, running my tongue over fuzzy teeth and tasting sleep in my mouth.

"Hello?" I almost never answered the phone in our house. I didn't like it, the way people breathed into the receiver, the clicking noises of tongue against the roof of the mouth, the long pauses between words. And after this call, I would never answer the telephone again.

SHE WAS ALMOST IN LUDLOW when it happened, heading toward the exit that would bring them home. Jonah had fallen asleep in Toronto; my mother had put him, face down, in the back of the wagon, covered him with a blanket. Up ahead on the exit ramp, a car braked, changed its mind, and began a fast approach in reverse, back toward the highway. My mother saw it at the last minute, swerved to the left to avoid it. One car slammed into the side of the Chevy, sending it spinning; a second, third, fourth, all collided. When my mother opened her eyes, lights flashed bright red, hurting her with every pulse. *Turn off the lights*, she remembered saying. When she asked for Jonah, they told her he'd already gone ahead to the hospital.

A doctor told me before I went in to see my mother, his wide hands failing to offer any comfort though they tried, patting my back. I pushed him away. My mother's face was white against the sheets, blood seeping through a bandage from her temple to jaw. She was cut, bruised, and had broken her arm in three places. Her head hit the side of the window; she had a concussion and twenty-eight stitches along the side of her face.

Jonah also hit the side of a window, but he shattered his skull. The rage would find me later. My mother opened her eyes, began to weep as I sat in the bedside chair, blank and dry-eyed.

I DIDN'T WANT A FUNERAL SERVICE, didn't want anyone to come, press damp hands against me, and whisper meaningless words—*at least he didn't suffer*—but they came anyway. Jonah was buried quietly, the frozen earth churned up and awaiting his coffin, a giant claw. Standing in the cold, my reddened hands turning numb, watching the coffin being lowered, I had the sense that the ground was caving in under my feet, pulling me down so fast that nothing I did could possibly stop its momentum. Imagining his small body alone, cold through the worst of the winter months, I threw myself over his coffin, willing the warmth of my body to force life back into his. Beside me, my mother fell to her knees in the snow.

Accused Hermit Odd, Neighbours Say

New details emerging about the life of a local woman facing assault and kidnapping charges have prompted questions about the woman's mental state. According to neighbours in Roseland, Belle Dearing, 51, lived without electricity or water since as early as April or May. "We'd see her sneaking around at night," said one neighbour, who wished to remain anonymous. "She'd steal anything she could, rifling through our garbage like a raccoon, taking scraps of food and newspapers. She lugged around these water jugs and filled them up with our taps around the side of our houses. Everyone knew. She wasn't exactly quiet about it, always singing or shouting weird stuff, poetry."

A *Lighthouse* investigation has unearthed relatives living in Toronto and in Vermont; all declined to comment and have had no contact with the accused for years. "She's been messed up for a long time," said one relative, who asked not to be identified. "But I don't believe she would ever physically hurt a child, or anyone else, for that matter."

Ms. Dearing was arrested three weeks ago on charges of possible sexual assault and kidnapping involving a six-year-old boy. A preliminary court date has been set for next week.

TWENTY

I never thought of my drinking as a problem, though I often wondered at the number of bottles stacked up in the mud room off the kitchen. But I have been known to wander the streets occasionally with wine in my hand, and I suppose most normal people don't do that often.

I kept all my letters on the top shelf of my closet in my bedroom, bundled and stacked and held together with rubber bands. Letters from my mother and Gardie when I lived in Silver Falls, from my aunt through all the lost years when I heard from no one else and made no effort of my own, and a few from Gema, who was much better than I at keeping in touch but who finally gave up when I left Silver Falls the second time. There was history in that pile of letters, pinpoints of time that have reference to someone, somewhere.

In 1989, Silver Falls blew up, did I mention? Only three hundred people lived there at the time or perhaps more would have died, been displaced. They think it started with a cigarette, carelessly tossed in an old mining building no longer in use, decrepit, dry in late August. I read about it in the paper, caught the small paragraph in the back pages. According to the reporter, the fire was small at first, easily ignored; by the time most people realized the danger (the dry, hot grass, the shifting wind), it was too late. And then that documentary on ghost towns I saw, the tremulous old lady interviewed. *It ate them all up*, she said, then paused to dab daintily at weeping eyes. *Everyone lost.* Strange that so much of my past could be erased in one burning rush.

I kept all my letters just as I kept the newspapers I stole from the front porches in the neighbourhood in the wee hours of the morning, and piled them high in the front room of the house. They are all concrete evidence that it all happened, that it was all once real. Without those written pages, what else could you believe?

AFTER JONAH DIED, everything just shut down and went underground for a long time. I hated my mother. That sounds terrible to say, even now after all these years. Almost unspeakable, the words, but they're true, or at least they were back then. I didn't want to talk about what happened or look at the pain and endless guilt in her eyes—I just wanted her to go away. If she couldn't do that, then I would disappear. And that's what I did; I withdrew until only a shell remained.

"You need to talk to someone," my mother said. "Just do it a few times. You can always stop if it's not helping." I went because I didn't care. I let her set up the appointment. She took the bus downtown to his offices with me and then waited in a coffee shop.

I expected the psychiatrist to look like Sigmund Freud (beard, long face, spectacles), imagined he would talk with an accent, stroke his face, cross his legs, as he asked me about my childhood and whether or not I loved my father, hated my mother. Dr. Armand was surprisingly normal, much thinner and smaller and quieter overall than I expected. When he sat back in his chair, it almost swallowed him whole. He did have an accent, but it was French, from Quebec City. When I asked how he wound up in Ludlow, he rolled his eyes and waved his hand dismissively.

"Long story," he said. He used the term *significant other* a lot, so I wondered if he was gay, studied the way he tucked one leg over the other, his slender wrists, thought of all the clichés.

I knew right away that Dr. Armand wasn't going to help; he wanted to discuss me and my life, and I didn't want to talk at all, at least not about important things. Instead, I talked about the stink of my shoes, how long I wore the same pair of underwear straight without washing it, how sometimes I found food in my hair that I'd eaten days before. He frowned a lot but didn't say much, just scribbled quickly on a notepad tucked into a manila folder, my name typed sideways on a white label and pasted (crooked) onto the tab. At our first appointment, I mostly just sat in silence, eyeing him, a staring contest. He looked away first.

It's funny, in a way. My mother wanted me to talk to someone and sent me to Dr. Armand; Dr. Armand wanted me to talk to my mother. But she and I never talked about the accident, never mentioned the Chevy that was hauled off for scrap metal or Polly's trip back east to live with Worthy in Newfoundland. The door to Jonah's room remained closed, his things untouched. Every day the same thing: the same three minutes spent brushing my teeth with my purple toothbrush, rolling up the end of the toothpaste tube when I finished; the same bus ride to and from work, my mother beside me on the plastic seat, our shoulders rigid but not (never) touching; the same number of steps from the bus stop to the factory gates. At work it was easy to disappear into routine, padded ear protectors wrapped around my head muffling all sound, the steady rhythm of conveyor belts and fans lulling. At lunch, I ate alone, avoiding my regular table, with well-meaning co-workers who dripped sympathy and sadness until I wanted to jab at their eyes with a fork.

And then the process reversed, counting steps back to the bus, back to the house, where my mother made dinner and brought up topics of conversation so quickly that I knew she'd made a list of things to talk about. I didn't answer, couldn't find the energy or will, just took my dinner into the living room and ate blankly until everything was gone. Sometimes even then I continued eating air, until the scrape of fork against plate made me look down in surprise. I never tasted anything. And then I simply sat smoking cigarettes down to the filter until my mother came in to get my dishes, not saying anything but looking at me sadly, collecting her letters from Vermont in the pocket of her burgundy cardigan. That face, drooping and lined, began to wear on me.

One evening she brought a damp cloth from the kitchen and wiped down the coffee table, sweeping my crumbs and dust into her cupped palm.

"Leave it!" I pushed her hand away from the table. "You're not my maid."

"Someone has to clean up the mess," she said. I watched her continue, the way she avoided my gaze and tried to ignore my dirty feet, shifting her hip to one side so that her body didn't touch mine as she came around the side of the table. And in that instant I needed to break through the pretence, wanted to injure.

"You know what Dr. Armand said?" I asked. "He said if you were more loving and warm after Father died, I wouldn't have felt so alone. *Alienated*, he said. It was always you and Gardie against me."

She flinched, wrung the cloth in her hands.

Dr. Armand had said no such thing, in fact. He did use the word *alienated*, but said I'd done it to myself with my choices, then looked outward for blame. He suggested I might want to look *inward* instead.

"Have you ever considered your role in everything that happened?" he asked as gently as he could. I told him to shove it. That was our last session together.

"Tell me what a terrible mother I was, tell me I deserved it. I know what you think of me," I said.

"Stop it," she said. "I don't want to fight with you."

"Well, maybe I do," I said. "Maybe I'm sick of you tiptoeing around as if nothing happened, when I know all along you're glad."

"You're out of your mind," she said. "Don't do this." She sounded too much like Theo then.

"Don't tell me what to do."

"Don't speak to me like that! I'm your mother," she said.

I let the silence between us stretch, long and sharp, then started in again.

"You never hugged us after he died," I said. "You never ever touched us. Or at least not me."

"That's not true."

"Yes it is. Maybe you hugged Gardie, but you sure as hell never hugged me. Never said, *I love you, Belle.*"

"But of course I did. You don't have to say those things all the time for them to be true. Of course I loved you. You both were all I had left. Still all I have." Her voice caught and she looked away. "I'm sorry," she whispered.

It wasn't enough for me. I didn't want her to be sorry, I didn't want her pity or her love anymore. I *was* unlovable; I caused pain to everyone around me, even Dr. Armand had said so, in a roundabout way.

"It's all a lie," I said. "Theo never died. How do you like that one? He never died. I don't even know that I ever loved him. I just hated my life, hated being a mother and a wife, and I hated that town where I lived. Worthy and Oscar and Polly and

Gardie, and everyone *needing* something from me but never giving anything back, never talking to me or asking me how I felt. The *only* person who has ever talked to me or listened to me or made me feel special was Father. I kept trying to find that again, but I never could."

"Oh, Belle." She was crying now, the tears cutting pale paths down her cheeks and dribbling into her mouth. She moved toward me, one arm outstretched.

"Don't touch me," I said. "Don't even come near me. You took him away from me, and I'll never forgive you. Jonah was everything, my life. I was finally happy, finally at peace with myself and all the mistakes I'd made. I was going to take him home, Mother. We were going to move to St. John's. I was going to make it all better again, with Polly and Jonah. My *children*."

The words were wrenched from me, deep in my chest. I knew she carried the guilt of Jonah's death, knew that it hurt every day, a single wound, festering and raw. I wanted to force it into the open, that pain, so that I would feel nothing but relief when she left.

"You killed him, you took it away from me, every bit of it." And then I said the worst thing I'd ever said, slowly, with venom, watching the colour vanish from her face and the grief and utter pain fill the lines and creases left behind. "I wish you had died instead," I said.

The terrible words hung between us for a long moment.

"How *dare* you?" she asked. She breathed fast, the fingers of one hand pinching her lips. "Everything I've done has been for you, can't you see that? But it's never enough, is it, Belle? You always try to hurt those around you. God only knows what your father and I did to you to make you like this. *You didn't hug me enough.* Is that what I did to you that was so horrible that you could say these things to me?"

I couldn't speak, let the angry words wash over me, welcomed them. Here it was at last.

"If you think that I don't lie in bed every night and cry for what's happened, you're wrong. You can't imagine how I feel. I've tried to tell you how sorry I am a million times, but it's never enough. *It was an accident.* A horrible accident that will destroy you and me and all of us."

I saw the veins on the back of her hands, her thin wrists and cheap blouse.

"You have no claim on pain, Belle. You, me, your aunt, even your sister—no one has had the easy life." She sagged, her neck bent low.

Ashamed, I wanted to sink down in front of her then, bury my head in her lap, beg for forgiveness. Instead, I closed my eyes and turned my head away, my tongue thick against the roof of my mouth, too weighted with anger and my own regrets. When I opened my eyes again, my mother was gone. Two days later, she packed up and moved back to Vermont.

AFTER MY MOTHER LEFT, the silence of the house crushed me daily until I felt so flat that nothing could slip in. I stayed in as much as possible that summer; outside, I was too vulnerable. I saw the house as others would see it: the uncut, half-dead lawn, the scattering of dried leaves from the previous autumn still collected in blown piles along the hedges and the side of the house, the rotting board on the steps to the porch. And I would blink, uncomfortably illuminated in the afternoon sun, conscious of my uncombed hair, baggy T-shirt from Goodwill, and peasant skirt from 1971, my feet bare and dirty, toenails in desperate need of cutting.

My aunt wrote me a single letter after that. *Who do you think you are, to talk to your mother like that?* she wrote.

You've devastated us. Your mother has lost everything—her husband, both sons, and now this. Please come to your senses and apologize. If you want to drive everyone away, that's your business. But don't do it, Belle. Don't lock it all away forever.

You might think I patched things up with my mother after that, might believe me to have a better heart than I do. But after Aunt Hannah's letter, I sat and drank more wine, one day melted into the next, and any good intentions I might have had somehow faded and slid back into memory. Everything was too twisted to unravel, or at least that's how it seemed to me at the time. *They're better off without me.* I'd destroyed everything in my path, crossed a line and couldn't go back.

At night I dreamed of my mother's face slipping and sliding down over her shoulders, her flesh melting. My aunt's words returned over and over again *(Who do you think you are?)*, night after night, the way the anger seeped like steam through the page of tight, hard writing. The harder I fought to push them away, the stronger they became, never letting go, twisting me this way and that, until my old self just came roaring back in self-defence.

Fuck you.

I would live my life how I pleased, and no one would tell me otherwise.

In LUDLOW, the university students poured in, set up residence in student houses scattered among the single-family homes. The city matured around me while I and my house fell apart. Windows broke and remained that way, paint peeled from windowsills, layers of grime accumulated on the walls, the floor. The green cushions my mother made were stolen, one by one, from the porch, and garbage rolled into my yard. I thought of Theo and the mess he created, left behind.

In the fall of 1988, I rented a car and drove up to Bressler, Ontario. On the back seat, a cardboard box held the shattered pieces of Theo's portable record player and a single envelope. I drove as fast as I could, cutting in and out of lanes danger-ously, swerving against blaring horns and middle fingers raised, unblinking. The highway, its snarl of frozen metal closer to Toronto, didn't scare me, but WELCOME TO BRESSLER, POP. 285,300 did. My palms sweated against the steering wheel.

There. A man by the side of a house with a burgundy front door and matching shutters, a man raking up soggy leaves left behind as the snow melted and bagging them, strong work gloves protecting his hands from branches and thorns of old rose bushes. My hands gripped the steering wheel, my tongue stuck to the roof of my mouth. Inside the car, the air seemed suddenly too tight, too close. If I didn't open a window, the door, I thought I would faint, but the handles burned into my skin and I didn't want him to see me.

I pulled from my pocket a letter—stained and creased—that had arrived a few days earlier, read it again for the fifth, sixth, seventh time.

I hope this letter finds its way to you, and I hope you are doing well. I kept the notes you sent (and the photographs) and used the return address on their envelopes. As you can see by my return address, I'm back in Bressler. My parents passed away last year, and I've come home to take care of their house.

A lot of time has passed, enough for the anger to fade. I never replied to your letters. In truth, I hadn't yet grown up and couldn't face what you had to say. You wondered then what would have happened if you discovered your pregnancy before you left. I don't think it would have changed a thing.

But now I write because I have grown up. I have a family of my own, and I look at my two boys and think of the third that's missing. It's too late for us, Belle, but I'd like to see my son, if you'd let me. I saved the photographs, showed them to my wife. A long time ago, she told me I should write, but I put it off. I'd like to be a part of his life now. I'm ashamed that it took me this long.

At the end of the letter, he'd added a PS: *What happened to my car and trailer? If you still have them, I'd like them back.*

I don't think I really have to describe how it made me feel, that letter. What struck me then was the lack of any kind of apology. I took a hammer from the basement, went for the first time since Jonah's accident into the trailer, barely breathed as I grabbed the record player from beneath the little table. And there in my driveway, not caring who saw, I smashed the shit out of that sucker, each blow making me lighter, as if taking away the rage and pain and forcing it into the open.

A small boy rode up Theo's driveway on a bicycle, another, younger, trailing behind. I slumped behind the wheel as I watched, my breath even, slow. I watched until it grew dark, the rake put away in the garage with the garbage bags, a woman (short dark hair, soft around the edges) briefly appearing at the doorway, then vanishing into the house again. I waited all night until the lights went out and raccoons darted across the street, illuminated by the street lights, their eyes glowing green. Only then did I open the car door, take the box from the back seat, and place it by his front door. A simple brown box, the pieces of our history, and a short note: *It's too late. Your car and trailer were destroyed in a car accident, and Jonah is dead. This is all that remains.*

I left Theo with his wife and his kids and his house in the suburbs and drove back to Ludlow, where I removed my mother's wedding band from my finger and returned it to the velvet box containing its larger, matching circle. I gathered up the rings and the glass jar with my father's ashes and placed them carefully on a ledge in the trailer, then closed the door. *Everything gone.* I let the rot creep up over the trailer, kept it parked in my driveway as a permanent reminder of all that I had lost. With the door closed to seal in the memories, my ghosts, I held them at bay, and I could go on.

ONCE A YEAR at Christmas, my aunt sent out a family newsletter, to keep me informed, I suppose, and would add at the very end: *Belle is still missing and missed. Please update us soon.* I never did.

How did all the years slip away? Easy. Think of a vacation you've recently taken, the way each day blended into the next so that before you realized it, it was time to go back. That's the way it happened for me. Each day was the same, with only minor variances—a trip to the grocery store with my small steel cart on wheels, a stray cat mewling at my back door, the crunching metal of a sudden car accident at the end of the street. I borrowed books from the library, romances like the ones I'd read in Silver Falls, but forgot to return them and then just didn't care, set them in a pile in my living room. I stole newspapers from my neighbours and read the obituaries first. And I bought wine and drank it, glass after glass, until my eyelids drooped over eyes filled with crushed sand.

I drank to cover the darkness and fill the empty spaces of the evenings, especially in the summer, when they became long and humid, and the voices of children could be heard even with all the windows firmly shut. After a while, my grasp of how much was too much slipped, and I took rambling walks through the neighbourhood holding a wineglass, one sock pulled up over the leg of my overalls, resurrected from the bottom of a drawer, my long hair half held up by elastic in an asymmetrical ponytail or lopsided bun. By the time the whispers and taunts and rocks thrown at my windows began, I no longer noticed or cared. And there I stalled, a fixture in an otherwise lovely neighbourhood, Theo's trailer parked and overgrown by a weeping willow. Nothing used, everything forgotten.

Twenty-one

I t must have been a while ago, the day I decided to start dying. I woke disoriented from a heavy, dreamless sleep, my eyes moving in slow, gritty arcs. When I blinked, it felt as if my eyelids would never have the strength to open, never regain their normalcy, and I knew that I was done. I pushed my comforter down to my ankles, watched the dust dance in the shaft of light shining through my bedroom blinds, cobwebs in each corner of the room. I would let nature take its course.

That day, I stopped going to work; someone else would have to pack up those damn candy canes. I stopped paying my bills, too, stacking them up one by one on my kitchen table, gauging their outrage by the colour of the ink on the outside: black and blue for reminders, red for final notices. I replayed the messages from the factory on my answering machine over and over again, cackling as the voice of my manager—first confused and questioning, then hurt and frustrated—cracked into fury. Finally he came and pounded on my door, a short man with chest hair that crept up onto his shoulders and neck, almost bursting out of a carefully buttoned collar shirt.

"Ms. Dearing," he said when I answered the door. Worthy and I had never officially divorced, not since I last checked, but I'd never taken his name, always kept Dearing for my own.

234

"Mr. Potter." I beamed, beckoned him inside. "Would you like a beverage?" I held up my wine, nearly toppled over.

He frowned. "It's eleven o'clock in the morning," he said.

"Too early?"

"Ms. Dearing, I came to see if you were ill. You haven't been to work in eight days."

"Yes, I am ill, Mr. Potter, as you can see. I suspect I'll never be well again." I kept smiling, watching his face.

He blinked, looked around my hallway, put his hand over his mouth. "You have a—a dead mouse there," he said, pointing.

I turned my head, saw the small rigid body only steps away, kicked it so that it slid down the length of the hallway.

"They come in with the cold," I said. "Poor little things."

Mr. Potter inhaled through his nose, backed up toward the door, his hand reaching out to steady himself. "If you're ill and planning on being off for any longer, you need to get a doctor's note," he said, forcing his words out formally, stilted, his eyes shifting back and forth from the dead mouse to me.

"Not necessary," I said. "I'll tell you right here, I'm not coming back. I don't see any reason to come back. I'm sick of the smell of candy, sick of waking up every morning to do a terrible job that's hard on my back, sick of watching you drink your coffee in your office and eat glazed doughnuts. Mostly, I just can't be bothered." He opened his mouth to protest, made as if to speak, but I waved my hand. "Don't bother," I said. "Glad you came by. Give my regards to the wife."

And I shut the door, fell against it laughing.

MOST DAYS, I woke in the early morning, watched the sun creep over the horizon. I made myself a cup of coffee, adding a dollop of vodka, just because, then had a cigarette. If the weather was fair, I stood on the front porch in my flannel nightgown and long johns, my feet in thick rubber boots, winter coat and hat and scarf all on to protect against the January cold.

"Morning!" I would call out to the neighbours starting their cars or retrieving the paper from their porches. Most of them didn't wave back, but what did I care? "How are you doing?" I would holler louder, sometimes cupping my hands around my mouth and practically bellowing the words, the cigarette dangling from one corner of my mouth and the smoke stinging my eyes, making me squint.

I knew things about them that they didn't know I knew; I saw things that went on when the lights went off. My next-door neighbour—university professor, two kids in high school—snuck out onto his back deck and smoked a bong late at night, almost every night, while his wife smoked cigarettes on the sly behind the shed where the kids (or her husband) wouldn't see. A shy woman who lived in the corner house—who kept her curtains drawn for most of the day and lowered her face when speaking to anyone—turned on the light in her bedroom, opened her blinds, and disrobed every night at eleven for all to see. Across the street, a recently divorced man picked up his morning newspaper wearing a pink woman's housecoat. Oh yes, he did. Pink with chenille edging.

BEFORE THEY TURNED the water off, I took a shower after my cigarette, letting the hot water pelt against my back until it became lukewarm. I closed my eyes and opened my mouth and just drank it all in. Sometimes I hummed bits of songs I hadn't heard in so many years. I'd think of Theo and the music he played for me, remembered the way his eyes darkened and focused until we were alone in the universe, the only ones who mattered. Felt the ripple broadening from my chest to spread across my shoulders, down my arms, body, legs, into the tips of my toes.

Everything seemed clear, as if I had woken into a new life. Nothing mattered; I would go as hard as I could for as long as I could.

By April my power was gone, but I'm not stupid; I prepared for my Armageddon. At the hardware store, I bought empty gallon jugs and filled each with water, jug after jug, and stored them in my kitchen, enough to get me through the rest of the winter. I bought carrots and potatoes and onions, canned goods (beans, fruit, beef, tuna), beef jerky, cookies, and crackers, stocked up on candles and matches, and cartons of cigarettes. I lugged everything home on the bus, small trips at a time. Readying myself gave me a purpose.

And then I suppose you could say I simply let go and sank down into the darkness of the house. How freeing it was to not care, to just *be*. I almost want to say those were my happiest months. I didn't think about Polly or Jonah, the ones I'd lost; didn't think about my family or the betrayals and lies and sticky webs. I reinvented myself all the time, gave myself a new history, a fresh heart, did my best to ignore the voices of ghosts that began to creep into my head.

Every morning, I loaded up a bag of candy canes and took the number 39 bus across town to the east end. I sat in the plastic moulded chairs with orange padding, bag on the seat beside me, a pair of fingerless gloves on my hands. People stayed away, as they always have (I didn't take regular showers anymore), but they glanced at me through narrowed eyes and muttered to their companions. If I caught someone staring at me directly, I'd lift a finger and place it up my nostril, rooting around for his or her benefit until he or she looked away in disgust. Oh, it was fun—I can't tell you how much fun it was. You really should try it sometime. My aunt was right, I *did* have to make my own happiness.

At the end of the line, I got off the bus and just wandered up and down the streets until I got cold. I passed others like me huddled in doorways, their faces lined and layers of grungy clothing thrown over stinking, wasted bodies. The forgotten ones. Many of them had nowhere to go, no home, only a cardboard box under a bridge or a bed with a stained mattress in a shelter. These were the ones I called my friends these days, though we hardly ever spoke.

At the corner of King and Main, an old man stood on a small wooden box, his arms spread wide, one hand waving a small book in great arcs, a laundry bag of belongings next to him on the stained concrete.

I celebrate myself;
And what I assume you shall assume;
For every atom belonging to me, as good belongs to you.

People on the sidewalk edged past, even crossed the street to avoid him, eyes downcast, but I stopped, the rhythm of his voice like a song.

And will never be any more perfection than there is now,
Nor any more heaven or hell than there is now.

He took notice of me, smiled, and stroked his yellow-stained beard.

"Beautiful lady," he said, and bowed. "My name is Whitman. Would you like to read my book?" He held out the small volume.

I studied the photograph on the cover, the name in bold black letters across the top. "You wrote this?"

"I did."

I looked at the back cover. "It says you died in 1892."

"Yes, but after three days I rose again, and now I sing my song for all to hear."

"You look a little worse for wear."

He smiled, lost the booming tone in his voice, and spoke normally. "Well, what can you expect?"

I saw Whitman nearly every day for a month, standing on the same corner, his hands red from the cold but still determined to spread his message, his voice a song in an April wind that hadn't yet shaken its wintry sharp edge. *I see, dance, laugh, sing.*

I STOPPED for a drink if it pleased me, or a plate of food. I had plenty of money; I'd worked for over twenty years and spent hardly any of it. So I walked and rode the bus, did whatever I wanted. When you look like you're homeless, people don't pay attention to you, at least not in a good way, and most people look away completely. I can't tell you how many times I sat on that bus or at a table in a coffee shop and overheard intimate conversations: secret lovers, infidelity, confessions of the most absurd kind, plots to steal or hurt. I heard girlfriends cry about cheating boyfriends, teenage boys detailing outrageous sexual conquests, men, women everywhere complaining about boring jobs and ungrateful children. I wanted to grab them all and shout *None of it matters!* in their faces with capital letters until they heard, really heard, what I was saying.

Instead, I recorded everything in a little notebook I took to carrying in my jacket pocket, all the little snatches of conversation and secrets revealed, and wrote *Confessions of a Dirty City* on the front. I mailed in the notebook to the newspaper, but they didn't print it with my name (Anonymous). Later I found a column called *Dispatches*, written by one Brian Muddy, and lo and behold, there were my stories—cleaned up and made nicer, but still mine. *Published, I am published.*

One morning in a coffee shop I saw something sadder than any conversation I'd ever overheard: a woman sitting alone, her head bowed, hair falling down across her face, a mug of steaming tea (tea bag left in, string dangling down the side of the porcelain mug) on a corner of the table. She didn't move for a long time. When she raised her face, her eyes were dark and deadened with such loss that it punched a hole in my chest. She stared at the mug of water, something building and rising up. Her face began to colour and change, her mouth pulled down, and with a violent jerk of her arm the mug flew from her table and shattered on the floor. The noise of chatter and spoons against cups and the *tk tk tk* of the cash register stopped. Calmer, she bent to sweep the broken pieces into her hand, put them on her tray, then wiped her bleeding fingers on her tan coat and stood to leave. Someone whispered, then laughed, and the normal morning routine of the shop resumed, closing in on itself and shutting out someone else's tragedy.

I HAD NO MORE WATER at the house, other than what I'd stored in the gallon jugs. You have no idea how much water you use until it's gone. I tried to make do with just drinking water, rarely washing my hands or face unless necessary. I did brush my teeth and flushed the toilet once a day, pouring just enough water into the tank to make it work. But I missed my showers, so every Friday I'd wander down to the YWCA, a towel, soap, and shampoo tucked in my bag. As long as I paid, they didn't mind.

At the beginning of June, someone stabbed dirty-bearded, homeless Whitman and left him to die near the doors of a bank. No one made much of a fuss; it wasn't even mentioned in the papers. Still, his blood stained the concrete sidewalk, and there, hidden in a pile of cigarette butts and empty coffee cups swept against the corner of the bank entrance, I found his book, spattered with droplets of red, and took it home with me to remember him by.

At night, before the shadows crowded in, I lit candles and read that book, and let me tell you, those words spoke to me and sang to my soul.

Not I, not anyone else can travel that road for you,
You must travel it for yourself.

I took to repeating them out loud, testing the words in all manner of voice. I found that if I shouted the lines, my chest loosened and my head felt lighter with a kind of euphoria. After a while I didn't need the book anymore, not for my favourite parts, and late at night, as the summer crept forward, my words could wake all the dogs on my street and set them barking. I stood under street lights as if in a spotlight and sang, watching windows fly open and hearing the angry shouts of my neighbours before bowing to them all and returning home.

In July, I siphoned water from hoses coiled against houses and sometimes stood beneath the spray, letting the coldness shock me into awareness. It was getting harder to hold on. It wasn't that I was drinking more than usual, though maybe I was, but the ghosts were pressing in no matter where I turned, until eventually I just fell, let them take me where they wanted. Drawn to Jonah's room, which hadn't been touched or visited since he died, I pressed my face into his little folded shirts and sleepers, breathed in musty and damp and tried to smell him again. I pulled his crib apart so that I could lie on his mattress, sleep in the sheets he last touched. I took his favourite teddy bear and wrapped it in a blanket, carried it around with me as if it were him, stroking its head and singing lullabies into its ear. For a few days I didn't leave the house at all but stayed close to Jonah, eating apples and beef jerky and opening my blouse to breast-feed. I woke with headaches that didn't go away, my mouth covered in woolly thickness, and drank to wash it down. Drinking, drinking, drinking.

When I came out into daylight again, my plastic bag of candy canes once again in hand, I had to blink against the brightness, the baking early September heat. My body didn't work as well as it used to; my arms and neck felt stiff and unused, my stomach ached and forced sour burps up the back of my throat, and my legs took odd, lurching steps that made me stumble. *Finally, finally*. I could sense the end of my road.

I rode the bus, but the voices around me jumbled together so that nothing made sense. Lips moved, opened in wide, gaping laughs; faces doubled, tripled in front of me. Off the bus, I tried to walk a straight line but failed, stopped in a bar for a drink. Pictured my organs shutting down, one by one, my palms sweating and chills making my shoulders hunch forward. Ate a banana from a corner shop that sold fruit and vegetables and flowers, then threw it up in a garbage can on the street, people walking by with twisted mouths, waving their hands in front of their faces to get rid of the smell. Knew I should go home to die but forced my legs to move along the sidewalk, Jonah's plump fingers patting my cheek, Polly glaring at a distance and then wrapping both arms around my knees. Hard to walk with both children clinging like that. Stop for another drink, maybe two, maybe three. Made it back to the bus, sinking into the air conditioning, forehead against cold glass smeared with fingerprints and what looked like a long line of dried snot. My stop. Heat closing in on me again, suddenly can't breathe well, and there, up ahead, the boy with his bicycle, poking at something on the ground. I focused on his eyes, the only thing I could see, tripped and sprawled, half on the sidewalk, half on my walkway, these very steps where Viola had died. The boy's face loomed, blocking out the sun. *Jonah.*

Twenty-Two

fter Lawyer Liam leaves, I sit for a long time on my bunk, hands held loosely between my knees. The telling has taken something from me, an energy I never knew still existed. This morning I read in the newspaper that Pierre Trudeau has died, and it seems to me now that the stories have all ended, come full circle. Now there's nothing left, no force to hold my head up on my shoulders, keep me from collapsing forward.

And then a near sense of peace lengthens my spine. I sit at my small table, pull a sheet of paper and a pen toward me.

No matter what happens to me, know this: I'm both innocent and guilty. I've had a lot of time to think about things in the past month, the way my life has veered and twisted and destroyed all in its path. Some people have asked me what I would do differently if I had the chance to do it all over. I can't ever answer this question. I can't erase what I've done, and even if I could, I'd lose so much of the good. But maybe I'd take a different approach, if not a different path. I hope you understand that I'm sorry for the burdens you've all carried. I'm sorry for the lies and betrayals, the pain I've caused. I pushed you all away, and now I'm paying the price. Nothing is more important than family, it's true, so now I'm trying to put the pieces back together again, to make you whole and new. Please forgive me for everything. Nothing was intentional.

I hesitate, wondering if it's enough, then fold the letter and tuck it in my pocket.

IT's EARLY OCTOBER, month of ghouls, skeletal leaves scraping across sidewalks. I've been in jail just under a month, not long by some accounts, but long enough to consider the possibility of a lifetime behind bars. Now I'm suddenly free, and it feels strange at first, so much space around me, as if bandages that have been holding me together have become unwound. My skin expands, plumps with the newness, letting the old tiredness seep from my pores. I take the bus across town, get off a few stops early to walk, the cold impenetrable, though I wear no coat. Lawyer Liam brought me a sweatshirt to wear over my T-shirt; it doesn't quite fit properly, but I'm grateful for its warmth. I'm aware of the impermanence of my sudden happiness but don't worry, don't stop to think or wonder *what will be*. Instead, I breathe in as deeply as possible, letting the fresh air brush through my nostrils, slide down the back of my throat. The ground beneath my feet feels different after all this time, softer. I'm breathing too hard, raggedly, and my feet drag a second too slowly.

Theo's trailer is almost a ruin, its outer aluminum shell somewhat protected by the inner branches of the weeping willow but dulled to an almost charcoal grey, covered in sap and broken branches and dried leaves. For the first time, I notice my house, the dirty windows, wires hanging from the roof, bits of garbage caught in the bushes that flank the left side. I pause for a moment at the front steps, picture Viola's terrible fall, her bare legs splayed. The paint flakes from those steps, exposing pale, sometimes rotted wood beneath; I see Brennan hesitating before following me to the trailer.

Footsteps scrape behind me, the sound of pointy toes pushing leaves off the sidewalk. I know before turning: Trina Allister, the boy's mother, the mayor's wife. Her blond hair is loose and tucked behind her ears, a long black sweater tied and belted around her small waist to keep out the chill. I used to look at her and see all the things I wasn't. Now I just see someone with her own problems, someone else just making her way down that road.

I wonder if she's come here for a fight. I have none left in me, not for her or anyone else.

"What do you need to say?" I'm so weary. "Just say it so we can be done with it. I have things to do."

I've caught her off guard; she hasn't expected this. She widens her stance as if to brace herself but says nothing, just watches me silently. And there we stand. She has no reason to look at me with such hostility, not after she suddenly dropped all charges against me. I've never lied about my innocence. *I never touched that boy.*

And now I understand that she doesn't intend to say a word. She's measuring, taking stock. And in her glance, I imagine a rainfall of accusations: *disgusting the way you live if I had any say you'd rot in jail no matter what my boy says I know you're guilty guilty guilty.*

When she walks away, her head bent forward, she reaches back to sweep her hair from her neck, her high-heeled boots clacking against the sidewalk, and I see small bones, the top of her spine. She doesn't look back.

UPSTAIRS, I stand in front of a full-length mirror for a long time, taking in my untamed hair with its streaks of grey and white, the skin that seems so lifeless and sags down my cheeks. I study my neck, chicken-like and lined, then the backs of my hands, wriggling my fingers; cords rise and fall, the veins pulsing blue and pressing urgently against my skin. *When did I get old?*

Articles of clothing drop to the floor, one by one: over-stretched beige sweatshirt, yellow T-shirt bearing one of those hideous (and slightly mocking) happy faces printed in black, long peasant skirt, panties that sag at the tops of my thighs, the elastic wasted and worn. Just like me, I think. *Wasted and worn.* I stand naked by myself, feet planted firmly on the floor in my room.

I TAKE THE LETTER I've carried home with me—sealed in its envelope and addressed to them all: mother, aunt, sister, husband, daughter—and place it face up on the kitchen table.

I line them all up in a row, the paper dolls of my past as they are today, according to my aunt's yearly updates and what I imagine must be true. Here are my aunt and mother, aging but still lively. My mother now lives with George Dillard at last; he suffered a heart attack last year but perseveres under her loving care. They've never married. Aunt Hannah returned to teaching years ago but has now retired; she sold the farm and moved into one of Lily's new condominium buildings this May. They've both been able to move on.

Here is Worthy, an insurance salesman in St. John's, Newfoundland. See his tie and shirt, his pleated khakis? Respectable. His accent has returned to tumble through his words, his memories are still sharp and bleeding, like mine. He sometimes travels to Halifax, where his brother, Oscar, lives with his wife and three children .

And here is Polly, who lived in the blue row house in St. John's with Worthy until the age of nineteen, when she moved back in with Gardie, the only mother she's ever known. Her scars aren't too deep after all, the damage minimal. She went to the University of Toronto, fell in love with her first-year history teaching assistant, and eloped to Las Vegas. She was married by Elvis. She never did graduate but says she doesn't mind.

Look at Gardie, dressed in black. Only a triangle of pale skin framing her collarbone and too-thin legs in shimmering sheer nylon break the solidarity. She went through a rough period in the eighties, our Gardie. Cocaine snorted in copious amounts, missed auditions, forgotten lines, bags under her eyes and crusted blood in her nostrils. One night she climbed onto the roof of a house at a party and removed her clothes, letting them dangle off her fingers before dropping them piece by piece into the pool below. Wrecked. Her friends pulled her, kicking and clawing and shouting obscenities, down from the roof, tucked her into a car, and she disappeared for a while. Now she's back in Toronto, sober and quiet and blank around the eyes, raw wet wounds. She's started over.

And finally, here is Theo, the shiniest doll of them all, the least touched or accountable. Though his sideburns have disappeared, his hair is still shaggy, but now streaked with grey. Lines climb from the corner of each eye when he smiles. Look away from the smooth skin of his neck emerging beneath the thick sweater and white T-shirt; don't let it suck you in. He is wearing a gold wedding band, has a wife, two kids, a white picket fence in the suburbs, a symbol of everything he once claimed to hate. If I had a pair of scissors, I would cut off his head.

MOST OF MY WALL HANGINGS—the maps, a few random pictures of Trudeau—were dismantled by the police; a stack of items, including my scrapbook, waits just inside the trailer door, sealed in plastic bags. I spread out a map of Newfoundland on the tiny table, find Placentia Bay, the smattering of black dots denoting towns and coves, some too small for names. And there, where we lived. How good it would be to revisit all that I have lost to pick up the pieces. But it would have changed now; things are no longer the same in the small settlements, the coves. All abandoned, the old fishing communities: outhouses tilted, stores padlocked, houses collapsing and pillaged of anything valuable. Ruins. I close my eyes and imagine human forms caught in solid, unmoving poses, as if lightning has flashed down, caught them all unawares, and stopped them forever.

In my vision, a road emerges, almost obscured by alder trees and bushes grown up without restraint for over thirty years, most of the buildings long gone or at least broken down bit by bit, some with one wall and a portion of the roof, empty windows gazing outward. A palpable loneliness. The houses have lost all personality, all sense of ownership, connected by crumbling wooden pathways, front doors padlocked or missing entirely, windows broken. I remember that morning, slippers on the creaking hardwood floors, the rocking chair, the sense of loss, helplessness. A family adrift after the father's death, Gardie's swollen eyes and luscious velvet dress. And there, the shelter by the sea where I escaped with Worthy for the first time, where I cried. My father was there; I could still feel him. This is where it began. Newspaper against the back of bare legs, cold sharpness of the rocks.

If I try to imagine it now, the church and graveyard remain, slightly battered by the wind, markers crooked, some pushed over, some missing. I would find my father's tombstone, kneel beside it, pull waist-high weeds until a path has been cleared, would close my eyes, place my palms down for a still moment. Then take the bottle from my bag, uncork, tip the contents over the ground, releasing him and freeing myself.

I KNEW THAT THE LITTLE BOY across the street wasn't really Jonah. My head knew it, at least. But when I saw him that afternoon in September, something about the way he straddled his bike and pushed himself along, head bent studiously to watch the line of ants, struck me, and in an instant it *was* him. No matter that this boy's eyes were brown instead of green, no matter that he was bigger than Jonah ever had the chance to be. Through the exhaust from the bus, I saw him clearly as he dropped his bicycle to the ground to peer more closely at the sidewalk. The bus hissed and roared away; he lifted his head and saw me too, eyes widening in what I took then for excitement, eagerness (and what I now know must have been fear). I moved toward him with a purpose that I hadn't felt in so many years, my bag of candy canes hitting the side of my knee.

But my legs became tangled in the spokes of his bike, I fell, and his face scrunched up in worry. He didn't know what to do, that I could tell.

"It's all right," I said, touching the scraped skin of my palms to my swelling cheek, testing for blood. "Am I bleeding?" He shook his head, finger crooked into a corner of his mouth. My plastic bag had flown from my hand when I fell, the contents scattering across the sidewalk and under the overgrown hedges. I gathered up what I could see, stuffed it all back in the bag. The little boy ran forward, palms outstretched, holding two candy canes he'd found by his feet. These he offered hesitantly, still unsure.

"Thank you, sweetheart," I said, "but you can keep them." He stood there, palms still up, as I walked up to my front door, dug in my pockets for a key. He would run away now, surely he would. I'd seen him before with his mother, shying away (cringing) from me, shuddering (like all the others) as he passed. Kids had done this to me for the last ten years; I was used to it. I heard the taunts, saw the way they crossed the street to be nowhere near me, heard the dares whispered among themselves. *I dare you to peek in her windows! Touch her front door! Ring the bell and run away!* More, I understood the shrieks when they returned from these courageous missions, sat in my darkened rooms and laughed to myself.

"What's that?" I almost didn't hear him, his voice was so soft. I looked to where he pointed.

"That's my trailer," I said.

He paused, curiosity tinting his brown eyes with an amber glow. "A trailer?" he asked.

I knew it was coming, turned and fumbled with my key. *Get in, get in.*

"What does it look like inside?" he asked.

The ground tilted; sky and clouds slid down in a rush, my skin clammy, cold.

"Do you want to see it?"

The trailer opened like a tomb, the door sticking and sucking as I pried it open. He looked around the small space, amazed, unsure where to look first, but still hanging back a little, unwilling to give himself up to it entirely. I breathed in the smell of my history and swayed, dizzy. Theo was here, along with Jonah and Polly, their own long-gone breath mingling with mine, passing through my lungs and tingling the edges of my lips.

"It's like a little house," the boy said. Slender, sloping shoulders, tanned flesh. A little girl in a long-ago dream offered up crushed flowers and whispered words I couldn't hear, breaking the silent heat that filled my ears with pressure until I couldn't stand it anymore and pushed open the door, lunging forward to let clean air into my lungs.

"Where are you going?"

"I need to put my things away," I said, lifting my bag so that he could see there were important matters to take care of.

"Can we come back after?" he asked. He wasn't afraid anymore, followed me closely up the steps to the house and inside, blinking a few times as his eyes adjusted to the dim light.

"Look around, if you like," I said. "Just be careful."

He roamed through the rooms by himself, exploring. I put my bag on the kitchen table and sank into a chair, massaging my temples, my throat dry. The boy reappeared, cheeks smeared with dust.

"Do you think that animals live here too?" he asked.

"Maybe."

"Which ones, do you think?"

"I don't know. A few cats. Some raccoons up on the third floor—if you listen hard, you might be able to hear them walking around."

He listened right then and there, cocking his head, the muscles of his face tensing and straining with the effort of listening *so hard*.

"I think I hear them!" he breathed.

My head began to pound and my eyes felt too heavy for the real world; the rooms lost their dusty veneers and became cozy, inviting. Lamps threw soft light on fat chairs. This was my false world of ghosts; in this world, cups of tea never cooled too much and the sun never sank over the horizon. Somehow the house and its hidden ghosts pressed down on my shoulders, whispering in my ear, a constant drone, until I could no longer distinguish the true from the untrue.

I moved my head from side to side, trying to escape the pressure.

"You have a lot of books," Jonah said, eyes wide as he took it all in.

"I like to read." I didn't really, but I took books from the library and never returned them, bought paperbacks at garage sales and stacked them in columns beneath the front windows. I always intended to read, had good intentions, but then the nights closed in with their shadows and something else consumed me entirely.

"Would you like something to drink?" My voice sounded raspy, odd.

He smiled, nodded.

"Juice?"

"Yes, please." So polite, that boy. I must have taught him that along the way; I must be a good mother. And look, in the cupboard, a sealed bottle of grape juice—everyone knows kids love that. I couldn't remember when I had bought it, but that didn't matter. I poured the juice into a new plastic cup—there were a set of four in the cupboard, all new and different colours (couldn't remember where those came from either)—careful to leave a few inches from the rim.

As I handed the cup to him back in the living room, my fingers brushed his, and I marvelled at how much he had grown. Seemed not too long ago that he was a newborn in my arms, little fist tightening around my index finger reflexively. I sat back and studied his face, searching for signs of Theo. Perhaps around the mouth or chin? His hair was lighter than expected, though, and (I frowned) his ears stuck out in a funny way. But so beautiful, so whole. The immensity of my love for Jonah surprised me, but I welcomed it, drank it in. I had never expected to be in love like this, thought Theo was the best I would have. I was so completely wrong.

"Can I see your trailer again?" He looked up hopefully, and I smiled.

"Be careful with your juice," I said, holding the front door open for him. He clutched his cup with both hands, walking slowly, eyes peering down, watching the juice jostle with every step. He made it into the trailer, smiled up at me proudly. The door shut behind us. His arm stretched forward to place his cup on the table; his foot caught the side of the bench and he stumbled.

"Oh, no!" Jonah spread his fingers, dismayed. "I spilled!" And he had, all down the front of his shirt and pants, a purple winding river twisting in drips onto the floor.

"That's all right, sweetheart. We'll get you changed into something else and then Mama will pour you some more juice."

Jonah wrinkled his nose, seemed confused. "My mama?" he asked. "Do you have little boy clothes?"

"Of course. Why wouldn't I? Silly." I knelt beside him, told him to lift his arms. His shirt caught on his chin for a moment. He struggled, blinded, before slipping it over his head.

"What's this, sweetheart?" A bruise, a bite, on his left shoulder.

He pulled his mouth down in a frown, strained to see what I saw, then shrugged. "A kid bit me," he said.

"Really? That wasn't very nice."

"I know."

He insisted on stepping out of his pants, one leg carefully following the next. And then his eyes flicked upward, catching in the light: brown eyes, not green. I was caught, his question—*You have clothes for me here?*—circling, repetitive. The *here* part didn't make sense, the surprise that I would have clothes *here* in our *home*. And then: *My mama?*

My head ached. I blinked, rubbed my eyes, and the web of time shifted forward like a wave and deposited me back in the here and now, where Jonah was dead and I was no one's mother. This boy standing in front of me was an imposter.

I grabbed him by his skinny shoulders, the seeping warmth of his skin making me grit my teeth.

"Who sent you here to trick me?" I shook him until he cried out.

"Stop, you're hurting me!" He pulled then, twisting his shoulders back and forth to break free, and as he did, his arms slipping from my hands, a great dim rage wrapped me in a cocoon. Overwhelmed, I tugged sharply, aware of life's unfairness. Why should it be right that this boy was living, breathing, in front of me while Jonah lay buried beneath the cold, hard soil?

The ghosts were back, their whispers rising to a constant hiss, loud enough to cover the boy's cries. My hands encircled his wrist; he clawed at my fingers, leaned down, and bit me hard. Every movement, every breath, seemed in slow motion. I watched distantly as I reacted, pulling back my hand in surprise and pain, then grabbing him again, leaning down, mouth close to the flesh on his shoulder, breathing in his scent.

And then.

And then.

He was just a little boy, real tears on his cheeks, his chest heaving. I let go abruptly, put my hands to my face, overwhelmed by my sudden sense of loss and failure. My Jonah was gone, Polly was gone, and I had destroyed my family. My breath caught and held deep beneath my ribs; coming back up, it shuddered and shook and released itself in a low keening sound.

Brennan looked at me in horror, then flew for the door, fumbling once, twice, before wrenching the door open. Down on the floor, the trail of his clothes, the spilled juice, plastic cup lying sideways.

I OPEN MY EYES NOW, fold the map carefully and place it on a pile with the others, and take a book of matches from my pocket. The flame catches the edge of the maps, holds, then grows larger, licking the curtains above the sink. Outside, I hear a group of young girls, imagine small hands linked as baby voices lift up in song.

Ring around the rosy,
A pocketful of posies.

I remember flowers in my hair, spilling from my pockets, crushed beneath a single, bare heel. Smoke rises, waves of heat singeing the hair on my arms. I have choices, but not for much longer. Two paths again, and which one would I choose this time? .

Ashes, ashes,
We all fall down!

The cabinets catch fire, blue-orange flames burrowing in corners and working their way inward. *You're strong, like me,* he'd said. *Not easily broken.* The fire gathers strength, surges forward in a hungry rush. The force of the heat sears my skin, but the pain doesn't touch me at all. I feel, instead, that familiar cold wind, a spray of salt. The weight of an arm presses against my shoulders, grey wool scratches across my cheek. He's here, or I'm nearly there. Something in me releases.

My life, my choice. *Make your own happiness.* I lean back against the red-and-white checked cushions, close my eyes, and wait for my answer.

Acknowledgements

I wish to express my gratitude to a number of people who helped create the final version of *Belle Falls* and who, ultimately, made the journey much less painful than it could have been.

First and foremost, I thank my editor, Barbara Berson, who pushed me farther than I thought possible, and my publisher, David Davidar, for taking a chance on a largely unfinished manuscript. I can't thank you both enough. I must also thank John Sweet for his insightful editorial eye and everyone at Penguin Group (Canada) who contributed to the production of this book.

I am fortunate to have a wonderful agent, Helen Heller, who has never given up on me and who always speaks the truth. I would never vote you off the island, Helen.

To the people who added layers and rich detail or otherwise helped in some way: Dawn Clarke-Martin, for sharing stories; Michael Crummey, for the brief review; Saskia Maddock, for reading and commenting diplomatically on an early draft; James Ramsay, for the names; David Seymour, for the brainstorming; and James Tennant, for all things musical. To the team of experts who took the time to explain criminal law and police procedures: Lisa Burgis, Beth Clarke, Ion Grigoriu, John Hobbins, and David Tano. You all helped enormously.

Special thanks to my friends and family, who have always supported and encouraged me, especially my husband, Charles, and my daughter, Sophie, who both probably suffered along the way.